"I wish I'd had this book before I returned to SF. After 10 years in NYC,
I didn't want to be the last single woman living there."
—Cecile Lozano

"This single woman says, 'Buy the book'.
If anyone's interested, I want the ring on the cover."
—Tara Marley

"My new bible. Single and staying that way."
—Mary Merkl

"I'm not the last, but the best. Not bragging, just saying. Read the book."
—Dale Grossman

"Career, love, and fashion, plus the Hamptons and Manhattan—
this book is the single woman's dream."
—Stacy Livingston

"Samantha's adventures in my hometown are the real deal!"
—Gigi Maguire

The Last
Single Woman
in New York City

The Last
Single Woman
in New York City

LORRAINE DUFFY MERKL

 Heliotrope Books

New York

For Meg and Luke

Other books by Lorraine Duffy Merkl

Fat Chick
Back to Work She Goes

"Those who stand for nothing fall for anything."
—Alexander Hamilton

"Feminism is about the ability to choose
what's right at each time of our lives."
—Gloria Steinem (*married for the first time at age 66*)

PROLOGUE

Three years ago

"Sam. Samantha. Hey, Dennehy."

Oh no, thought the twenty-nine-year-old executive hurrying down Fifth Avenue; her red-bottomed shoe had just touched the corner of 51st Street, where St. Patrick's Cathedral loomed large. Today was not the day to get held up by a former Columbia classmate, who, as Sam recalled, could talk a blue streak bragging all the way.

"Hi, Amy. Long time."

"How've you been?"

"It's all good. I'm kind of in a ru—"

"You went into advertising, right?"

Sam gave a nod to her agency's portfolio while shrugging her black Goyard tote up onto her shoulder. She began to take baby steps away from her fellow alumna, who was a lot blonder, more skeletal, and harder-looking than Sam remembered.

"I did indeed. And I'm headed to a meeting. Good to see—"

"I'm going in your direction," said Amy as though it were a happy accident. And so began their hurried Aaron Sorkin–like walk and talk.

"Whatever happened to that guy you used to—"

"We're still together," Sam assured Amy.

"Married?"

"No," Sam said, losing patience.

"But it's been—"

"Eleven years."

"Oh, honey," Amy condescended with a gentle rub to her former class-mate's upper back. "If, after all that time, some man didn't want to marry me, I mean, heave-ho."

As she'd met with this judgment before, an unfazed Sam responded as indifferently as if she were directing a tourist to the nearest subway station: "We're getting married in the next year or two. We put the whole 'piece of paper' thing on hold 'cause...never mind. Anyway, a lot of women our age aren't married; I work with plenty who don't even have boyfriends, so . . . um, I've got to get going."

Sam indicated with her portfolio that she needed to hang a right at 50th Street toward Rockefeller Center. "My agency is pitching NBC."

Not to be one-upped, Amy spit out: "I'm about to become the most fa-mous editor in New York. My publishing company is doing a book-signing event in front of 30 Rock. We're going to the exact same place."

"How 'bout that."

Sam began to speed walk like a woman trying to escape a stalker, hop-ing Amy, in her much higher heels and tight pencil skirt, wouldn't be able to keep up the breakneck pace and speak simultaneously.

"So, let me tell you about the book. You've heard of Hannah Ran-dolph—"

Before Sam could say no, Amy added, "If not, you're about to. She's the single woman's most sought-after guru."

I don't care

"Her goal is to ban marriage."

Dear God. "Is that so?"

"She started out doing these TED-type talks and branded herself 'The Anti-Wife.'"

Look at all these people. Move. You, with the camera and the map. Move.

Suddenly, as though her thoughts had sway, there was a break in the promenade crowd, and Sam zipped around the plaza, which, in the winter months, looked over at The Rink. Regardless of how focused Sam was on her destination, Amy remained so close by her side that Sam felt as though they were in a three-legged race.

"Then Hannah wrote it all down and got an agent. That's where I came in. I was fresh off my divorce and couldn't have been more pro being an 'Anti-Wife.' I fought for the book, and our sales team backed me. They had Walmart and Target begging for it. This title is going to blow up."

Mercifully, Amy had run out of wind and simultaneously exhausted her career coup by the time they'd reached *The Anti-Wife* happening, which had been set up where the famed Christmas tree would stand in a few months.

"That's Hannah over there," Amy pointed out. "Come. Let me introduce you."

Sam looked past the young blonde woman Amy was gesturing to and saw her agency colleagues waving frantically at her from in front of the revolving doors of the art deco landmark.

"I'd love to, but I can't. Good luck."

"Wait. Here," offered Amy, as she grabbed a copy of the book off the display, "take one."

"No, that's okay . . ."

But Amy had already shoved it in her chest.

Without even looking at the cover, Sam acquiesced, "um, sure," slid one strap of her Goyard off her shoulder indicating that Amy could place it in her bag, and as she hurried toward her now downright pissed off co-workers, Sam hollered back, "thanks. Bye."

1

Present Day

"'With this ring, I thee wed. I promise to love, honor, and cherish everything we registered for on BrideMe.com.' The commercial then goes on to show all that can be had on the site at prices that won't break the bank of the happy couple's friends and relatives. The spot ends with the bride throwing her bouquet at the camera, aka TV audience, and it freezes. The logo and tagline pop on across the flowers: BrideMe.com— We promise you everything."

Another positive presentation, acknowledged the thirty-two-year-old president of Dennehy Consultants as she regarded the client-side of the table and saw three heads nodding so vigorously they belonged on a car's dashboard.

BrideMe, which was getting lost in the glut of wedding-related sites, which all took sanctimonious approaches, led Sam to pitch a strategy using humor to cut through all the preciousness. There would be the platforms of social media, of course, and magazine ads, but Sam thought a television commercial on shows like *The Bachelor, The Bachelorette, Marriage Boot Camp,* and other relationship-centric programs would be the lynchpin. Clearly, her current boardroom audience agreed.

So much so that Sarah, her former colleague from McCann-Erickson, responsible for bringing Sam in to help the company, got up and began to run—not walk but run—from the conference room to get BrideMe's CEO.

Since her arrival in NYC a decade ago, Sarah had worked hard to suppress her South Carolina drawl, yet when emotional (for better or worse), the account executive couldn't help but fall back on the expressions that made no mistake from whence she came.

"Y'all, I'll be back faster than a hot knife through butter."

Sam smiled and nodded, not surprised by Sarah's reaction. In the past, the two hotshots had operated well together because both women had the same strong work ethic, each always at her desk an hour before even the few who chose to show up at nine on the dot. Their professional similarities though, never led to a personal relationship outside the office.

Sarah, whose cascading hair was the color of marmalade, and alabaster skin had never been kissed by the sun, was a sorority-cum-party girl who knew her way around a Jell-O shot and how to use a tabletop as a dance floor. Her once-prized possession was a neon blue tank top that read: So many men, so little time. In the summer, when casual Fridays ended at 1:00 p.m., Sarah would change into it, along with her Daisy Dukes, and do a lap around the office before catching the Hamptons Jitney.

Sam never partied hard, or at all, really, not in high school, or even college, let alone in adult life. She'd long ago made peace with her lack of a sow-your-oats social life during her early years and now saw it as a plus; she looked younger than many of her peers whose skin and hair suffered from too many late nights. Sam also was neither in any type of twelve-step program, nor conversely did she rely on a bottle of chardonnay or a joint to unwind at the end of the day. In fact, she attributed a lot of her success unapologetically to her homebody ways. Best of all, Sam the Man had liked her that way.

*****

Samantha Dennehy and Samuel Winston III met in line at registration on their first day at Columbia University and were a couple by the second week after their first date at a dorm party.

By the end of the evening, he observed: "You look as good now as you did when we got here."

"Uh, thank you?"

He then nodded toward a co-ed, who was passed out in a corner; another who was dancing with abandon with her button-down unbuttoned; and others who needed to be held up or carried out by their escorts.

"Well, I don't drink, so . . ."

"You're dignified. I like that."

And Sam liked him.

Everyone, including the twosome, got a kick out of the fact that they had the same nickname but agreed it was monotonous to always have to clarify which "Sam" was being referenced; hence the moniker Sam the Man was born.

The Upper East Side of Manhattan scion loved it because it made him sound even cooler than he already was; although she did a lot of eye-rolling, Sam secretly liked going out with the cool guy who held court wherever they went.

Their campus couple status continued even after sophomore year when The Man left the renowned institution to pursue his career dream of being a chef.

"I never wanted to come here in the first place," he ranted while tossing textbooks he was going to sell into a box and term papers into a Hefty bag. "I only did it because my dad put his foot down, and my mother guilted me into 'not giving him a heart attack.' It's time I take my future into my own hands, you know? If I stay, I'll only end up running a hedge fund like my brother. Ivies, college in general, are overrated."

Spoken like a legacy accepted before he even filled out the application, thought Sam. Although she supported her guy's decision, she could not disagree more with his philosophy.

The Bronx girl from modest means had worked herself into a frenzy to get accepted into the only Ivy League college in New York City. Regardless of its fluctuating *US News* ranking, Sam always believed it was the best, with the added plus that the school was close to her outer-borough home; she could not move that far away from her family responsibilities.

That was one of the reasons she encouraged her boyfriend's transfer to the Institute of Culinary Education; at least one of them should have the courage to cut family ties. In fact, she took a bit of credit for putting the idea in his head.

When he made her a meal, Sam would always say the same thing after taking her last bite: "Imagine what you could do if you did this professionally."

The two Sams graduated from their respective programs at the same time, and their gift to each other was to support one another's careers. They both reached their goals two years ago, then began planning their long-delayed wedding that stopped short of the rehearsal dinner.

After eight post-grad years of putting off marriage so they could focus on their professional lives, the newly minted marketing entrepreneur and the executive chef were on the cusp of tying the knot when he sent her an email that read, "I already blasted this," referring to the attachment. "You can forward it to your guests. I suggest ASAP."

Even before she clicked on the PDF that would change the calculus of her life, Sam knew almost verbatim what it said: "Dear family and friends, the wedding will no longer take place. We know you saved the date to celebrate with us. Apologies for the inconvenience and short notice."

She dialed his number, and Sam the Man answered without a salutation: "I'm sorry," then proceeded to mansplain.

She could hear his voice but not make out a word he was saying. Like a boxer knocked for a loop by an opponent's blow to the head, Sam felt unsteady, and her ears had begun to ring. Every now and then, a phrase would get through. Something about never having had time to be by himself, and then, she thought she heard something about Europe. Opening his own restaurant? She wasn't sure and didn't want to know.

As the bride-not-to-be hung up, the first person she thought of strangely enough was Sarah, whom she hadn't seen in years.

When they were at McCann, if something went wrong and everyone was running around like Nancy Drew trying to find out whodunit, Sarah would announce: "Who cares how the cow got in the ditch? Let's just fix this." An unfamiliar reference to a native New Yorker, but one that Sam appreciated and agreed with all the same.

What an odd thing to remember just as life as she knew it had disappeared with a ping. Indeed, what difference did it make how Sam the Man's change of heart came about? He was humiliating her, and if he was leaving, she wanted him to go out of her life that second.

The outside world would never see her cry over him, just as Sam had never seen her mother Evelyn shed a tear over Sam's errant father. This helped her bury her emotions down into a place so deep it was as though they had decomposed.

She was celebrating her company's second anniversary with impressive results. After all, Sam had been working in advertising for a decade, so she had lots of contacts. And, of course, her reputation didn't hurt either.

Sam had made a meteoric rise to the level of senior vice president/creative director by age thirty, with impressive credentials garnered from her staff jobs at some of the most established agencies in New York City.

Hence, everyone was shocked when Sam traded in her prestige for her freedom.

Even though she knew, as did others, that she had the stuff to be a She-EO of one of the big firms, Sam wanted to work for herself, as it offered more flexibility. At the time, she was thinking like a wife-to-be, one whose financé—just tapped as executive chef at The Water Club—didn't work traditional hours, so she didn't want to either. The couple also had agreed that Sam would be a stay-at-home mom. Owning her own business would let her have the best of both worlds.

But that was then; this was now. And in the now, Sam just wanted to feel in control of her life.

****

Sarah returned trailing after her boss, Eileen Smythe, a business mogul in her forties with a Park Avenue pedigree and a half-dozen marriages behind her.

Sam put her whole presentation on again for Eileen, who resembled Meryl Streep in the movie *Manhattan*. She was tastefully dressed in a sleek beige pantsuit, with her straight, butt-cheek-length platinum hair swept over one shoulder like a flaxen scarf. She continually stroked it as though it were a pet.

Eileen was neither embarrassed nor ashamed of her marital failures. In fact, she fancied herself an expert in the field. "If you like something, do it a lot," she'd say, and Eileen did like anything wedding-related, rumor had it, more so than actually being married.

Since graduating from FIT twenty-odd years ago, she had worked for her famous father's fashion house, Smythe Designs, renowned for knocking off red-carpet creations at affordable prices. Eileen though was always coming up with offshoot companies of her own to run, and always focused on bridal. To date, she had a line of shoes called Aisle Take Those and an all-natural, moisture-drenched cosmetic brand: I Dew. BrideMe was her latest venture meant to take the registry sector of the industry by storm.

The queen of the runaway brides tapped her reading glasses on the mahogany conference table and stared down the storyboard. All the while, her minions, who had been so enthusiastic less than ten minutes ago, were now sitting stoically. Sam broke the ice and braced herself to be thrown under the bus.

"Let's start by addressing any quest—"

"So, you think the sacrament of marriage is funny?" challenged Eileen.

Sam's poker face did not betray her thoughts: *Did she just not only take a tone but refer to the institution in the religious sense? This woman was probably one floral arrangement away from dumping groom number seven and has essentially made a mockery of the "sacrament" by "doing it a lot."*

"I think the market . . ." began Sam, continuing to defend her strategy with facts and figures as well as examples of what rival companies were doing. It was clear she knew what she was talking about and even more evident that Eileen was not listening.

"Are you married?" the CEO demanded.

"I don't see . . ."

"It's not a trick question. You either are, or you aren't."

"No," she answered as her lips pursed.

Faster than you could say engraved matchbook covers, Eileen's tone changed from confrontational to condescending.

"You obviously put a lot of work into your presentation, and I've got a lot to digest. I'll read over everything you prepared and let you know shortly about next steps."

Sarah followed her two sycophant co-workers who were rushing out behind their boss like solicitous bridesmaids and mouthed for Sam to meet her in the lobby in ten minutes.

After half an hour and several urgent text messages, Sarah hurried out of the elevator and signaled for Sam to join her in the building's Starbucks packed with the lunchtime crowd.

"I know, I know. That woman is enough to make a preacher cuss. I'm sorry, it's not going to work out. I'll make sure your invoice gets paid. I promise," said Sarah, all in one nervous and embarrassed breath.

"Slow down. What happened?" asked Sam, trying to gain the upper hand of the conversation.

"I really have to get back upstairs," said Sarah, and turning über-professional, announced drawl-free, "We're going in a different direction."

Sam sidestepped her and attempted to remain composed as she insisted upon the truth. "Look, stop with the party line and tell me."

"Eileen pitched a hissy fit because you're not married. She thinks that anyone who isn't . . . well, she compared you to one of those TV match-makers who claim they can set up anyone, except they can't find a man for themselves." Then, with genuine consolation in her voice, Sarah added, "I know I roped you into this and really admire that you took the assignment after what you went through, bless your heart."

"There's no need to bring my personal life into this, although clearly, your boss has."

"I realize I just gave you the ammo to sue us, but please, I'll make sure your invoice gets paid," Sarah reiterated as though it were a bribe.

Sam was now bored and exhaled in disgust. "You already said that, and I'm not suing anyone. I have a lot of clients and work to do. I only took this project as a favor to you. And yes, you will pay me for my time and efforts. But one more question: How come she lets you work there? You're not married."

The southern belle held up her left hand and gave Sam the finger—the fourth one, which sparkled. Her two-carat diamond was stacked atop a simple silver band.

"When did this hap—why didn't you say . . .?" But Sarah's look gave her the answer. Sam responded acerbically: "There was no need to postpone your joy. I could have handled the news."

Sam gathered her things to leave the coffee mecca and mirrored her former colleague's previous professionalism as she offered, "Congrats on your marriage and good luck with your new direction."

Sam was not posturing when she enlightened her almost-client that she had other work on her plate, and as would soon be the case, more on the way.

2

Sam's cell rang as she turned the corner of East 86th Street, only steps from her apartment on East End Avenue. The number was not only unfamiliar but turned out to be a business call; shocking if only because it was the first post–Memorial Day Friday afternoon when most offices, as well as the city in general, cleared out early.

"This is Barry Rogers' office."

The Applause Television Network honcho wanted to meet with Sam on Monday at 11:00 a.m. to discuss a "major venture."

As the head of production and development, Rogers had been responsible for some of the best Emmy-winning scripted shows on TV. Even so, this master-of-ratings gold had not been able to get a foothold into reality programming, the likes achieved by Bravo and WEtv; at least, not until now.

The assignment involved the darling of the literary world, influencer and disruptor Hannah Randolph, whose self-help book, *The Anti-Wife*, had debuted three years ago as a bestseller and had been one ever since. Apparently, she was getting her own show, and Rogers, having heard great things about Sam from mutual contacts at NBC, was considering her to spearhead the marketing.

"I can send over a copy of the book by the end of the day," volunteered the executive secretary.

"No need," said Sam. "I've already got it. (*Somewhere.*) I'll see Barry at eleven on Monday, and please thank him for the opportunity."

One of the great things about consulting was that Sam could call it a day when she felt like it. And she felt like it right that second. After all the work she did for BrideMe.com and energy she put into the dog and pony show for Sarah & Co., plus having to do it again for Eileen, ending up with nothing to show for it was more than aggravating, but at least the workday was finishing on an up note.

Sam entered her high-rise and was greeted by the ever-cheerful Jimmy, her boyishly handsome, thirty-something doorman, who offered, "TGIF. Right, Ms. Dennehy?" as he handed her letters and some packages.

"You said it, Jim."

Even though her co-op apartment was located only twelve floors up, today's elevator ride reminded her of the time her third-grade class visited the Empire State Building, and the journey to the top seemed never-ending.

When Sam finally entered her two-bedroom, she dropped her trusted Goyard as well as her leather briefcase and mail on the red oak entry hall table, kicked off her black Louboutin pumps, and headed back out into the hall to the adjacent studio apartment—her former home after she was able to escape the Bronx—that was now her office. Even though it was only next door, the one room allowed her to feel like she was going to work each morning, as well as help separate her personal and professional lives.

Sam's current main living space, decorated with classic Ethan Allen furniture and antique shop accents, was once where Mr. and Mrs. Winston would live. The Man called her real estate coup "brilliant" when bragging to friends about how, after they got engaged, his wife, as he started calling her in advance of the ceremony, "just rang the neighbor's bell and said, 'Wanna sell?' Just like that. Who has the nerve to do that?"

The chef told Sam that he could not wait to move in. Long ago, they had agreed not to live as though they were married until they actually were. They both wanted their life as husband and wife to be new and different from their long dating relationship.

In the meantime, The Man divided his time between his 48-foot Albin North Sea Cutter that he docked at the 79th Street Boat Basin in the nice weather and The University Club during the winter. Of course, he often stayed in Sam's studio. Then when they bought the bordering apartment, even though he didn't live there full-time, The Man offered her well-needed decorating advice. The antique touches were his, a taste acquired when he was still in short pants at St. David's, and he used to attend auctions at Doyle's on East 88th Street with his grandmother.

Sam had grown up in a home where the kitchen chairs had masking tape covering the rips in the vinyl, and pillows hid the sofa's threadbare holes. She didn't know from interior design and bowed to The Man's suggestions.

Sam had gotten accustomed to the pre-owned tchotchkes, hence the reason they were not thrown out the window five minutes after her last phone call with her ex-fiancé.

Her office, on the other hand, was sleek and contemporary, modeled from an article she'd seen in a magazine about making the most of small spaces. She bought two glass-top desks and Lucite chairs, plus two small square Lucite tables in front of an off-white sofa, which had a chrome standing lamp on either side of it. The walls were linen white with a satin finish, and, adding a personal touch, she'd hung framed black and white photos she'd taken with her phone of the Chrysler and Flatiron Buildings, Central Park, and the Washington Square Arch; a makeshift view of all her favorite icons.

Sam wanted this one room to feel as large and airy as possible. Although she left the bathroom intact, she stripped the galley kitchen bare except for the sink, which sat in the center of a long white and black granite counter. Along one side of the basin was a microwave and Keurig coffee maker; on the other side was a multipurpose copy machine and more workspace. Underneath the counter were a mini-fridge and file cabinets. The other two walls had shelves for storage.

Not willing to wait until next week, when her assistant Katie returned from vacay, Sam opened PayPal and invoiced BrideMe, if nothing else than as a symbolic gesture that she was scraping them off her plate like wedding cake crumbs.

Back at home, she shucked her navy Ralph Lauren suit and pulled on her Levi's and white J.Crew t-shirt, then phoned Lena.

The two women had met a decade ago at Sam's first staff job at Ogilvy and hit it off immediately; Sam gravitated to the olive-skinned, raven-haired art director in her flowy thrift store garb that made her look like a gypsy fortune-teller because she was cooler than anyone Sam had ever known. Lena, in kind, thought the preppy-ensembled Sam was the most together person she'd ever met.

3

S am walked from the Upper East Side to Lena's West Village apartment, desperate for a nice head-clearing sojourn, as well as to get in that day's ten thousand steps (and the next day's as well).

She mapped out her route so the late afternoon constitutional would help her get the utmost of Manhattan's hustle and bustle: down York Avenue to 57th Street, across 57th to Fifth Avenue, then down Fifth to 9th Street, where she'd hang a right for the last blocks of her journey. At a brisk pace, the five-mile walk would take about ninety minutes.

When she was growing up in the Bronx, Sam used to watch a lot of Turner Classic Movies to appease her grandmother. She fell in love with the ones set in New York City during the forties, fifties, and early sixties, particularly when the opening credits included a frenetic, whimsical overture to denote the fast pace of Midtown.

Sam decided somewhere around fourth grade that she would someday escape her outer borough and live "downtown" as Bronxites called Manhattan. She wanted to be in the thick of it.

That day, her end game was to arrive at One Christopher Street free of all memories of the newly married Sarah, the ever-married Eileen, and all things bridal, having worked up an appetite for dinner with her bestie.

"Sam?" asked the woman who tapped her shoulder while she waited for the light at the corner of 57th Street and Lexington Avenue.

"Yes."

Who was this person who could have easily been cast as the suburban soccer mom in a Subaru commercial?

"It's me, Maura Murray."

Sam fully expected that the next time she saw her high school classmate, Maura would be wearing some variation of a nun's habit; instead, she was dressed as though she'd just stepped out of a Talbot's catalog.

Through the grapevine, Sam had heard that after college Maura, who used to do a killer imitation of their principal Sister Teresa, the strictest, most dour woman on the planet, had joined the convent.

"Maura, of course, how are you?"

"I'm great. Pregnant and starting to deal with morning sickness, but great."

Pregnant? Was this the immaculate conception, or had she joined some really progressive order?

While Sam stood with her mouth open and a furrowed brow, Maura continued: "I heard your wedding—"

Sam cut her off: "Yeah, yeah, but you know, God closes one door and opens another."

She hoped that because she was talking Maura's language, her former school chum would get the hint and go along when Sam changed the subject.

"So, what's this about?" She pointed to Maura's barely swollen belly. "I thought you became a nun?"

"Oh, you didn't hear? I never actually went through with it."

No, Sam hadn't heard, and now for some reason, she was annoyed. Was there no one who committed to anything they promised?

"So, when you're supposed to get married to God, and you change your mind, how? What hap—?"

"He lets you keep the ring, and you can go on the honeymoon with your girlfriends."

Maura's straight face gave Sam pause, but when she caught on, they both burst out laughing and the tension Sam felt guffawed away.

"I was teaching and living at the convent as a novice," the mother-to-be explained, "but as the time got closer to take my final vows, one of the older sisters took me aside and said, 'I really believe you should rethink what you're doing.' I was rather confused until she pointed out how, whenever I heard someone was pregnant or engaged or potty-training their toddler, I'd always say things like, 'Well, that's another thing I'll never do in my lifetime; that's something I'll never know about.' I guess I was in denial. I told her, 'Oh no, I'm kidding,' and she reminded me that behind every joke, there's real meaning. I took her words to heart and left."

"How did you get back into the swing of things?" Sam wanted to know out of curiosity and for personal reasons.

"I continued teaching, and there was a single dad with a daughter in my class. He asked me out. I had always thought he was attractive, but, of course, put any thoughts like that out of my head. As soon as school ended and his girl wasn't in my class anymore, I said yes to coffee. He was the one, though, so now I have a stepdaughter, plus we then had a son, and we've got another on the way."

Maura patted her stomach again, leaving Sam at a loss. Even someone who was living as a nun could get a man to say "I do." Her face started to feel really hot, as though someone had turned up her internal thermostat, and suddenly, even though she was pleased that things had turned out so well for her one-time friend, Sam just couldn't stand there a minute longer. She announced her departure with the rat-a-tat of a machine gun: "It was so good to see you, and I'm so glad you're happy and have such a beautiful family, but I really must run because I'm late meeting a friend."

Her hug goodbye was more like a chest bump, which knocked Maura back a step, then Sam was off to Fifth, walking faster than she had ever intended to when she'd left the house.

By the time she reached Fifth Avenue, a thirty-something man and woman exited Tiffany's where he dropped to his knee in front of the iconic jewelry store and proposed to his girlfriend with the contents of his little robin's egg blue bag. The other pedestrians formed a circle around the happy couple, offering applause, yips, and shouts of congratulations.

Is the universe antagonizing me? Sam thought, trying to ignore the Insta-worthy moment.

Suddenly, she found herself reminiscing about her own engagement, grateful it was not on public display but for an audience of two in her apartment.

After they'd finished the pan-fried lamb chops with a homemade onion and mushroom sauce, garlic mashed potatoes, and green beans topped with sautéed bread crumbs prepared by The Man, he got up from the table to what Sam believed was clear the dishes. Just as she was about to offer to do it, since he'd cooked, after all, Samuel knelt before her and slipped his family heirloom, two-carat halo antique emerald-cut diamond ring on her finger.

"He's a chef, and he didn't hide it in the Crepe Suzette or anything?" asked someone she couldn't even remember.

"That's right, he didn't, because he knows what's good for him," was her retort. Stunts were for guerilla marketing, not real life—at least not hers.

Forty-second. Thirty-fourth. Twenty-third. Fourteenth. Her hurried trek between these major Manhattan streets was all a blur, except she did notice every single twosome holding hands while window shopping and sightseeing.

When did the whole world become a couple?

The 9th Street sign indicated that the last leg of her personal marathon was literally around the corner, and Sam started running as though she were being chased by an angry mob carrying pitchforks and torches.

When she arrived at Lena's digs, Sam was out of breath and appeared as though she'd just stepped from the shower.

4

*L*ena opened the door, yogurt in one hand and the spoon, which she slowly removed from her mouth, in the other. She gave Sam the once-over, seeming genuinely alarmed.

"You know I don't know CPR. Should I call 911?"

Sam, leaning on the door jamb, held up an index finger to signal she needed a minute.

"My walk," she wheezed, "turned into a run when I began to feel outnumbered," still panting. "The second person in one day has told me," she exhaled, "she's married, and one of them was a nun. Oh, wait. Let's throw my sister in there for good measure and make it three. She's coming up on her year anniversary."

"I thought running was supposed to lessen your anxieties? If you were a drinker, I'd say a shot of bourbon might do the trick."

Sam moved into the entry hall and held up her hand again, indicating she indeed needed yet one more sec. She was already feeling calmer just being in her friend's shabby chic wonderland. Even though Lena made good money as a freelance art director and occasionally sold a sculpture, she still lived as she had when she was a teenager, like a Bleeker Street bohemian: no-frills tables and dressers painted in distinctive shades and covered in colorful sheer scarves of various sizes, some embroidered, others bedazzled with crystals and sequins.

Lena did insist, though, that her living room chairs and sofa be new but found a store in SoHo that duplicated overstuffed retro "grandma" furniture. Of course, her mattress was new as well, but her brass bed was antique and an amazing street find.

Lena Kent was ten years older than Sam but didn't look a day over thirty. She'd been a rock wife, married the year she woulda-coulda-shoulda graduated high school. Her saxophone player husband was in a band that never achieved a status beyond opening act but did studio work and sometimes toured with big names.

"He hung out with Madonna?" Sam once asked with superfan excitement. "The Madonna?"

"No, Madonna the mother of Jesus." Then Lena proceeded to let down her friend by clueing her in to the reality of being a professional musician.

"And he didn't hang out with her. He stared at Madonna's back for two hours every night—twenty feet from stardom, as they say. After the show, the Material Girl got in the limo, and everyone else got on the bus," so ending any residual junior high fantasies that Sam had about concerts, the music business, or going out on tour having any glamour whatsoever.

After leaving school in tenth grade and becoming an emancipated minor, Lena eked out a living using her innate talent painting murals on the walls of Greenwich Village eateries, designing the menus, and offering decorating ideas. This continued even after she got married at seventeen. Six years later, someone of consequence actually took notice of her handiwork. A C-suite Madison Avenue guy inquired of a Spring Street café owner, "Who did this?" as he pointed to the establishment's takeout brochure that was more cleverly designed than most. He called Lena, and without asking for a CV or portfolio (neither of which she had), he offered her a job on the phone. "There's no need to meet first. I know talent when I see it. Start tomorrow."

It was just the break the boho hippie chick needed: the perfect marriage of art and commerce, which countered the imperfect union she'd entered into on a whim. Advertising gave Lena a steady paycheck as well as real structure during the day, while her husband was either touring or at home asleep, resting up to play sax at some dingy club until the wee hours.

This new opportunity also gave her a way to escape the stigma as a high school dropout who saw only cashier or bartender in her future. It was also a way to break free of a life of groupies and gigs and a guy who was gifted musically but had absolutely no talent for being a husband.

After several years of working as an art director, a twenty-seven-year-old Lena flew to Reno and got what she called "the most efficient divorce in history." The next time she saw the man she had been married to for a decade, he was in the morgue, having OD'd on the road in a Motel 6.

When Lena met Sam, the seasoned art director was thirty-two and, although she still believed in love, had no affinity for sanctioned relationships, making her own the quip coined by the brazen 1920s actress Mae West: Marriage is a great institution, but I'm not ready for an institution.

Lena and Sam were immediately drawn to each other. It was a big sister/little sister dynamic at first, which Sam seemed to like—finally, someone looking out for her for a change. But it was abundantly clear to Lena that despite the age difference, they were equals, as Sam was mature beyond her years.

In the beginning, at least, Lena lived vicariously through Sam, who had accomplished so much more than Lena had ever even dreamed of. Not only had Sam graduated from Columbia, but she was considered a rising star at the age when Lena was still offering to sweep out the back room of Fanelli's on Prince Street and mentioning that she could "paint something cool on the wall or jazz up the look of the menu for a few extra bucks."

Lena also envied Sam's poise; she was so polished and commanded respect the minute she walked in the room, whereas Lena was an acquired taste. Her tell-it-like-it-is quality, unruly curls, and Coachella-like ensembles were something that people either loved or hated. So many colleagues hadn't understood how these two possibly got along, albeit became friends. Some thought it was the novelty of opposites attract. Only Sam and Lena understood that they were spirit sisters from another mister.

****

When Sam finally caught her breath and was able to speak in her normal tone, she confessed, "I'm starting to feel like one of these days, I'll turn around, and everybody will be a real, real housewife of New York City, except for me, the last single woman. Even you've been married."

"Don't remind me."

Lena enjoyed likening herself to Goldie Hawn and her long-time love,

Ben to Kurt Russell. They didn't need some license to validate their relationship. Lena believed that the lack thereof was the reason hers and Ben's relationship had lasted longer than some marriages, including her own.

"Yeah, but at least when you die, you can say that you were married."

"No, when I die, I can say I was divorced. Now, that's enough. There will be no more talk of marriage in this house."

Feeling herself getting her second wind, Sam changed the subject: "Oh, Barry Rogers called me."

"The TV bigwig?"

"He's doing a reality show he wants me for."

"*Real Ad Execs of Mad Ave*? And how, pray tell, will you use your new platform? To peddle a cookbook? Moderately-priced handbags? Or perhaps your own line of mocktails? No table-flipping, though. It's been done."

"I'll be behind the scenes, thank you. He wants me to market his new show. It's with that author, Hannah Randolph."

"Oh, there was an article about 'Disruptors of the Decade' in last month's *Harper's Bazaar*. She's the Wife-Hater or however she brands herself."

"*The Anti-Wife*. That's the name of her book, and her alter ego. She's been on the cover of *Forbes* and *Entrepreneur*."

"Well, whatever. I refused to read that thing."

"But you know, she professes the same anti-marriage stance as you."

"Be that as it may, once I saw that every chick on the subway had a copy, I revolted. You know how I am about bandwagon-jumping."

"You jump the other way."

"As though it were an Olympic event."

"Well," confessed Sam, "I have a copy; a freebie I got from the editor, a woman I went to college with," to which Lena viewed her friend as though she'd been hiding some deep dark secret. Sam redeemed herself immediately with, "But, I never read it. Since, you know, I was still pro-wife at the time. I guess I'll have to zip through it this weekend since the meeting's Monday."

Lena saw a hint of water welling in her friend's eyes, a sign that Sam had been triggered to think of Sam the Man and what might have been.

"Why don't we take a break from talking? I'll make us some iced tea."

With that, Sam sank back into one of her host's over-pillowed chairs and allowed it to envelope her like a pair of loving arms as she obeyed Lena's additional instructions to breathe in four beats, hold for four, and breathe out for four more.

As Sam watched her friend putter in the kitchen, she dabbed her eyes as she willed herself to stop crying.

When Lena's phone rang, she assured her guest, "Whoever this is, I'll make it quick," to which Sam waved her off with a cheery, "Take your time. I'm so comfortable I might just doze off before we go to eat." But only the first part was true. Sam did want Lena to take as long as possible, but not for a nap; Sam needed time to pull herself together, as the day's events had brought to the surface what she worked so hard on a daily basis to stuff down.

****

The Dennehy-Winston nuptials were not going to be the Park Avenue version of the Royal Wedding—much to the chagrin of Sam the Man's mother. The couple would marry in St. Paul's Chapel at Columbia University, then head down to the Water Club, where The Man's boss was gifting them a small reception for twenty family members and friends. The successful twosome also eschewed presents, informing guests that if they chose to bring a gift, "Please make out your check to the American Cancer Society," a charity close to the groom's heart as that is the disease to which he'd lost his beloved grandmother.

Sam chose not a traditional wedding gown but the white Tom Ford dress with an über chic cape that Gwyneth Paltrow wore to the 2012 Oscars, which she was able to procure from Rent the Runway. After the celebration, the newlyweds were to head to the Winston family's summer home on The Vineyard for a short but quiet honeymoon.

"Tasteful. Unfussy. Straightforward," was how Sam would describe her special day when people asked, "Are you having a big wedding?"

But one day and six hours before the rehearsal dinner, the infamous email showed up with the phone call chaser, which was still a blur.

Sam had dialed the phone as she paced around her living room, but then for at least twenty minutes after she'd hung up on The Man, her jilted self just stood frozen, staring out the window, her eyes the only moving body part darting from her view of the Bronx down to the 59th Street bridge and sometimes laser-focusing on a pane smudge.

The whole time, her mind was racing, thoughts tripping over each other: *All this time together for nothing. How did I not see this coming? I should have broken up with him years ago. I should have never started going out with him in the first place. What was I thinking?*

Sam then went from paralyzed to moving at what felt like warp speed. Running to the computer and realizing that Samuel's e-blast covered all their friends, Sam need only give the head's up to Lena, Evelyn, and her younger sister, Evelyn's namesake forever known as Little Evie.

Realizing once these calls were made, the situation would be out in the world, and all too real, the heart palpitations began, which led to the most, or perhaps only, irrational thing she'd ever done. Sam went to the closet to grab outerwear. She then sat by the front door next to the intercom in her Burberry raincoat, so when the heart attack kicked in, she could call Jimmy to have him call 911, and she'd be ready to go when EMS got there.

Even though it wasn't cold in her apartment, she pulled her coat around her as she used to when she and The Man would use his family's season tickets to go to Giants games—sometimes when it was snowing out and below freezing.

What do I do now? Sam kept asking herself. There had been a plan. She would go to college then into business. Get married, have a happy home and children. *Once you make a plan, you don't deviate. What am I supposed to do now? Find someone else? Where? How?* The Man had been the only relationship she'd ever had.

Embarrassment began to set in. She had been so smug. So many women she knew didn't have relationships. Others changed guys the way Sam switched lipsticks. She may not have been married, but she had a committed relationship. Initiated by him. Fostered by him. Sam let him take the lead because it was all new to her. And he wasn't going anywhere. He told her so. She was the one. *What do I do now?* Then, she did what women so often do, taking the blame for the behavior of the men who've let them down: *How could I be so successful in my professional life yet such a failure in my personal one?*

After an hour of, once again, staring into space as her thoughts swirled like water going down a drain, and not having gone into cardiac arrest, Sam's need to move soared back up to Mach 5.

She packed up her rented dress post-haste so Katie could return it the next day and readied her engagement ring, which The Man was having picked up by messenger. In situations such as these, the bride gets to keep the ring, but it was a family heirloom, so in exchange, Samuel was going to give up his half of the apartment and pay off the mortgage from his trust fund.

She handed the ring box, now inside a manila envelope with The Man's name scrawled in black magic marker, to Jimmy without engaging in their usual exit-the-building pleasant banter and went for a walk; if one can call storming down York Avenue a walk, scowling at everyone she encountered—*these people and their goddamn dogs only a shade less annoying than the goddamn people with baby carriages, who are a cut above the couples who can't let go of each other's goddamn hands to let someone get by*—while tears streamed down her face.

When Sam got to around 68th Street, she once again felt as though she couldn't breathe and grabbed onto the side of a bus kiosk to steady herself because she feared she'd faint in the middle of the sidewalk. Just as the light was about to change, she darted across the street to New York Presbyterian Hospital and prayed she'd make it around the circular driveway to the emergency entrance. But once inside the ER, instead of heading to the desk and screaming, "Help me," she realized she was indeed breathing and just sat down. Simply being in proximity to medical professionals who could "save her," from what she wasn't exactly sure, had a soothing effect. So much so, that after about twenty minutes, Sam experienced something else that was new to her: feeling stupid. As she was about to slink out, the EMTs brought in on a stretcher a thirty-something brunette woman, who Sam believed to be her doppelgänger. The woman was crying out as well as thrashing about. Sam swore she heard one of the staff use the term "psych consult."

Sam couldn't tell if her resemblance to the incoming patient was real or imagined, but what she witnessed was very sobering. *That's how I'll end up if I don't get it together*, she thought, followed by, *I won't let him do that to me*, which she recited over and over again as she walked back up York and one block over to her building (and continued to do so during the following months until the phrase was inculcated in her mind.)

By the time she arrived home, Jimmy reported that her envelope had been picked up. As though he'd referred to something work-related, Sam responded, "Thanks for letting me know," and got in the awaiting elevator without missing a beat.

She entered her apartment, feeling numb and ready to move on to the next phase in the breakup process. As she did when she was about to make a business call, Sam poured herself a glass of water over ice and began to dial.

"Mother, the wedding's off."

There was no reason to soft-pedal it. The two women had never had a heart-to-heart in their lives, and Sam was not about to start now. She held the phone as far from her ear as her arm could stretch and let Evelyn carry on about how she "knew this would happen because no good comes from dating someone that long." There was a comment about "rich people not caring about anyone but themselves" and other things that Sam tuned out.

"I really don't want to talk about it. I'm just letting you know."

"Don't let it make you bitter, Samantha."

"I'll do my best. Goodbye, Mom." And she was onto the next.

"You mean I won't get to be a maid of honor?" whined Little Evie, sounding more twelve than twenty.

Yes, let's make this all about you.

"No, I'm afraid not this time."

Sam had to let her sister stand up for her, and Lena was fine with that. "The only things worse than marriages are weddings." But Sam told Little Evie that the job was hers on the condition there be no bridal shower or bachelorette party; the former because the couple needed nothing, and the latter because Sam didn't need one last hurrah, as she never hurrah-ed in the first place. Again, the bride-no-more explained that she didn't want to get into it.

"I'm sorry, Sammy."

"No need. Sometimes things just happen, and you move on."

The call to Lena was less stoic, but Sam would not let her emotions get the best of her. She was determined to stay strong, even in front of her best friend. Sam shared the multiple anxiety attacks but left out the parts about sitting with her coat on and going to the ER, both of which were too embarrassing to re-live. If she was going to get over that The Man—the one thing in life she considered a sure thing—was gone, she would have to not dwell on it.

This did not stop Lena though. "You know, I never liked him," began her tirade, and Sam let her friend continue saying all the things Sam felt but knew if she let loose, she'd lose her mind.

"We need to go out, like tonight, and find you a Mr. Right Now," the wing-woman concluded.

"No, if I'm going to get through this, it'll be my work that'll do it. 24/7."

"Having something else to focus on is great, but I really think you need to feel your feelings and . . ."

"I've been feeling them all day, and well, they feel pretty awful. I can't feel awful. I won't feel awful," Sam said as her voice began to break.

"Okay, let's take a cleansing breath. Four beats in . . ."

"No, I don't need to breathe," Sam countered, swallowing every ounce of emotion. "I need to work. From now on, I'm all business."

By saying it aloud, Sam made it so.

5

*D*inner with Lena on Friday evening was followed by up and at 'em on Saturday to get chores out of the way. Sam needed to go full steam ahead, preparing for her Monday morning meeting by speed-reading Hannah Randolph's manifesto about doing away with marriage entirely, so people could actually relax and enjoy the solo life and unpressured romantic relationships.

Before hunkering down with the page-turner, Sam found herself examining the cover for almost too long. The title spread across the top of the book jacket, with the author's name taking up the bottom real estate. Between this typeface sandwich was a closeup shot of the Anti-Wife. It reminded Sam of a magazine skincare ad. Hannah's translucent face dominated the page, and her cascading yellow hair made her appear absolutely beatific. But it was her eyes, sapphire blue and staring directly at the reader, that were the clinchers. Sam had never made such intense eye contact with a live person, let alone a two-dimensional one. So much so, she had to force herself to look away before she could open the book and begin to read.

As Sam suspected, the contents were the kind of rhetoric that could captivate a large audience of single women tired of dating men who didn't want to get married. The Anti-Wife herself saber-rattled all the usual stuff about not ever wanting to be tied down, being one's own person, and living on one's own terms, but she did it, remarkably, not in a man-distaining way; she loved men it seemed as well as sex. Hannah was only marriage-adverse.

The bestselling author/guru hated the institution, and not in the tongue-in-cheek way Lena did, but in a well-researched, "See, marriage was never really about love, blame it on Hallmark" way that Sam found sort of interesting—unrealistic, but interesting.

How, though, would or could she ever promote a show devoted to doing away with an ages-old ritual attached to a current billion-dollar industry?

No one loved a challenge more than Sam, so she'd just have to see what Barry Rogers had in mind.

Sam began her workweek by entering her office before the usual 9:00 a.m. start time to find Katie already at her desk.

The assistant's white Lily Pulitzer shift dress showed off beautifully her tan as well as her twenty-four-year-old sinewy arms and legs. Sam considered Katie a find, not only because she was smart and conscientious, but because her preppy subordinate reminded the executive of herself, socially, academically, and especially physically.

"I like your J.Crew suit," Sam had said as she nodded in approval two years ago to the recent NYU grad who sat before her for an interview.

"Thanks. How'd you know it was . . . ?"

"Kate, I am J.Crew."

And as Sam and her brunette mini-me with blue eyes laughed at their devotion to what would most likely include madras, seersucker, and Nantucket Red anything, a work marriage was born.

"Hey, good to have you back, especially bright and early. I'm meeting with—"

"Barry at Applause. I saw the calendar," said Katie, who had the instincts of "Donna" of the now defunct *Suits*; she always knew what Sam was going to say even before she said it.

"How was Bora Bo—?"

"I got engaged. Look."

Sam thought her eye was going to be poked out by the small yet tasteful diamond jutting from the rose-gold band that was a mere centimeter from her lashes.

Dear God, you too? she thought but said, "Oh my, how wonderful. Best wishes."

She then simultaneously pulled her head back and pushed Katie's hand away, pretending the gestures were only so she could get a better look.

"Here, now I can really see it. Lovely. And it's the perfect fit for your delicate hand. Wear it well."

In another time and place, an office manager would have arranged the obligatory cake-in-the-conference-room, and in order to appear the team player, Sam would have attended and listened to queries about honeymoon destinations, the dress silhouette, and bridal party headcount. Sam was never so glad her one-room office had no separate meeting area, and when it came to milestones, the tradition between her and her right hand was a simple, "Congrats," "Good for you," or "Happy birthday."

There was something a little disconcerting about finding out that someone younger was going to be further along in life, but even harder because Katie and her boyfriend, now fiancé, had been college sweethearts, same as Sam and Sam The Man. But she would survive hearing each day about the dress, the cake tastings, the band versus DJ conundrum et al. involved with Katie's special day because she could survive anything after going through Little Evie's engagement and shower with the ceremony chaser.

****

"If she were only taller, she could be a supermodel," was the de rigueur praise people used to offer about Evie.

Whereas Sam sported highborn features and smarts, Little Evie got the looks of a 1940s movie star: flowing, golden blonde hair a la Jean Harlow, complemented by big blue saucer eyes, and skin that sent a subliminal message to get a bowl of peaches and cream. Even in Sam's hand-me-downs, she had always looked like a just-unboxed doll. What she made up for in beauty, though, she lacked academically.

Besides doing her own school work, Sam tutored Evie because "you will not 'just pass,' not on my watch. You will get a good mark." But eventually, the elder sister realized "just pass" would be the gold standard.

As high school graduation approached, Sam thought her sister too immature for the working world, and Evie was as much college material as "Penny" on *The Big Bang Theory*. Sam researched trade schools for everything from catering to cosmetology, but Evie had no real interest in any kind of career.

She took a job as a receptionist at a medical office, then after two years, Dr. Joseph Barnett, MD, joined the practice. He was slightly older than Sam and fell in love with Evie on sight. Their romance was whirlwind, and before you could say, "The doctor will see you now," he was asking Sam, not Evelyn (at Little Evie's behest), for her hand. Sam gave her approval based on a Spokeo search and her gut.

Next thing, Little Evie was sporting a diamond as big as the pretend sparkler she'd worn the Halloween she donned a black wig to be Kim Kardashian for trick-or-treating.

"We're doing it right away," Little Evie said of her wedding. "And no, I'm not pregnant. We just can't wait to be married. And you'll be my maid of honor, right? I mean you'll be okay . . . ?"

If ever Sam needed to be okay, it was right then, even though her sister's big announcement happened on the heels of Sam's lowest moment.

"Of course, I'm going to stand up for you. If you asked anyone else, I would have to tie her up and shove her in a closet to take her place at the altar."

Little Evie bounced up and down on her toes, like a child spilling the details of her birthday party, as she shared her future plans as a Mrs.

"I'll still work at the practice," she told her older sister, "so me and Joe can be together all day."

"Joe and I," corrected Sam.

"Oh, right, Joe and I."

Evie still had that baby voice from the days when teen Sam would play Barbies with her. Evie also still had a little girl's vision of marriage—Cinderella and the prince living happily ever after.

The newly betrothed then added, trying to sound more adult, "Until I get pregnant, and then I'll stay home and take care of my babies."

Sam smiled and nodded, then hugged the younger woman while saying a silent prayer this would all work out for Evie as it had not for Sam or their mother.

She then chose to look on the bright side. Little Evie was someone else's charge now.

****

"You. Are. Kidding. Me. Right?" Lena barked at Sam, who was fingering her pearls like worry beads as she shared her sister's big news. "I know she's your sister, and you're her second mother, and blah, blah, blah, pull at everyone's heartstrings, but I want to kick this girl's ass. I know she's young, but how insensitive can she be? I suppose you're footing the bill for the shindig."

"All right. Calm down. It's not as bad as you think. First, they're not having a wedding-wedding."

Lena did a double-take.

"I know. Of all people who you'd think would want little birds to dress her like a Disney Princess and arrive at a castle-like church in a horse and carriage . . . but instead she wants—don't judge—to get married at City Hall in a white vintage suit, then go eat lunch at a diner, like—don't judge—Carrie and Big."

Even though *Sex and the City* had ended years ago, thanks to its prominent place in pop culture and reruns galore and cable's never-ending programming of the two movie versions, new generations of women were still following the escapades of the four friends with Manhattan as the fifth character.

"And Joe is picking up the tab for everything," Sam assured her protective friend.

"Fine, I won't kick Evie's ass, and I'm glad you only have to deal with a meal and not a four-hour reception, but they couldn't have waited until your breakup wasn't so raw?"

"You know, I can't say the same thing hadn't crossed my mind, and I know you don't believe this, but it's for the best. Now with Evie having a husband to take care of, and my mother still working and still able to take care of herself, I am finally free to live my life. Not as I had originally planned, of course, but to live it just the same."

Lena nodded and smiled in agreement.

"Before you exhale," said Sam sheepishly, "I'm throwing the shower."

"You're killing me."

****

At the bridal shower, pulled together with the momentum of a shot-gun wedding, no one dared make one of those passive-aggressive, "You must be happy for Evie, yet sad that your younger sister is getting married before you, especially since you were left, not quite at the altar, but close enough" comments.

First of all, no matter how refined, accomplished, and Upper East Side Sam had become, everybody knew she was still a Bronx girl on the inside. There's something about growing up in the "outta" boroughs that gives people a tough-as-nails quality that comes through even when they're not even trying. No one would start with Sam if they knew what was good for them.

Since Sam was unattached, her only request of the bride was that she be able to bring Lena as her plus-one. It was the least her sister could do, and of course, Little Evie agreed.

At the luncheon, after the short ceremony, Lena leaned over to Sam and said, *Sex and the City*, huh? So, if she's Carrie, who does that make you?"

"Charlotte. During her hiatus between Trey and Harry."

6

As Sam sat in the palatial receiving area at Applause awaiting her meeting with *the* Barry Rogers, she smiled to herself and decided that devoting herself to ramping up her business had really paid off.

She'd been thinking of late, though, that it was probably time to get back into the game. There would be, however, no Match or swiping right or going out to bars. And definitely no Tinder. She would only meet someone who was introduced to her by someone she knew. References were how she had the most success in business, and so that would be the technique she'd use socially.

Her cyber footprint included LinkedIn, of course, and had Facebook and Twitter accounts for professional purposes, which Katie handled. As a rather private person, however, she never had the inclination to blast her personal life over the internet. Besides, Sam the Man, who was more of a showoff than her, had posted, often under her protest, enough of their goings-on for the both of them. Perhaps she'd have to reconsider her social media position but that would be for another day and her always-growing to-do list.

****

Sam's meeting with Barry couldn't have gone better. The 50ish silver fox who made up for his humble Lower East Side beginnings by dressing in

Turnbull & Asser, with many of his pieces bespoke, was impressed with her credentials and couldn't wait for her to start steering the marketing ship of the Anti-Wife's reality show.

"I'm flattered, but my understanding is that your in-house marketing department is strong."

"Don't get me wrong. My team is top-notch but busy promo-ing all our other fabulous shows. Plus, 'reality' is virgin territory for us, and we all agreed fresh eyes would serve us best."

His answer hadn't made sense to Sam since she had no more experience in that arena than his staff, but hey, he wanted her, and it was a high-profile, if not lucrative, gig.

On his end, Rogers believed he had responded truthfully, even though he failed to mention that all his people had met the abrasive ("It's my show, done my way or the highway") author, whose loud mouth had the disruptive power of a jackhammer, and those in a high enough position to do so, either politely declined the assignment or vehemently refused to work with her in the "I'll quit if I have too" vein.

The Anti-Wife herself had had more give-me, where's-mine, I-want de-mands than any bridezilla, which Barry had promised to accommodate. Since her book became a runaway bestseller, Hannah's people had fielded offers for her to do a network talk show, a Netflix sitcom based on her book, as well as an AppleTV+ hour-long drama. Her vision, though, was a combination of Anti-Wife rally speeches, where she preached her mar-riage-is-a-dinosaur concept to the converted, and footage of her living her most fabulous unmarried life. "Living by example" was how she described it to those who already had a toe-hold in reality TV, but they gave her pushback. "We have a formula that works," she was told, and well, she told them where they could stick their formula.

Hannah chose Barry's network because, as she was quoted in the press release, "They're letting me be my most authentic self," aka do whatever she wanted.

Half the footage was already shot, and the rest would be filmed at her upcoming Ben Hur cast of thousands, crowd-pleasing lecture, and camer-as had already begun following her summer fun in the Hamptons.

The first question out of Barry's mouth to Sam was, "So, you read the book?"

Sam drew out the answer for emphasis: "Ab-so-lute-ly."

Although this was true, she was self-conscious about her tone, up-talking and smiling a very toothy smile because she knew she'd have to finesse her answer to what Sam was sure would be the follow-up question.

"And? What'dja think?"

This was the maddening part for her, having two conversations at the same time. The voice in her head was saying "unrealistic," while from her lips came words like "the most modern take on relationships."

"I couldn't agree more," said Barry to Sam's well-rehearsed assessment of what he was sure would be his latest windfall venture. So in love with Hannah's controversial shtick and the dough the company would potentially rake in from it, Barry picked up the book and began reading the flap copy. Sam got the impression this was something he did frequently during the day; like an opioid addict who keeps popping pills, she envisioned Barry speaking the tome's description to get high off the success of the future TV version.

"Marriage is dead," he read aloud, starting out in a monotone and building to a dramatic crescendo. "In fact, it's an institution that should have never seen the light of day. A construct to keep women low on the totem pole, marriage never had anything to do with hearts or flowers. It was bartering daughters for pigs, land, or cash. In more civilized times, it became about showing up friends and frenemies; who could throw more money at the wedding industry for an expensive dress only to be worn once, a giant party most people don't even want to attend, burdening loved ones to buy you gifts and secretly resenting it, then having to apologize to everyone, especially your parents who paid for the fête, when the marriage goes kaput. There's only one reason to get married: social pressure.

"They call it 'tying the knot' for a reason: it resembles a noose. Be independent. Take care of yourself financially and emotionally. Then when you are with someone, it'll be because you want to be, not need to be. With your untethered life, you can walk away anytime."

Then, like an actor who had diligently memorized his lines and was self-assured enough to go off-book, Rogers looked up from the inside cover and recited the last bit while looking Sam directly in the eye: "On the flip side, if your 'love' leaves you, it isn't high and dry. You have already cultivated your own life, which you will keep living."

He then closed his eyes as though he were having a religious experience. Actually, Barry's ear-to-ear grin was due to his envisioning a high dive into the pile of money he would undoubtedly soon garner.

Even though Sam could relate to that last part of the jacket copy, she just couldn't buy into the Anti-Wife philosophy, but she'd have to start pretending.

"Well, if that's not the new mantra for the modern woman, I don't know what is."

"That's it," said Barry as he slapped the desk with what had become his bible. "Now you have to take this job because you've just given me the show's tagline. Ads. Billboards. Everywhere. *'The Anti-Wife*. The new mantra for the modern woman.'"

"The modern woman's new mantra." It's shorter and quicker.

"You. Are. So. Hired."

7

*T*here is not enough money in the world to make dealing with some people worth the effort.

That was Sam's initial impression of Hannah Randolph, and it came to her five minutes into their FaceTime conversation.

She, however, was going to make every attempt to forge a relationship, with her first line of attack being a bonding sesh over their mutual colleague.

"So, I actually went to Columbia with Amy."

"Who?"

"Your editor, Amy."

"Oh, her," said Hannah as she flipped back her bouncy curl blowout. "She bit the dust long ago. I couldn't stand her. I mean, she acted like she was the one who wrote the damn book. I told the publisher it was her or me."

There was no love lost between Sam and her one-time classmate, but she was extremely put off by how cavalier Hannah sounded about taking another person's job away, especially since, if she recalled correctly, Amy had been the one who got her published in the first place.

Sam attempted to get out of her mind the mental image of Hannah racing through the publisher's halls like the Queen of Hearts in *Alice's Adven-*

tures in Wonderland, shouting, "Off with her head."

Now that her go-to strategy had bitten the dust, Sam switched gears and focused on explaining how important it was for her to meet with Hannah, feel her out, and get a firsthand impression of her before designing the marketing program for *The Anti-Wife* show.

Hannah, as Sam was quickly finding out, always had another idea from what was being presented to her, and it didn't even matter from whom the idea was being generated. No matter what anyone came up with about anything, even choosing a shade of lipstick, Hannah's next sentence would begin, "Yeah, but what if . . . ?"

The budding reality star had already flat out vetoed Barry's suggestion for a sit-down in the Applause conference room with Sam and the team, where they would watch and dissect the current show footage while eating a catered lunch.

Sam's first assignment for this project was to turn that "no" into a "yes," but was unprepared for what Hannah's "yes" would entail.

"I don't want a meeting with the team. I want you—doing a deep dive into my day-to-day."

Sam would be required to shadow her, the reasoning being that only then would the marketing consultant be able to understand the guru, her credo, and the Anti-Wife movement.

Sam translated "shadow" in a wishful-thinking way, meaning "spend a little time," and tried to negotiate a few dinners peppered with *SATC* girl talk-cum-talking points that could translate into ad copy, but the Anti-Wife again was having none of it.

"So, starting Monday, you'll stay at my house in East Hampton for a couple of weeks."

"Ex-excuse . . . I mean, what a generous offer, but—"

"No buts. I host these dinners with a different bunch of friends; each group is an eclectic mix—actors, models, politicians, business people, artists, writers. I invited my mail carrier once and had one of the cater-waiters join in another time. We talk about the movement and the reality of marriage as opposed to the fantasy most people have. Everybody agrees that marriage adds an unnecessary burden to life. I love getting feedback from everywhere and everyone."

Sam thanked Hannah Randolph for the chance to learn her business in-depth, then asked if she could call back to confirm.

Seconds later, Sam turned into a whirling dervish screaming for Katie to "get Rogers on the phone," her sense of urgency usually reserved for a 911 emergency.

"Sounds fun," Barry said nonchalantly upon hearing of the invite. "You, though, sound upset. Don't you like the Hamptons? Don't you like Hannah? Don't you want this job? We already signed a contract."

In lieu of a paper bag, Sam breathed into her cupped hand while Katie laid a cup of ice water in front of her using her left hand and momentarily blinded Sam as the sunlight reflected off her diamond ring.

When the entrepreneur took the assignment, she had no idea how all-consuming it would be and feared that what was turning out to be a glorified babysitting job would cut into and perhaps jeopardize the work she needed to do for her other clients.

"Of course. I guess I was just taken aback. She's a bit much."

"No, she's too much. And that's why Hannah Randolph will make great TV; that's why everyone who works on this potentially rewarding project will placate her."

The exaggerated way he said "everyone" made it clear that Sam would need to pack her bags for the East End. And as Katie noted: "Buckle up."

8

*H*annah was a pretty, sunny blonde with a toned size-four body. She had a natural, no-makeup makeup, Southern California look she modeled after Jennifer Aniston's, and wore exclusively Tory Burch to come off boho casual yet polished.

Everything about her was a far cry from her humble beginnings.

Hannah Marie Randolph was born a brunette in South Philadelphia to a gracious homemaker mother and a good-natured lug of a dad, a Mr. Fix-it who embarrassed the family, or at least Hannah, by keeping all his half-completed projects all over the front lawn, driveway, and backyard. "Everywhere you looked, there were parts," she would say in interviews when asked about her upbringing.

Where other families on the block had hedges, bushes, and trees, the Randolph's landscaping consisted of desperate-to-be-mended furniture, broken washing machines, dishwashers, and other disassembled appliances.

She had one older brother and was the youngest of five sisters, the older four all beauties, accomplished in academics as well as athletics. "College material, unlike you," her father would remind her every time she stumbled in past curfew.

In high school, Hannah partied hard on school nights, more so than some people did on weekends. Whereas her sisters had met their future husbands in either secondary school or university, Hannah was always being broken up with. "Demanding," "bitchy," "you've got such a 'tude" were just a few of the go-to adjectives the guys would use as their exit excuses.

"You're not the boss of me" was a phrase she learned when she was three, and it had become her catch-phrase way into adulthood.

Unlike other girls in her crowd growing up, she never planned her yet-to-come wedding, designing bridesmaids' dresses in her mind. Hannah stopped believing in the Disney Princess future before it even started, thanks to her parents. Theirs was her example of marriage: grade-school sweethearts, who, when not arguing, lived separate lives. If their relationship discouraged Hannah, her sisters' unions bored her; their existences with husbands, kids, and carpools struck her as nothing shy of a snooze. (She believed in her heart, they thought so as well.) Even her brother, whom she described as "the most easygoing guy on the planet," was divorced.

Hannah made up her mind even before she graduated from high school that she would never get married. She didn't understand it. Marriage guaranteed nothing; not loyalty, not everlasting love, not support—emotional or financial, nothing.

And she liked sex and was not ashamed to admit it. Hannah heard from many sources, even her sisters, that after a while, that part disappeared from marriage. That alone was enough for her to say, "I don't."

Of course, when her father agreed with her and called her "not the marryin' kind," it was her innate need to do the opposite of whatever he said and prove him wrong at every turn that caused her to wonder if maybe she could be. So, with a fervor she never gave her schoolwork, Hannah started researching marriage, its origins, and how it developed over the centuries. Afterward, for the first and last time in her life, she had to concur with her dad. She indeed was not the type to marry, so she stuck with her original plan and said, "Pass," not that anyone was asking, just to the general concept.

Hannah then decided that the institution was not only not for her, but for no one; she shared (read: commandeered every conversation with) her philosophy—first, with friends and acquaintances, then professionally, taking up stand-up comedy and branding herself the "Anti-Wife."

Club patrons wanted to laugh, not be preached to, so Hannah started offering herself gratis to groups who needed a serious yet entertaining speaker.

This, of course, required a more grown-up look than the jeans and rock 'n' roll t-shirts she'd worn on stage at the comedy clubs where she first professed her POV on being un-wed. Thumbing through one of her sister's fashion magazines while babysitting, Hannah saw a picture of Tory Burch and decided, "That's how I want to look."

As her birthday was nearing, Hannah bought a box of Clairol Nice'n Easy Ultra Light Blond and put the word out to her sibs, parents, and pals that she didn't care if gifts of "Tory anything" were procured on sale, came from Century21 or even Goodwill, that's what she wanted. No substitutes accepted.

Repackaging herself as well as switching her Anti-Wife message from humorous routine to life-choice crusade for which she began charging served Hannah well. A book agent who caught one of her talks encouraged her to "write this down." And she did.

Because in the world of celebrity reason and logic have never reigned supreme, Hannah, the overbearing, attention-seeking, know-it-all, then-twenty-four-year-old had a newly minted book deal and more disciples than Jesus.

****

Sam had worked weekends and holidays for clients. She had sat through excruciating lunches and dinners to serve their needs; attended meetings that could only be described as a long day's journey; traveled, literally, to the ends of the earth to tour their facilities to see how the sausages were made; and was given an office at companies, so they could get even more work out of her. Never, however, had she ever had to move in with one until Hannah Randolph demanded Sam do "a deep dive into all things Anti-Wife."

9

S am stepped off the Hampton Ambassador—the first-class version of the Jitney—onto the East Hampton sidewalk and got an unexpected pang for days gone by.

Long Island's East End was where she and Sam the Man spent many a summer weekend, except farther out—in fact, at the farthest point, in the more rustic fishing village of Montauk.

As the bus pulled away, Sam whispered into the air, "Siri, kill me. Kill me, now," as though the virtual assistant was omnipresent and could accomplish the task which would put her out of her misery. She nodded at who had to be Hannah's chauffeur because he was standing by a black Mercedes and holding a sign with her name on it. The thirty-something man with the physique of a bodybuilder and the face of a '50s matinee idol approached and took her bags.

"Hello, Miss Dennehy. I'm Carl." His passenger was taken aback, as his voice did not match his appearance. Carl sounded a touch like a punch-drunk boxer.

Sam knew there were people who would give a spray-tanned leg to be limo-ed around this rich person's warm weather playground for a two-week stay in what she knew to be a mansion on the ocean, yet she couldn't help but feel that this was a pretty big ask even for heavy hitters like Hannah and Barry. In the end, *The Anti-Wife* was just a TV show, and like all of the most popular ones, if it was good, viewers would find it and come back for more, regardless of what the ads did or didn't promise.

Carl had a just-doin'-my-job demeanor and only spoke when spoken to. This served Sam well. A natural introvert, she welcomed the silence. Given what she had already experienced with Hannah, Sam figured this was the last bit of quiet she'd know for the next fourteen days and wanted it to last.

"She . . . lives . . . here?" Sam asked, to which Carl just chuckled.

Sam went from not wanting to talk to physically struggling to blurt out that sentence as they rolled up the driveway. She had seen the spread in an article about Hannah in *The New York Times Magazine*, but nothing prepared her for the real-life version that conjured the word "extra." If God was going to live on earth, he'd live here.

The *Times* had called the estate Chez Randolph and wrote that the ten-thousand-square-foot home began at the top of two flights of steps resembling the famed ones in front of The Metropolitan Museum of Art, which led to a fire-engine-red front door.

The description pointed out a large living room with a stone fireplace, formal dining room, media room, a study, and gourmet eat-in kitchen. The place had seven bedrooms, all with French doors that opened onto terraces and nine and a half baths; the bedroom on the first floor had been turned into Hannah's office, the second-floor master was hers naturally and boasted a fireplace. In addition, there was a separate four-car garage, guesthouse, pool with spa, and a gas fire pit on the patio.

Too big for its lone twenty-seven-year-old owner? For sure. But Sam's understanding from Katie's research was that Hannah was rarely without an entourage, so the house almost seemed too small to accommodate the intimidating fortress of friends that was said to swirl around her.

Sam's time in East Hampton, it seemed, would be spent not only with Hannah but Hannah & Co. The hot author-cum-reality star was not just anti being a wife; she had developed a rep as being pro-woman to a maniacal degree, surrounding herself with those as powerful she, as well as what she called "STRAYS"—She Tried Relentlessly And Yet Struggled. These were women whom Hannah read or heard about on the news and was touched by their the-struggle-is-real tribulations, undoubtedly at the hands of some man who had abused them personally or professionally, and no matter how hard they tried, they just couldn't get back on their feet.

Their new guru would take them on a vacation, pep talk them, find them a job through her many varied connections, or offer seed money to help them get a business venture off the ground. Hannah wanted her gender to not only have a rightful place in the world but rule it. All for the purpose of not needing a man to save them via marriage, you know, before she had a chance to abolish it.

Carl brought Sam up the front steps and into the house where he handed her off to the housekeeper, Inez, a diminutive fifty-ish woman who seemed to make a point of holding her head high; carrying herself with such dignity, the gray and white uniform Hannah had her wear came off as couture.

Inez took Sam's bags and asked if her employer's guest wanted to see her room. Before Sam could answer, Hannah's assistant, Allison, white-knuckling an iPad like a mother clutching her child's hand in a crowd, appeared as if by magic and eclipsed her co-worker.

The twenty-something had the body of a fashion model, her rather plain face camouflaged by makeup and more contouring than a Kardashian. Sam couldn't figure out how it all didn't melt off in the summer sun.

She had to admit though, Allison knew how to make herself look attractive with her professional-casual meets beachy-chic wardrobe, and honey blonde highlights that danced on her meticulous blowout when the sun streamed through the foyer's skylight.

The super friendly, fast-talking drinker of the Anti-Wife Kool-Aid and liaison between Hannah and the world greeted Sam with a kung-fu grip and a soupçon of importance. She began the first-floor guided tour before Sam could say, "Pleasure to meet you, too."

"So, let me give you the lay of the land," said Allison, which commenced with her own place in it. "I'm a local girl, born and raised in East Hampton. My parents are in real estate and actually sold this house to Hannah. When I graduated from Farmingdale two years ago, I went into the family business and hated it until I worked on Hannah's deal. Meeting her was a dream of a lifetime. When I heard her mention to my mom that she was looking for a new assistant who'd live in and be on call 24/7, well, how could I not jump on it? As well as being her executive assistant, I'm also the director of social media for Anti-Wife, Inc. and in charge of monitoring e-commerce, as well as the content director for the website." Then she took a beat for a humble brag: "I know my job is cray, I can't believe I haven't gone insane."

"It's quite a lot to stay on top of."

"Actually, everything is farmed out, but I oversee and facilitate. Of course, Hannah has the last word on everything."

"Of course; now, about the website. I searched for it but couldn't find—"

"It's a subscription. You pay three hundred a year, and after you're vetted, we send you a link and the passcode to get on, then you can benefit from Hannah's wisdom that even the people who go to the rallies aren't privy to. Business is booming, but still, tell a friend. Well, enough about that. Let me show you around."

Allison's delivery wasn't the only thing that was faster than a speeding bullet. Sam had to run to catch up as her tour guide bounced like a pinball from the grand entrance hall with an imperial staircase to the living room that could double as a ballroom into the walls-o'-books library, which also housed a rather grand Steinway.

"Does Hannah . . .?"

"No," Allison jumped in. "Hannah doesn't play, and she also doesn't have time to read."

Sam surmised she wasn't the first to ask. Because Allison didn't want her boss labeled a poser who wasn't a musician or intellectual, yet wanted to give the impression she was, the loyal sidekick added, "Hannah isn't trying to show off eruditions she doesn't have. The room is set up for guests to entertain themselves if the weather's inclement or they've just had too much fun in the sun."

As they left the library for a spin around the dining room with a never-ending rectangular table that seated twenty comfortably, Sam snuck a text to Katie: *Ur Donna on Suits title stripped—HR's asst makes u look dim LOL can u say OFFICIOUS?*

There was a detour into the media room replete with giant TV and rows of recliners for the full movie theater effect. The last stop was a chef's kitchen that rivaled some restaurants, with double doors that led out to a sprawling backyard with a view of Block Island Sound beyond the Olympic-size pool.

And there they were. Hannah and her mixed bag of devotees jumping from the roof into the pool with the reckless abandon of drunk frat boys, chugging rosé from the bottle, which Sam assumed would continue "all day," and many could be overheard reciting Hannah's anti-marriage bombast like cult members, one knee pad away from genuflecting at the mention of the Anti-Wife.

Sam flashed back to Hannah's shelves of bestsellers and classics alike, wondering who in this bunch ever accepted the invite for some reading-is-fundamental entertainment, then she envisioned a cloud of dust emitting if any of the book spines were ever cracked.

She began texting both Katie and Lena: *died n went 2 Hannah hell—looks like the spring break I gratefully never went on.*

Just as her iPhone started to ping with their responses, Hannah's head popped out of the water and she yelled, "Hey, Sam," which sounded more like a taunt than a greeting. Then to the DJ: "Hey, cut the music." Then to the crowd: "Hey, everyone, this is Sam, the marketing genius in charge of promoting my show." Who knew the word "genius" could sound like a dig?

The entire backyard shouted, "Hi Sam," then laughed in unison.

Sam had never felt so mocked. Like the new kid in fifth grade standing in front of the room full of smirking cliques while being introduced by the teacher, the usually confident exec wanted to find her seat and die.

10

*H*annah climbed out of the pool topless but did Sam the courtesy of wrapping a plush bath-size towel around herself before she approached.

"Welcome," said the immodest host as she sized up her latest guest. "You're wearing a suit. This is the Hamptons, gurrl. Loosen. Up."

"Well, I am here on business, so that's what I dressed for." Then, looking around, she continued, "But I see—"

"You brought other stuff, right? Like beach clothes?" Hannah cut off her guest because she really never had time to entertain anything anyone besides herself had to say.

"Of course. In fact, why don't I excuse myself and go change." Any reason to remove herself from this pseudo-orgy.

Hannah screamed out, "Inez, show Sam to her room."

As everyone did when Hannah barked, Inez appeared and obeyed.

Within minutes, Sam found herself upstairs in a spacious bedroom decorated all in white, right down to the bleached wood floor. She immediately kicked off her heels in fear of getting dirty the purity beneath her feet. Through the French doors that opened to a small terrace overlooking the ocean, a light breeze floated in and made the floor-length sheer curtains billow. Suddenly the poolside raucousness below and around the bend was forgotten.

As she switched outfits, Sam couldn't help but admire how un-hospital room this colorless space seemed. "Maybe I'll do this to my bedroom," she thought aloud, then considered buying *Architectural Digest* and the like to get ideas before deciding to copy the taste of her celebrity host.

Sam's life had changed abruptly so many, many months ago, yet she allowed her environment to stay the same. Perhaps she should start to bedeck her home to reflect her taste alone and rid all influences of Sam the Man, no matter how nice they were.

She took a look at herself in white capris, black Jack Rogers sandals, and a pink and white striped Vineyard Vines button-down shirt left unbuttoned to expose her pink bandeau bathing suit top by Solid & Striped. She was still overdressed by the standards of what she saw around Hannah's pool, but Sam felt the need to be modest because she was there for work, as she had reminded the Anti-Wife.

Before heading back down, Sam wanted to call and check-in with the office, but Katie reached out first.

"You read my mind, as usual," said Sam, then went right into a rundown of other clients and what she wanted emailed, FedEx-ed, and handled. The overachieving exec, of course, brought work with her, as she had assumed that Hannah kept business hours, and when her host was taking care of what did not involve Sam, Sam would take care of the rest of her workload. And then there were the evenings when the houseguest figured she'd be off duty.

"Okay, now that all that's out of the way, dish," said Katie.

"It's that frat flick *Neighbors*, except Zac Efron's part is played by a woman."

"I heard she's badass. I mean clearly, I'm not down with her philosophy but . . ." said the almost-wife.

Sam could not contain herself: "Well, I can't attest to how 'bad' she is, but at first blush, 'ass' could describe her, but another part of her anatomy would be more accurate. She came over to introduce herself to me half-naked. Who does that? Granted, by the time we were face to face, she'd covered up, but the sheer inappropriateness. Seriously. I'm not her friend. I'm a business associate."

"The Anti-Wife sounds like the anti-Sam. So, what are the other guests like?"

"It's such a cast of characters, and there are just so many of them. I saw some famous faces; no one really famous, more like 'Oh, wasn't she on an episode of *Blue Bloods*?' There are some standouts, like a drag queen or two, but the general vibe is average with a twist of purposely kooky for the sake of it. I hope they all go home after dinner."

"I read in *People* . . ." began Katie, but Sam's attention was stolen away by a rock that came through the open French doors and landed in the middle of the room.

"Hold on."

She walked tentatively toward the terrace to investigate and saw a smiling, again half-naked Hannah surrounded by a few laughing friends.

"What's taking so long, gurrl? Get down here. Join the party."

"Oh, dear God," Sam said under her breath as she smiled and waved. "On my way."

Then she backed into the room, where her face, head, and shoulders dropped in unison as she exhaled so profoundly, she wasn't sure if it was her wind or that which was coming off the ocean making the curtains flutter.

"I've got to go." She rolled her eyes as she added, "The client wants me."

"I heard. Bye, gurrl."

Sam just hung up but laughed to herself, at first at Katie and then at the absurdity of what was sure to be the next fortnight.

Back once again amongst the partiers, Sam noticed the fabric on the lounge chairs and cushions of the seating around the tables was identical to the white with green leaves pattern at The Beverly Hills Hotel. This was in contrast to the black and white stripes chosen for the chaise lounges that surrounded the pool. The cushions on the straight-back chairs and umbrellas that sat in the middle of the poolside tables were that color combination as well. It didn't match, but somehow it went together well.

Because the patio was covered by an awning, which also donned the BHH pattern, Sam chose to stay there and used the excuse that she wasn't a sun worshipper. It was her way of joining in without actually doing so.

"Okay," said Hannah, once again covering herself for Sam's sake, "what can we get you to drink?"

"Cranberry and club soda with lime, thanks."

"You don't want a drink-drink? I mean, I heard your 'I'm here on business' rap, but . . ."

"I don't drink alcohol."

"Ever?"

"Ever."

"Are you . . .?"

Ah, the proverbial question. "No. I'm not on the wagon. I just never acquired a taste."

Hannah looked at Sam as though she'd just announced that she didn't breathe air. "I thought all you sorority girl types..."

"Nope. I was never one of those either."

The hostess shrugged, signaled for the waiter, and said, "To each her own."

Hannah gave the now-hovering server Sam's order, then gave him the international gesture for a refill: rattling the ice in her empty scotch glass at him.

While they waited for their beverages, Sam took the opportunity to at least try and pin down Hannah about the assignment.

"So, when do you think we can sit down and discuss . . . ?"

"We are sitting down."

Oh good, we're going to play the smart-aleck game. I already have a little sister, sweetie.

"We are, but we're surrounded by lots of people at, what I must say, is quite the bash. What I mean though is sit down in a setting more conducive to discussing . . ."

And then Sam spied the cameras.

"Are we . . . am I being filmed?"

"Oh, yeah, I forgot. They show up whenever so they can have footage of my fun single life. You have to sign some waiver for Applause. I'll have Allison—"

"No. I'm not part of the show. I will not be seen on camera."

There was only so much she would do to mollify this woman. Living in this adult day camp was already enough.

Hannah was used to getting her way but secretly enjoyed it when someone dared to push back. There was nothing more satisfying than the challenge of getting that person to bend finally to her will. But, there was something about Sam. Hannah could tell, if pushed too hard, the ad exec would have no qualms about walking away.

"No problema. I'll tell Allison to tell the crew not to film you, and if you should show up in a scene, they're to blur you or whatever they do."

Before Sam could declare victory and thank her client for understanding, Hannah screamed, "I can't believe it," with the incredulousness of someone being offered the contents of a Brinks truck and jumped up, letting her towel fall to the white, hexagon patio tiles.

"I made it," said the guest, who was swinging a bottle of Prosecco over her head like a lasso.

"It's a model with a bottle," acknowledged Hannah, arms now outstretched.

"No, two bottles," said the Hadid wannabe, as she then whipped out a spare from behind her back to present both to her host. "One for each of us."

Sam was not sure which Hannah was more excited to see, the woman with the *Vogue*-cover face or the booze. Either way, the Anti-Wife took a moment to turn back to Sam with the reminder: "You're here for two weeks. There'll be plenty of time to work. Relax, gurrl. Enjoy."

Sam did not know how long she could deal with being called the elongated version of "girl," but after a few hours of observing Hannah interacting with the other partygoers, she realized that the Anti-Wife referred to everyone that way, even the guys. Perhaps, decided Sam, it was easier than having to learn people's names.

By the time night fell, the tiki lamps were lit, and the DJ had cranked up the tunes for the musical enjoyment of everyone on all of Eastern Long Island and perhaps the borough of Queens. It became clear that the festivities were not going to end anytime soon, and from the canon-balls-in-the-pool contest initiated by the home's owner, maybe never.

After Hannah abandoned her for the two-fisted catwalker, Sam sat for a while, texting Lena about the antics and updating Katie, until Katie texted, *join the party gurrl —dive. I know u want 1-on-1 with HR, but who knows what u'll find out from the masses?*

Katie was right and wasn't telling her superior anything she didn't know. But this was not Sam's scene or how she normally did business, and she had been taking this passive/aggressive approach to let Hannah know it. *Grow up, Dennehy. Show Hannah you're interested in her movement, and if deep diving means an impromptu focus group with these out-of-control adults living their second childhoods, then so be it.*

"So, how did you meet Hannah?" "Are you here for the barbeque, or are you actually part of the movement?" "Hannah wants marriage done away with. Do you really think that's plausible?" Sam's conversation starters had the potential to reap valuable information if they had not fallen on the ears of people who had been literally swimming in vodka since a pool game they were playing required losers to have a bottle of Stoli poured over their heads.

In response to her queries, Sam listened to slurred jokes that had no punchlines and stories that seemed to have no conclusions. And although everyone had nothing but good things to say about Hannah and proclaimed to be pro her Anti-Wife philosophy, no one was in any shape to discuss it intelligently. Sam's patience well only went so deep before burnout set in.

Since everyone, especially Hannah, was concerned only with his or her own good time, it was easy enough for Sam to slip upstairs to her room. Even though there was no escaping the thumping of the DJ's tracks, the crashing of the waves was what she chose to hear. She didn't even bother to turn down the luxuriously fluffy comforter. Sam just fell onto the queen-size bed and went to sleep in her clothes.

11

"She's where?" Sam demanded.

The reluctant boarder could feel her ire in her toes, then like ivy crawling on a neo-Georgian building, it made its way up her legs, then torso, and settled in her temples, which began to pulsate.

Sam managed to contain herself and realized that although Allison was an assistant, she was not Sam's assistant, so the executive cleared her throat and rephrased her question in a less strident, more professional way.

"I apologize, Allison. Now, you said Hannah is in Manhattan at a meeting with Barry Rogers and left me here?"

Allison stared sheepishly at her ever-present iPad as Sam questioned her. She, though, was used to dealing with people whose tolerance was worn thin by Hannah's behavior and had a lyrical way of talking them down by treating her boss's I-do-what-I-want-when-I-want conduct matter-of-factly.

"Yes, what you just said is correct, but please allow me to clarify. Part of Hannah's success is based on the fact that she really does operate on her own terms. For example, she never went to sleep last night. She partied till 5:00 a.m., then took a super-hot shower followed by a deep tissue massage, had her hair blown out, dressed, and got in the car by 8:30, where she went right to sleep. Carl will wake her up right before they go through the Midtown Tunnel so she can have her face done by her hair/makeup person, Greg, who's doing a ride-along. By the time Hannah reaches the Applause offices for her lunch meeting, she should be wide-awake and refreshed. And that's pretty much how she rolls."

Allison wrapped up her soliloquy with a shrug and a dinner invite.

Sam's mouth hung open in amazement as Allison spoke, then shook her head slightly to awaken herself from her stupor.

"But I mean, shouldn't I be in that meeting? I should call Barry now to tell him to FaceTime me when . . ."

"Um, yeah, no. If Hannah wanted you there, you'd be there."

"She never even mentioned it or the fact that I'd be here without her. I'm going to have to demand her schedule for the next two weeks so I know what's what."

Allison smiled and nodded as though she were pacifying a demanding child and pivoted.

"Anywho, while the cat's away, this mouse can't play. I've got lots to do, so I will be in Hannah's office getting it done. Oh, did I give you my cell number? Here, let me."

She took Sam's phone right out of her hand and added her info to Sam's contact list.

"Add Hannah's too, if you would, please."

"Again, if Hannah wants you to have her private number, she'll give it to you. Until then, please go through me."

Allison handed the cell back and, before zipping away, offered, "Buzz me if you need anything. And FYI: some of last night's guests are still passed out by the pool. So, you might want to lay on the beach."

"Thank you. I'll take that under advisement," seethed Sam to Allison's quickly disappearing back.

Sam headed into the kitchen with all its top-of-the-line appliances and marble-topped center island, her scowl still intact. She didn't even care that there seemed to be nothing to eat for breakfast since finding out that she would be wasting another day not being able to get into Hannah's head about her book, show, or philosophy made her lose her appetite. She did help herself to one of the Keurig cups on the multi-tiered carousel, figuring since Hannah prided herself on being the hostess with the mostest, nobody would mind that she was taking liberties with the coffee.

When Inez walked in, Sam felt suddenly a little self-conscious, but the housekeeper was nonplussed. She was used to non-residents making themselves at home in her employer's domain.

"Would you like me to ask Chef Kenny to make you something to eat?"

Sam grounded herself before answering. Although she had distanced herself successfully from her Bronx roots, she never forgot where she came from. Back in her outer borough, Inez could very well have been her neighbor as well as the mother of a classmate. She knew that for the duration of her stay, she'd probably speak to the housekeeper with more respect than perhaps she would even bestow upon the lady of the house herself.

"Thank you for offering Inez, but I'm good with this," she replied, indicating the mug from which she was about to drink.

"Next time you want coffee, tell me. I'll make it for you fresh. Those cup things . . ."

Her sentence trailed off as Inez shook her head and waved her hand as though she were shoo-ing away a fly.

She then said that at around 1:00 or 1:30, she would be more than happy to bring Sam a crab salad sandwich and large bottled water.

"Where will you be staying?"

Without thinking twice, the visitor resigned, "My room."

Sam entered the space reserved for her and gave the door an ever-so-gentle slam, not enough to call attention, just hard enough to let out some of her frustrations. Yes, she was angry that Hannah was in the city at a meeting in which Sam believed she should have been included, but more than that, Sam was irritated because she felt like she was being played.

The usually early riser had awoken from one of the most beautiful, peaceful slumbers she had known since her breakup; sea air filled her lungs, and the sunlight streamed through the open terrace doors, giving the room a slightly yellow hue, making her question for a moment whether she had actually fallen asleep in someone else's suite. A quick scan, spying her suitcases and some personal items she had unpacked the day before, countered her fears.

Feeling invigorated and ready to begin the workday, Sam checked her phone and saw something she could not fathom: it was 10:00 a.m. For someone who usually got up before six each day, this was more than just oversleeping; she felt like Rip Van Winkle, her thoughts migrating to the valuable time that had been squandered.

Grateful that her room had a private bath, she had gotten out of bed, walked, and stripped at the same time, all the while believing that Hannah was downstairs tapping her flip-flopped foot and thinking that Sam was taking advantage of her hospitality, not unlike all the other hangers-on.

In an effort to seem relaxed and going with the flow, especially after Hannah's sartorial comment the day before, Sam put on a pair of Lily Pulitzer white shorts paired with her Rowing Blazers hunter green cropped polo shirt. No sooner had she slipped into a pair of navy Havaianas and barreled down the staircase like a co-ed late for the chem final, with every intention of apologizing for sleeping in, did she run into iPad Allison, carrying a coffee mug with an Anti-Wife logo and wearing an ear-to-ear "isn't-life-grand?" grin on her face.

"Good morning."

"Well, late morning," replied Sam.

Shaking her head and checking her iPad, Allison respectfully disagreed: "No, it's only 10:30."

"That may be, but usually I'm up at dawn and by now would have written an entire client strategy brief. I'm a productive person. I never sleep this late, not even on the weekends. If you would please tell me where Hannah is so we can get down to business, I'd really appreciate it."

And kaboom. That's when iPad Allison dropped the bomb that it was Hannah Takes Manhattan day, but she would be back to host an intimate dinner party that evening, and of course, Sam was invited.

"I was actually just about to send you an email," said the assistant. "It's an eclectic group of people. The invite will let you know who all will be there."

Even though Sam heard what Allison said, she was still a few beats back, focused on the fact that Hannah was out, and reacted accordingly with the "she's where?" screech.

WTF, texted Katie after receiving Sam's run-on message about her day thus far.

Indeed, thought Sam as she sat at the table on her terrace. Rather than text back, she hit the FaceTime app.

"I just needed to see a friendly face," she told Katie, who proceeded to smile broadly.

"Now, let's talk about what needs to be done for the other clients. I'm going to treat this like any other business trip where I find myself with downtime, and just stay in my 'hotel' room and work on whatever matters are at hand, for people who actually respect my time and efforts."

The more she talked, the more Sam generated a real head of steam.

"In fact, when I hang up with you, I'm putting a call into Barry and demanding to know why I wasn't—"

"Don't do that," interrupted Katie.

"Excuse me?" *Who's giving whom orders?*

Although Sam had grown to rely on her and valued her a great deal, considering Katie more of an assistant account executive rather than just support staff—a title bump she was going to make official as soon as payments from the Applause job came in and she could give Katie a raise—there were times when she felt that the younger, less-experienced woman was overstepping.

"Just hear me out. You told me that Barry already expressed to you how he feels about Hannah. They didn't forget to extend an invitation to the meeting; he didn't want you there. I'm positive it wasn't a slight. In my humble opinion, it sounds like a maintenance visit; he just likes to have one-on-one time with her, you know, to schmooze, keep her happy and let her talk about herself, her big dreams for her book and who knows, her next book, and, of course, her TV show.

"That being said, you're right. She should have given you the head's up. You're also right that it's probably a better use of your time to keep up with your other clients. At least you'll be doing so at the beach."

Sam was impressed. Katie had turned that around quite nicely, even if she was in agreement with Allison.

"Good call, Kate. Expect some PDFs I'm going to need you to proofread and send . . . well, you know what needs to be sent where."

"I'm on it, Sam."

In the spirit of camaraderie as well as proving she did have a sense of humor, Sam signed off with, "I know you are, gurrl."

Shortly after hanging up, Sam was pleasantly surprised as well as grateful when Inez remembered to deliver what turned out to be the most delicious crab salad sandwich she'd ever had, along with a liter of sparkling Poland Spring, a tall glass, and a bucket of ice.

It had ended up being quite a constructive day in a more serene environment than she usually experienced in her office, which was on a block that never met a police or fire truck siren it didn't like.

Sam was so pleased with all she'd accomplished that she had stopped resenting Hannah, even choosing to enjoy her surroundings with a late-afternoon walk on the beach.

About half a mile down, Sam was taking in the vastness of the ocean and warmth of the sun. She began picking up iridescent seashells and ruminating about what to do with them. Could she delicately poke holes in them to create a piece of jewelry? Or perhaps glue them around a frame and place in it a selfie taken on the balcony with Hannah's ten-million-dollar view in the background? Sam wasn't really into arts and crafts, but her walk had put her in touch with a different side of her creativity. Until, that is, Sam ran smack into a wedding party taking photos.

There is just no escaping this, she thought to herself, followed by, *Who gets married on a Tuesday?* before realizing it was a magazine photoshoot.

She stopped in her tracks to observe the "bride" in traditional white while her attendants were wearing beige linen dresses with a three-inch Nantucket Red ribbon around the waist. The groom and groomsmen's jackets matched the dresses, while their Bermuda shorts as well as ties, layered over white button-downs, matched the ladies' faded pink/coral sashes.

Long ago and far away, whenever Sam and Little Evie came upon a wedding at their church, Sam would lift her sister up for a good view, then they would comment on how pretty the bride looked and give a thumbs up or down to the style and color of the bridesmaids' dresses, pretending they were members of the *Fashion Police*.

That day, Sam turned on her heels and headed back, letting out her annoyance by throwing her shell collection back onto the sand while commenting under her breath, "You'd think if they were going to make the color scheme Nantucket Red they would have had the common sense to shoot on Nantucket."

Relieved did not describe how Sam felt when she arrived back at Hannah's patio and saw that all the party-attendees from the previous day-cum-night had either left or been kicked out by Allison.

Sam gave one of the poolside black and white striped lounge chairs a try, but just as her eyelids were about to flutter closed, she was jolted back to consciousness by the ping of her iPhone. As expected, the ever-efficient iPad Allison had emailed not only the list but also the bios of Hannah's other four dinner guests.

Sam—As promised, the others you will be dining with tonight at 8:00 sharp:

Susie Fitzsimmons (Actress)—Not quite a household name, but a familiar face. You've probably seen her on episodes of *Law & Order: SVU, The Blacklist*, etc., as well as her starring role in the short-lived network drama *Downtown Blue*, where she played the only detective with a conscience in a corrupt precinct. Susie is married with three kids. Very down to earth. She's also Hannah's BFF. We love her.

"I guess that means I love her, too," mumbled Sam.

Britney Swanson—(Neighborhood babysitter/cheerleader/Ross School eleventh grader)—Britney is a lovely young woman who Hannah hired as a mother's helper last summer when Hannah's sister came to stay and brought her two kids. Hannah may be followed by hordes of grown women, but she's really now tapping into Gen Z, represented by Britney. Hannah finds her mature for her age.

Sam exhaled deeply and went from covering her mouth with her free hand to using her thumb and index finger to pinch the bridge of her nose and massaging it vigorously until the throbbing in both her eyeballs dissipated.

Bobbie Jones (nee Bobby Jones—Trans Rights Activist/former tennis pro)—You may remember her from before she transitioned and won the US Open men's division two years in a row, did a Nike commercial, and had several failed marriages to prominent starlets. Now, she is a leader in the LBGTQ community, and Hannah always welcomes her voice at the table.

Brett Randolph (Accountant/Hannah's brother)—As handsome as Hannah is beautiful, Brett is a year older (Irish twins, if you will) and close to his sister. He is divorced with no kids. FYI: It's best to make an effort with him, as Hannah values his opinion.

And with that last nugget of information absorbed, Sam's hand, which was propping up her head, gave her temple one last good rub, while the one holding her smartphone fell gently to her side, and the sounds of the surf lulled her to sleep.

****

"Hey gurrl."

Sam was having one of those awake dreams. Someone was calling her "girl" and prodding her. Even though she was technically no longer asleep, her eyelids refused to lift themselves. It was that delicious moment between slumber and rejoining the world, and Sam did not want it to end; the jabbing, however, was another story.

Where was she? How old was she? Was she in high school when each Saturday morning Little Evie would come into her room to wake her up to play by climbing on her bed and poking her face with a tiny toddler finger? "Sammy, get up and play with me. Play with me." Poke. Poke. Poke.

"Cut it out," Sam uttered as she opened her eyes. But, she was not in her teen bedroom, and the offender was not her little sister.

"Well then, gurrl, get your ass up. Company's coming."

And with that, the reality that Hannah had returned was as clear as the ice in her glass of what Sam had come to learn was Johnnie Walker Blue.

"Oh my, what time . . . ?" She asked as she checked her phone.

"Time for you to get going."

"They'll be here in fifteen minutes? I have to shower and change."

"For what? It's totally caszh. I'm not changing. I'm wearing this."

"This" was the epitome of casual boho chic: a Tory tunic and white pants, each Sam guesstimated at almost three hundred dollars at Burch's store on Madison Avenue.

"Well, there's caszh, and there's sloppy, which is how I'm feeling. So even if there's no time to shower, I prefer not to meet your company in clothes that I've not only been in all day but recently slept in. I'll be right down."

After splashing water on her face, applying makeup, twirling her hair into a simple up-do, and putting on a coral, belted J.Crew V-neck jumpsuit, then slipping into her navy-with-white-trim Jack Rogers, she was ready to be a gracious guest and engage with the others.

Sam hit the bottom of the staircase just as the bell rang. Hannah waved off a dutiful Inez to open the door herself.

"Look who I found," squealed Bobbie as she let Susie go in ahead of her.

"We pulled up at the same time," announced the actress, who, just like every character Sam had ever seen her play on TV, spoke in a monotone with an expression that gave away she was tired, in an existential way.

Right then, Sam began to wish her life away. *Please let this be over soon.*

Please let them all need to go home by ten. Next time I look at my phone, please let it be 10:01.

Just then, a man in his late twenties came sashaying out from the direction of the kitchen.

"Look who the cat dragged in," said Hannah, stepping aside so he could greet Bobbie and Susie with a kiss on the cheek. When he turned, the gentleman noticed Sam and began to walk toward her. As Hannah hustled her two friends in the direction of the backyard, she tossed over her shoulder, "Oh yeah, this is my brother, Brett."

"You must be Sam. I've heard all about you," he said.

"It's a pleasure."

"Okay, everybody," announced the boss/hostess, "let's go have cocktails on the patio before the kid gets here. Allison said that because we're going to have a minor with us, we shouldn't drink with dinner."

Everyone seemed to agree, but then from what Sam could tell, everyone always agreed with whatever Hannah said.

"But after dessert, I'll send her home, and we can break out the Chardonnay."

Bobbie, Brett, and Susie cheered and applauded theatrically, and Sam, seeing her hope that this evening would end early disappear like a boat in the Bermuda Triangle, realized she better go along to get along and also pounded her fists against the air.

"But you don't drink."

Her less-than-gracious host felt the need to call her out.

"No, I don't, but I'm excited for you all." Lame, indeed, but the best response Sam could come up with on the fly.

"Well, all right," shrugged Hannah.

Since when is it appropriate to put a guest on the spot and make her feel awkward? thought Sam. Isn't it the job of the host to make everyone feel comfortable?

"Anyway, bottoms up," said Hannah after the waiter passed out mojitos to all, assuring Sam that hers was virgin. Hannah added with a wink, "See, gurrl, I gotcha covered."

Sam nodded in appreciation and realized that this seemed to be the Anti-Wife's schtick: A slap then a kiss.

She had witnessed this the day before at the pool party between Hannah and iPad Allison. The boss calling the subordinate an idiot for forgetting to give something to the mail carrier and screaming at her in front of a backyard full of guests to "run," only to have a beleaguered and humiliated Allison take off like Flo Jo to catch the postal worker before he got back in his truck.

A few hours later, though, a still-wounded Allison gushed on the verge of tears when Hannah took brand new, thirteen-hundred-dollar Alaia metallic studded sandals, sent to her gratis by the company after she spoke at one its employee retreats, and presented them to her flunky.

"Here. If you're going to run my errands, you're going to run in style."

Allison fell into her employer's open arms, and the whole party exploded in yelps and hand-clapping. Sam just sat and stared with her mouth agape, guessing those tiny moments of recognition made the ill-treatment worth it; the "kiss" being the gateway drug to the really addictive one which was Hannah herself.

"Hi, is it okay to come out?" said the young girl hovering in the doorway that divided the kitchen from the patio.

The hostess hopped up to greet her.

"Of course, you're my special guest."

And with that, a loving caretaker appeared where a snarky, smug mistress of ceremonies had once stood.

"Everybody, this is Britney. Britney, this is everybody. Introduce yourselves, people." And they, including Sam, followed orders.

"Dinner is served," announced the server.

There was nothing "caszh" about how the formal dining room was set up.

Sam had been to weddings that were not as finely appointed. An ecru, antique tablecloth with silver and gold embroidered leaves swaddled the circular mahogany dining table, which had been swapped out for the rectangular one that was there when Sam got the grand tour. At each place was a Hermes H Deco dinner dish atop a silver charger plate, accompanied by Christoffel silverware and Waterford Crystal, and antique napkins that did not match the tablecloth but complemented it all the same. Five small floral arrangements formed a circle in the center of the table. The light from the chandelier made the whole room seem magical.

If her crab sandwich at lunch was any indication of Chef Kenny's culinary skills, the repast would do justice to the décor.

Even though it was clear that Hannah was going for a Knights of the

Round Table vibe, where everyone was supposed to be equal, there was no doubt that wherever she sat would be its head.

"Well, first, I just want to thank you all for coming to my little soirée. Most of you know that I like to surround myself with different kinds of people who have different ideas, even though mine are the only ones that are right."

At that, she threw back her head and laughed, as did everyone else. Sam chuckled along with the group but didn't believe that Hannah was joking. Sam was actually shocked that Miss My-Way-or-the-Highway would allow into her home anyone who dared to have an opposite thought to hers.

To make it through the evening, Sam decided to look at this dinner as a real focus group. Much to her disappointment, however, there was no talk of the Anti-Wife movement, not during the refreshing watermelon salad appetizer or even the soup course, where they were served Cioppino—calamari, mussels, clams, shrimp, and lobster in a tomato broth. Nor during the main course. Sam was actually quite full by then but somehow found room to devour the toasted scallops with sides of roasted baby carrots and cauliflower.

While dining, Hannah wanted to hear people's opinions on current events and asked Britney to lead a discussion on education in America. Granted, no real problems were going to be solved at this beautifully decorated table, and no one was more informed than any other average Joe, but it was lovely dinner conversation, and Sam held her own without saying anything controversial that could turn pleasant banter into an unpleasant heated debate.

And then came dessert. The coconut cream pie had barely hit the table when Hannah announced: "Let's talk marriage; not just the institution but the stuff that goes with it. I can't think of anything more stupid than buying a dress you're only going to wear once. I mean, you can't even cut the thing down and wear it as a cocktail dress because it's bright white. Even if you dyed it, it'd still end up looking like a tinted wedding dress. It's like the aisle of the church is one giant red carpet. You have this wedding so that you can show off you got a new gown. I just don't get it. Britney, weigh in here."

Sam, who had not relished the idea of spending her evening with a teenager, was actually quite impressed with the high school student. She was poised and confident without being self-satisfied or rebellious in her opinions. Sam also liked her look: surfer chick.

Britney was a natural beauty—no makeup enhancement necessary, long straight dirty-blonde hair, and a lean, almost boyish figure. To attend the evening's festivities, she wore the teen version of dressed up: pressed wide-leg blue jean pleated trousers and a white, short-sleeved t-shirt bejeweled at the neck. Her only actual jewelry were these rope-like bracelets worn by those who hang ten.

"Well, I know weddings are like a tradition and stuff, but I don't know if people my age are into it the way people in previous generations have been. Like, my mom told me once that when she was my age, she already knew what kind of wedding dress she wanted and what color her bridesmaids were going to wear, and even who her bridesmaids were going to be. I mean, I don't even think about that stuff, and really, neither do my friends. Like, I want to be my own person and, you know, have my own job and rely on myself and then, you know, if I meet somebody, that's great. If we decide to get married, I guess that'd be okay too. But maybe we don't even have to do that."

"Bingo," said Hannah as she slapped the table hard enough that the silverware jumped, and Bobbie and Brett both reached for their stemware to make sure the shaking table wouldn't cause any liquid to spill.

"Out of the mouths of babes. I've been saying this forever, and everybody always glared at me like I was talkin' crazy. I'm so happy that young women can finally say what Britney just said and have it considered normal."

The others responded with things like "absolutely" and "definitely" with a "you said it" chaser and Britney smiled like a Miss America contestant pleased with her answer to the "How would you bring about world peace?" stumper.

All Sam could think was, good for Britney that she values independence, but one Long Island teenager, regardless of how sincere, saying exactly what her host wanted to hear, did not the voice of her generation make.

Because she just had to know, Sam risked the wrath of her host by infringing upon Hannah's role as moderator to address Susie.

"You're married, correct? But, yet you're a proponent of the Anti-Wife phenomenon."

Sam used that grander word instead of "movement" in the hope that it would stroke Hannah's ego enough to let go of any resentment she might feel that Sam could be trying to take over the discussion.

Hannah started to snicker, and Susie nodded her head. Apparently, she'd had to explain herself to others before.

"I never wanted to get married," began Susie. "In fact, I was against marriage after watching my parents turn every day into a battle royale. When I met my husband, I thought he was a great guy, and I liked hanging out with him, and I was more than happy to keep doing so because, quite frankly, I didn't like dating; you know, telling my story to different people over and over and over again. I figured, *I've met this person who I could stand for more than ten minutes,* so we kept hanging out, then he wanted us to live together. At first, I really didn't want to do that, but then I found out I was pregnant, and because raising a child alone is a hard gig, I took him up on his offer. The next thing you know, we had a house, and it seemed super important to him for us to make it official. I went along with it. But really, I never had to be married, and don't get me wrong, I don't regret my children, and I don't regret my husband, but I agree with Hannah—when marriage is not part of the equation, there's just less pressure on the relationship."

"Just to piggyback on what Susie's saying," Bobbie chimed in, "the whole idea of marriage and who can get married should just leave this earth completely. I mean, gay couples, interracial couples, interfaith couples—they fall in love, everything is good, then they announce they're getting married, and hell breaks loose; family members won't come to the wedding, or some government worker won't give them a marriage license based on the person's religious beliefs, or somebody won't bake them a cake—I mean, honestly. All that kind of discrimination would go out the window if marriage didn't exist."

Even though the other guests had valid answers, Sam still had many questions: What about people who want to get married? People who are married and make it work? Sam could've started asking, but she realized it would only protract the group conversation. The fact was, she didn't want other people's POVs. She wanted the answers to come from the Anti-Wife herself, preferably in a one-on-one interview.

Suddenly, Brett raised his coffee cup, and that was everyone's cue to do the same, except for Britney, who held up her tall glass of cold milk.

"To my sister, the perfect hostess and feminist role model; a great example to women who want to live their own lives."

"Hear, hear," and "cheers" came from the group, and then Hannah lifted her cup and said, "Here's to leaning in to your own life."

By that time, it was 11:00 p.m., and the doorbell rang.

"That must be my dad," said Britney.

Susie got a text from her husband saying that one of their kids was under the weather, so she hit the road as well. Bobbie said she had an appointment in the morning, so she'd be running along, too.

Sam's original wish that the evening end sooner rather than later was granted, but what still lingered was the question as to whether Hannah was going to make her sit and watch her and Brett drink the Chardonnay.

Hannah bid goodnight to her guests, shut the front door, and turned to Sam and said in the same flat tone she often used with iPad Allison, "I need to talk to my brother, so see you in the morning."

Sam smiled and said, "Thank you for a lovely evening," but Hannah was already walking toward the library with Brett and could not have cared less about what Sam thought about what transpired during the previous few hours.

Heading up the stairs delighted to be released, yet disturbed at being dismissed in such a "you can't sit with us" way straight out of *Mean Girls*, Sam texted Katie: *dinner over #relief still don't get HR or alter ego AW.*

12

Sam stood stone-faced. Like Bill Murray's character in *Groundhog Day*, all she could think was, *This again?*

iPad Allison had just informed her that on this day three of her unjust incarceration, Hannah would again be unavailable.

Sam had gotten up at eight, still two hours later than usual. That salt sea air was really knocking her out. She wasn't even ready to admit it to herself but getting this kind of REM sleep was doing a lot for her psyche.

When Sam arose, she pulled on a pair of red J.Crew capris and a three-quarter sleeve light blue cotton top from Vineyard Vines and went downstairs. Today was the day that she and her host would get down to the nitty-gritty, she determined, but just as the day before, Sam reached the foot of the stairs and ran into Hannah's henchwoman and her ever-pinging Apple product.

"Where is she today?"

"Actually, Hannah is in residence all day, but she's taking a mental health day and does not want to be disturbed under any circumstances; even I'm not allowed into her suite, unless, you know, the building's on fire or someone died—and, of course, then it depends upon whom the deceased is."

"Why am I here? Why did she have me come?" Sam stipulated.

"Well," Allison said, "so that you could do a deep dive and really understand . . ."

Ah, the party line.

"Okay, how am I deep-diving into the movement when the person who runs the movement does not make a move to speak to me? Why do I have to be here for two weeks or at all? I mean, I could be ignored just as easily in my own home or office via phone or Skype or Twitter or any of the other many forms of communication available to us, thanks to modern technology."

The easy smile of the person usually as solicitous as a geisha dissipated, and iPad Allison stared at Sam as if to say, *Seriously, just get with the program.*

"At Hannah's level of fame and success, she wants what she wants when she wants it, and she gets it. She wanted you here for two weeks. I really don't know her reasoning; she doesn't explain herself to me. All I can say is this is the most beautiful house that any of us have ever had the opportunity to step foot in. We have a four-star chef who makes us three-course lunches or, if we prefer, just a sandwich. Inez is a house-managing magician, and Carl will drive us anywhere we want to go if Hannah doesn't need him. You can swim in the pool, walk on the beach, read every first-edition book in her library, and if it suits you, bang out a song on the Steinway. You took the job with Barry Rogers. This is the job." Then, with a tilt of her head, Allison's Stepford Wife–grin reappeared: "Why not just enjoy?"

Right there, Sam remembered two things: a) when she was talking to Allison, she was talking to Hannah, and the Anti-Wife would hear every single word of every single conversation with her assistant, so Sam needed to watch herself, and b) iPad Allison was right.

"I understand completely. Thank you for your candor. I actually have plenty to do. I got a lot accomplished yesterday and will do so again today."

"I just love conflict resolution," chirped Allison. "Oh, and I'll send you an email about tonight's dinner and who the guests are, just like I did yesterday."

Another dinner? But instead of reacting with an eye-roll, Sam said a gracious thank-you before heading to the kitchen to take up Inez on her previous offer of a cup of her special brew.

"It's only my third day here, and I feel like I'm on week three," Sam said to Lena as she strolled along the sand, sipping the most savory cuppa Joe she'd ever had.

"Well, I just got a freelance job. It's six months' worth of dough. I can do the designs from home, but a couple of times a week, I have to go in for status meetings; today's one of those days. It's a nice agency, but it's still got walls and fluorescent lighting, so it's a little hard for my heart to bleed for somebody who's working from the seashore."

"I hear ya."

"You know, Sam, you really never gave yourself a break after what happened. I mean, you went from not having your own wedding to attending your sister's, which, for me, was a little too *27 Dresses*, then diving into work, which I totally understand, but why don't you consider this a working vacay—power down and breathe."

"You're the second person to give me that advice, and it's not even 10:00 a.m.," said Sam.

"Well, why don't you run it by Katie, and if she agrees, then perhaps three times is the charm?"

With that, Lena said she had to go. Her MTA app was reporting the trains were a mess, and she'd probably end up walking to Midtown. That was all Sam had to hear to appreciate that she'd rather be rambling on the yellow sand.

After her head-clearing walk, Sam returned to her private terrace, sat with her feet up on the table, and swigged from the bottled water Inez had waiting for her. After she gave Katie the play-by-play of last night's dinner and that morning's newsflash, her assistant chimed in.

"You know, not for anything, but if I were you, I'd consider this a pretty lit opportunity. Take a mental health day as well. Everything's under control here; all your memos and strategies and proposals and what-have-you are out to all your other clients. We're just awaiting feedback. From past experience, we both know it might take a day or two or longer for anyone to respond. I mean, it's Wednesday—hump day—use it to recharge your batteries."

Indeed, three times was the charm.

Sam knew better than to go to Hannah's office and disturb Allison, undoubtedly hovering over her iPad, doing what Sam put under the über-heading of "Hannah's bidding." So, Sam texted her.

Is it OK if Carl drives me into town?

Within seconds, Allison answered, *He's pulling [car emoji] around now. [Smiley face emoji]!*

Carl dropped off Sam at the East End shopping mecca: Newton Lane. She popped into Madewell, AERIN, Club Monaco, as well as Hannah's go-to Tory Burch. She strolled Main Street, home to Intermix, J.Crew at the Beach, Hermes, and Ralph Lauren. Sam also made her way over to the area called The Circle to take a look at what Blue & Cream had to offer and treated herself to a floral-patterned, navy-blue maxi slip dress, which she'd wear to that evening's dinner party.

Yes, the Hamptons had all the same stores that she had back in Manhattan, but she found it much more relaxing and pleasurable to shop in them between bouts of sunshine.

Sam was considering where to get a light bite before she called Carl to take her back to Chez Randolph. Perhaps she'd head back to Newton Lane and treat herself to an omelet at Babette's, but her decision-making was interrupted by the ringing of her cell, which displayed a number she didn't recognize.

"Samantha Dennehy."

"Hi, it's me."

"Excuse me?"

"Sam, it's Sam," said the male voice she thought she'd never hear again. "How've you been?"

How've I been?

"I've been fine, thank you."

Her silence indicated that she would not be asking him how he'd been doing, so Sam the Man cleared his throat and got to the point: "Okay, then, I wanted to see if you could come down to the restaurant for lunch. It's probably too late today; you've probably already eaten. What's your Thursday look like?"

Oh no. Sam had already seen this movie, where, by the end of his proposed lunch, she would be channeling Meg Ryan's "Sally," crying to Billy Crystal's "Harry" because her former boyfriend "Joe" was getting married.

"Congratulations. Good thing I sent you back great-great-grandmama's ring."

"Wait, what?" stammered The Man.

"What's her name, you know, the woman you're engaged to?"

"Who told you?" he said, like a criminal demanding from the detective sweating him the name of the skell who dropped a dime.

"No one. I'm telepathic. Seriously, you're not that hard to figure out.

You never were."

"Can we not . . ."

"First of all, I'm on my way to lunch now, so yes, today is too late, and my Thursday is booked. I'm not even in the city. I'm sure you think inviting me out to tell me you're marrying someone else makes you a 'good guy' who's 'manning up' and doing the 'right thing,' with no regard to what it would be like for me, not to mention a waste of a good meal."

"You know, some guys would do this over text."

"You mean the way you told me we were no longer getting married? Oh, forgive me, that wasn't a text, it was an email."

"To make up for that, I wanted to tell you about this to your face."

"Well, then your call could have been via FaceTime." She addressed his exhaustive sigh by adding: "There is no need to tell me anything at all about your life since you're not in mine anymore."

And with the swipe up on her iPhone's screen, she made him disappear.

Sam texted Carl who responded immediately: *b there in 10.*

It was a beautiful seventy-two degrees with a cool, light breeze, yet Sam began to feel as though she were burning up. As much as she wanted to blame the sun, she knew this sensation that she was on fire came from the inside.

The once-jilted bride sought refuge inside the first store she saw, hoping a blast of AC would douse the internal flames. Sam never moved past the counter nearest the door, though, indicating to the attentive sales professional that she was "just looking."

She stood staring at the same shiny objects in the display case for what seemed like an uncomfortably long time, yet if anyone had quizzed her on what she had been looking at, she would not have been able to tell them. In her peripheral vision, she could see a trio of employees watching her and commenting to each other. This gave her the incentive to check her phone and realized that Carl's ten minutes were up.

She smiled at the sales clerks who wished her a nice day, heard Lena's voice in her head tell her to take a deep breath—four in, hold for four, four out—and pushed open the door. With her head up, she breezed out to the curb just as Carl was driving up in Hannah's Mercedes. The timing was as perfect as a routine choreographed by Bob Fosse. She slid into the back seat, and as they took off, the only thing Sam hoped was that everyone on Main Street who saw her believed the fantasy that all was right in her world.

That bit of superficiality was what she needed at that very second to get her through the ride back to her temporary home without imploding.

They pulled up and around the circular driveway, and Carl had yet to come to a full stop before Sam swung open the door. The alarmed driver slammed the brakes and shouted, "Wait," as he turned to look incredulously at Sam, who had literally hit the ground running.

Halfway to the front door though, civility eclipsed her frenzy. Sam turned and quickly hurried back to the car and knocked on the passenger window. As it began to descend, she said sheepishly, "Thank you, Carl. And, um, sorry," then spun around and scurried into the house, hoping to avoid Allison and her mighty iPad and even kindhearted Inez.

Sam took the stairs as she used to as a teenager: two at a time. Now, just as back then, she couldn't get to her bedroom, with its promise of privacy and solitude, fast enough.

She locked her door and exhaled at the same time, then dropped her Goyard and shopping bag to claim her seat at the edge of the bed. She needed to process what had happened, but all her thoughts were swirling like sand during a windstorm. There was only one person who could help calm her mind and make sense of this.

"Hey, hey, hey. How's the beach?" Lena said in lieu of hello.

But just as Sam opened her mouth, the words she thought would shoot out like the contents of a shaken soda bottle could not find a place on her tongue. Perhaps she was hesitant because if she put out into the universe that Sam the Man was engaged, it would become all too real; or maybe she just wasn't ready to listen to Lena rail against what an asshole he was; or maybe, just maybe, the news wasn't as worth sharing as she thought initially.

Instead, Sam opted for the adage, "When in doubt, do nothing," and responded to her friend with, "I took your suggestion and carpe diem-ed. Let me tell you about the dress I bought at Blue & Cream."

The gal pals chatted for about an hour, covering everything from that evening's dinner event ("Maybe there might actually be some interesting men for you this time, and no teenyboppers," injected Lena), to how the usually on the ball Allison had yet to send the guess-who's-coming-to-dinner email, to Lena's freelance assignment.

Attention then turned to the upcoming weekend.

"I'll still be here," sighed Sam.

"Once again, let's remember where you are, is where a lot of people wish they could be. I'll be in Vegas, though, so I'm not jealous."

"Fulfilling your dream to see Celine Dion, perhaps?"

"Feeling lucky and trying to beat the house at The Bellagio," laughed Lena, who then explained, "Ben has business there. He's leaving tomorrow, and I'm going with him. While he's in his meeting on Friday, I'll do my layouts, perhaps even by the pool. Then we'll stay the weekend just for fun. Maybe we might even actually see Celine; I hear she puts on quite a show."

Sam wished her friend a great vacation, but before they hung up, she seemed to be starting to say something else.

"What?" asked Lena.

"What, what?"

"You sounded like you were about to say, I don't know, what?"

It had been Sam's last chance to share the news about Sam the Man, but for a second time, thought better of it. She signed off with, "Throw a dollar in one of the slots for me. Baby needs new Manolos."

****

Sam got ready for Hannah's dinner party with the giddiness of a high school senior dressing for prom. Even though that afternoon's news still had her feeling not her normal self, she actually preferred this high-anxiety buzz to hang-dog depression.

True, she hyperventilated twice during her shower, once while blow-drying her hair, and, even though she only applied a light touch of makeup, it took almost a half-hour to put it on because she needed to go out on the terrace every five minutes to breathe—in with the good ocean air, and out with the bad. She was glad, though, to attend the festivities with a lot of, albeit manic, energy. Sam had to admit that at the previous evening's dinner, she'd been a bit too low-key. She didn't even mind that Applause would be filming. Without the waiver, they couldn't use any footage of her, so she would just ignore them.

As she admired herself in the floor-length mirror and liking what she saw, Sam was glad to have blown three hundred some-odd dollars on the slip dress. Stepping into her navy Jack Rogers completed her boho-chic ensemble, which was quite the departure from her usual fashion trifecta of J.Crew, Vineyard Vines, and Polo, with Lily Pulitzer making the occasional appearance as the fourth musketeer. The lifelong preppy looked like someone else, and that's how she wanted to feel.

Unlike every other time since she'd arrived, Sam walked slowly down the staircase, trying to appear regal, wanting to make an entrance. With each step, she ran down the guest list Allison had sent her: Mimi Granger, an up-and-coming standup comedian/actress; Mike Bennigan, a local school teacher; Ted Baldwin, an entrepreneur; and back by popular demand, Hannah's brother, Brett.

Instead of the dining room, they would be feasting on the beach. A tent had been set up, a quartet was playing softly in the background, and the funky, eclectic, and colorful decor consisting of a table cloth with Moroccan-designed embroidery and vibrant cushions sealing the deal made Sam think Lena would be right at home there.

Brett and a woman Sam assumed was Mimi were standing to the side of the tent, looking at the red and orange sky. Sam felt confident approaching the others, not only because she already knew one of them but because she felt she mirrored Hannah's usual upscale caszh.

A Luxor forty-two-inch freestanding charcoal grill off to the left caught her eye, though, and there in the flesh was Chef Kenny behind it, working with the intensity of a mad scientist.

The almost-wife knew those moves. For a minute, Sam imagined that she was watching her ex flipping, seasoning, and flame-broiling. But that moment passed in an instant, thank goodness. Sam laughed to herself, *How could I confuse the two guys?*

At a statuesque five-eight, Sam always had felt dwarfed by six-two Sam the Man, who looked like he stepped off a New York Fashion Week runway. Hannah's chef had a pudgy, pleasant, but plain, everyman face, thick black-rimmed glasses shielding puppy-dog eyes, and curly red hair set atop his no more than five-six frame.

A light breeze sent the aroma her way, and it was just too enticing. Sam dared to take a detour for a sneak peek. Fresh lobsters? Shrimp on the barbie? Her mouth was watering before she even spied the food. It took everything she had to wipe the disbelief off her face. Tonight's menu would be the basics: hamburgers and frankfurters with grilled corn on the cob.

Sam knew, though, from personal experience that in the hands of someone with true culinary skills, even a hard-boiled egg could taste like heaven.

Chef Kenny became aware that his cooking space had been invaded and gave her a look that said, *May I help you?* in the most inauspicious of ways.

With a wink, Sam said, "I bet these will be the best burgers and hot dogs any of us have ever had."

Kenny winked back and said, "I try," but like any kitchen autocrat, he broke eye contact and went back to his fare. *You can go now* was implied and respected by Sam.

While she was preoccupied with what was for dinner, the two other male guests had joined Mimi and Brett. Sam was only about ten feet away from turning the group into a quintet when Hannah came out of nowhere.

"Okay, you losers, let's sit down."

Seriously, this is how she speaks to her visitors? More confusing for Sam was her host's choice of wardrobe: A Grecian-inspired, cold-shoulder gown in ivory crepe, accessorized with a pair of low-heeled satin slides with a cascade of resin pearls embellishing the white, beige, and gold brocade pattern. Around her neck was a long, gold chain, and Hannah wore a gold cuff bracelet on each wrist a la Wonder Woman.

Okay, so let's get this straight, mulled Sam. *For the formal dining experience, she wore a sophisticated, yet nonetheless pedestrian, shirt and pants, whereas, for this backyard BBQ on the sand, she's gussied up like the East End's answer to Helen of Troy?*

Sam guessed that throwing people off-guard was one of Hannah's power moves, and on some level, scratched the Anti-Wife's look-at-me itch.

"Hi, I'm Mimi," said the bubbly blonde. Both Mike and Ted made their way over to Sam to introduce themselves before taking their seats. Brett gave a friendly wave.

"Good to see you again," said Sam as she waved back.

Hannah took her rightful place at the head of the table and announced they'd be eating family-style. Just then, platters of burgers, franks, corn, as well as bowls of salad, fries, and onion rings plus condiments were laid before them.

It was fun passing the food while listening to Mimi talk about her upcoming gig: "It's a good nervous, you know what I mean?" and having Ted explain how he picks people's inventions to finance, like a judge on *Shark Tank*. It turned out that as well as being an English teacher, Mike was shopping his historical novel about Sir Thomas More.

Before Sam could tell them about herself, Hannah began reciting her business associate's CV almost verbatim. She built up the ad exec so much, even once again bandying about the word "genius," that the others sounded like a Greek chorus cooing "Wow," in unison.

Their awe seemed genuine, and just the reminder Sam needed that even without Sam the Man or any man, she was indeed "wow."

What would an evening with Hannah be, though, if she didn't steer the conversation to marriage and the Anti-Wife philosophy, and Sam watched as the others were more than happy to oblige. After all, cameras were rolling.

This night, though, Sam listened with more interest. Not only for professional reasons, but personal ones as well. Everyone at the table was in their late twenties to early forties, as well as single, which it seemed was how they wanted to stay. The narrative thread they all tugged on was "alone and happy."

Like a spectator at a sporting event, Sam found herself almost unable to keep track of which player's turn it was; looking from Mimi to Ted to Brett, then back to Mimi to Hannah to Mike, her head swiveling to catch the richly embroidered story, the I-can-top-that interjection, the clever comeback, and here-and-there a nugget of wisdom. The conversation was so fast-paced, with everyone often talking over each other, that Sam suffered from FOMO even though she was entrenched in the exchange.

The banter-a-thon began with Hannah. "I don't want to be someone's wife. It makes the inevitable breakup so much more convoluted."

"Marriage drives people to want to kill each other. You know how on *Law & Order* if the dead person is married, the first suspect is always the spouse?" said Brett.

"I'm so glad those days are behind me—when every guy I dated made me say, 'Am I gonna marry him?' Yuck," offered Mimi.

Hannah added: "Truth is, I'm happy AF when I'm focused on my career and those I care about."

"Up until last year," said Ted, "I was living with this stigma of being over forty and unmarried. By the way, this idea that people look at single men as carefree bachelors is false. The only men who are viewed that way are like Clooney pre-Amal or a post-divorce Brad Pitt. If you're a regular guy, people think there must be something wrong because no woman is trying to lock you down."

"What happened last year, though?" inquired Hannah.

"All my friends who had been riding me to man-up and wife-up started getting divorced," answered Ted. "Turns out, I'm not such a loser after all."

"As an adult male, I hate the infantilizing feeling of 'being in trouble,'" began Mike, "and my observation of married men is that they're always on the verge of having a finger wagged in their collective face."

"Always one dirty dish away from being in the doghouse," added Ted.

"I was married," admitted Brett.

"Just so everyone knows, he's not bragging. Trust me," noted Hannah with a smirk.

Brett raised his eyebrow, and they began to have some unspoken sibling conversation that Sam imagined went something like:

Shut up, smartass, and stop interrupting me.

No, you shut up, and I can say what I want.

The older brother cleared his throat and continued, "I realized, thank goodness, sooner rather than later, that I got married not out of love, but fear that I would be alone forever. Being 'on call' day and night, though, made me want to be by myself more and more. When that need for solitude became the norm, there was no longer a reason to stay in it. I'm sorry to say I didn't get much out of the union."

"Oh, Brett," said Hannah. "What does anyone really get out of marriage except the optics of having a legal partner?"

"You don't have to be married if you're emotionally woke," announced Mimi, not changing the subject, just the focus away from the quibbling siblings.

"Men don't want to be married," chimed in Mike. "They just want to keep the woman they're into from being with other guys, so they acquiesce."

"I hate when people say, 'But if you don't get married, what happens when you're old?'" griped Hannah.

"I'll hire one of those eldercare companions," shot back Mike.

Brett piggybacked with, "Right, like is that really the selling point for getting married? When we're sick, wrinkled, and toothless, we can take care of each other?"

"But the reality is that women outlive men," Hannah added, "so my husband would be dead, and I'd end up alone anyway."

Then Ted shared, "I've been seeing this woman for years. She lives in LA, and when we see one another, we're a couple, and when we're apart, we're not a couple. And she, even more than me, thinks it's great. We're both out there living our lives, and we don't have to worry about each other. We still feel connected, yet there's no guilt if we're with other people."

"I'm involved in something similar," said Mimi. "When we're together, it's awesome, but I don't think of him when we're not together. And if I ever meet someone who I want to be my regular hang, I can say buh-bye to my long-distance friend. Until that day comes, I just like having the option to see him."

Heads were nodding in admiration, and Sam, for some reason, chose that moment to join the dialogue: "And you never have to care when he tells you he's marrying someone else."

Suddenly there was silence, except for the echoed screeching of some distant seagulls.

As they all stared at her and each tried to formulate a response, Hannah jumped up and yelled a string of expletives at the sight of a ketchup glob that had dripped onto the bib of her gown.

Sam surmised that somewhere there was a stabbing victim rushed into the ER who was not getting triaged with the hypervigilance being paid to this woman's Tory evening attire. The group acted as though the ketchup was blood, and even Sam called out for club soda with the urgency usually reserved for the directive: "Get me an IV, stat."

Hannah screamed for the crew to stop shooting, then took the liberty of taking her aggravation out on her guests. She shoo-ed everyone away from her and said half-jokingly that the men were using the spill as an excuse to touch her breast. Then she stomped back to the house, declaring she had to go change.

There was then a definite shift in the mood of the evening. With no cameras to play to or Hannah to show off for by pledging their allegiance to her no-marriage mindset, the once-lively discourse transformed into natter, with benign comments about how nice their host's house was, how peaceful the ocean seemed, and how brilliant Hannah was, not to mention generous.

"I had quite a stretch where I couldn't book a gig if my life depended on it," confessed Mimi. "Hannah paid my rent for almost six months."

"For my wedding gift, she bought me a house, which my ex still lives in," offered Brett. "After the divorce, she let me live here, then bought me another house. She also bought a new house for our parents and all my other sisters."

"I asked her to donate some signed books to my school's fundraiser," said Mike, "but instead she came, and at the end, she matched the two-hundred-thousand dollars we'd raised with the silent auction. Handed the principal a check right there."

"I lost my shirt on a deal about a year ago. You know, the sure thing that turns out to be anything but. Hannah gave me seed money to help me get back on my feet," revealed Ted.

Sam's head was spinning but was able to catch words like "angel," "fairy godmother," and "good people."

If she wanted to be cynical, she would've thought, *No wonder everyone lionizes her and lets her call them losers; she gives them money.* But having enjoyed the company of these lovely people whose energy buoyed her and salvaged her day, after enjoying a simple yet delicious meal, which indeed included the best burger she'd ever eaten, Sam began to mellow. She now saw the Anti-Wife as the successful yet uncouth relative who likes to share the wealth to feel simultaneously generous and superior.

After about an hour, they all decided to get the hint that their host would not be returning, so the group made its way back to the house. When the rest left via the front door, Sam climbed the stairs.

She checked her phone, which she'd left charging on her bureau, and there was a text from Allison: *Thurs 8am sharp meet H in foyer.*

Finally, day four would give her what she came for: Sam and Hannah head-on.

13

The alarm went off at six, and for the first time that week, Sam anticipated a normal business day.

She got up, showered, did her hair and makeup, the whole time "in the
zone," ready to plow full steam ahead into her meeting with Hannah. Even
though they were indeed still at the beach, Sam put on her lightweight,
navy Ralph Lauren suit with a white cotton tee for just a hint of caszh, then
slipped on her nude Louboutin heels that made her feel appropriate yet
sexy and powerful at the same time.

She had yet to close the bedroom door behind her when she heard the
din coming from the first floor. Before going down the stairs, Sam walked
to the banister and peered over to find so many people crowded into the
foyer that it reminded her of the first day she got there when Hannah was
presiding over her frat house kegger.

Sam backed away a little confused and texted Allison: *on way down 4 8
sharp meet with H-hope I can find her thru the rabble ???!*

A nano-sec later, Allison replied: *EVERY 1 WAITING 4 U COME
DOWN PLS NOW*

Waiting for me? That's not a phrase that Sam understood. She didn't do
"late," and besides, it was 7:55, so technically, she was still early.

Sam was starting yet another day aggravated, once again thanks to iPad

Allison, who, from the all-caps tone of her text, thought herself one salute away from being the drill sergeant in *Full Metal Jacket*. The captive exec barreled down the staircase, briefcase in hand, and went gunning for the wayward assistant. Instead, she found herself toe-to-toe with Hannah, looking her most professional self in Tory beige trousers, a gunmetal silk tank top covered by a beige, dark and light gray striped cardigan with beige fringe along the hem; the kicker: the same exact shoes as Sam.

"Oh, there you are," said Hannah, like a mother admonishing a teen who almost missed curfew. "We've got to go. You're in car two."

Hannah pushed past Sam like a rush-hour commuter about to miss her train because a clueless tourist was in the way.

"Where? Where am I going?"

"You know, I don't have time for this. I need to be in my head." Then Hannah yelled out, "Allison, take care of this."

Like a woman on a mission, the Anti-Wife marched out of her house and into her Mercedes, or as it would be known that day: car one. Accompanying her would be Allison and her iPad, and Greg, her hair and makeup wizard, who jumped in the front with Carl.

Because she hadn't realized she'd be leaving the premises, Sam had to fly back upstairs and get her purse. By the time she ran back down, fighting the urge to slide down the banister to make better time, the place was empty.

Inez had made what Sam had come to describe as her magnificent and robust blend of coffee for the trip and poured it into an array of silver travel mugs that carried the Anti-Wife logo and set them up on the art deco inlaid wood round table in the middle of the foyer. When Sam first peeked over the balcony, she couldn't decide whether it smacked of a store display at Starbucks or some abstract installation at The Whitney. Now, though, there was only one mug left, which Sam grabbed as she bolted out of the house, hoping the caravan had not left without her. Good thing she took her coffee black, as the milk and sugar had disappeared as well.

As she was approaching car two, Sam's phone pinged: *anti-wife rally speaking event Long Island University's Riverhead campus.*

Okay, well, at least now Sam knew where she was headed. Too bad iPad Allison didn't add that little tidbit to last night's text.

Sam got in the vehicle, which, to her surprise, included *The Anti-Wife* showrunner, Dave, who could have doubled for a little boy on his way out to play in a striped Polo shirt, khaki shorts, and Chuck Taylors, as well as the network's suited and bespeckled marketing executive, Bob, and his assistant, Mindy, who ended up sitting up front with the driver, Beverly.

After greeting them politely, she just had to know, "Who are all the other people in cars—actually minivans—three, four, and five?"

Mindy had the 411, as assistants usually do: "Car three contains what's being called 'Friends of Hannah.'" Sam translated that to mean some of the sycophants who mooched off their idol and hung by the pool. "Cars four and five are superfans." Mindy explained that the guru/author/soon-to-be reality star had Allison keep a list of die-hard disciples who got free tickets to the usual four-hundred-dollar-a-pop events. This guaranteed Hannah would have avid supporters in the audience reacting with unbridled enthusiasm at everything she said.

Sam started texting Katie to keep her abreast of today's agenda: *Circus is mobile.*

After Katie responded with a question mark, a more detailed explanation followed, as well as a little venting: *Surprise AW rally [red face with steam coming from nose emoji].*

The beauty of seeing Hannah in action was not lost on the marketing exec; she just could not deal with being blindsided all the time, constantly feeling out of the loop, like a tagalong rather than a valued member of the team. Sam took a momentary break from texting, looked up, and noticed that Dave and Bob were looking at her impatiently.

"Do you need me?"

"Um, yeah," said Dave.

"Dave and I thought we could use this opportunity to talk about the show," added Bob.

Did they now?

Bob inquired if Sam had been getting their emails. She confirmed that she not only got them but read them and was on the same page as everyone so far. Sam made it clear that after her in-residence research and eventual (she hoped) sit-down with Hannah, she'd devise the blueprint for the creative teams at Applause to follow in order to promote the show.

"I thought we all agreed that was the plan."

Proactive Bob added: "For sure. Barry, though, shared with us the tagline you had come up with in your first meeting with him, 'The modern woman's new mantra.' I already have our designers coming up with logos incorporating it, but I also have our copywriters coming up with some alternative lines, you know, just in case."

Trapped in this confined space unprepared to see anyone from the network, let alone participate in an impromptu meeting, Sam decided it was not the best use of her time to debate/argue.

"Great," Sam humored. "When you've got something you like, just send it all my way."

Then, saved by the bell.

"This is my assistant," Sam announced, referencing the ping of her iPhone. "Excuse me."

Katie said that another client had responded to a proposal, and with that, Sam buried her face back in her phone and proceeded to reel off a list of things she needed Katie to do, as well as people she wanted her to reach out to in order to move other projects to the next phase.

The trip was an hour in light traffic, but unfortunately, tie-ups were more on the heavy side that morning, and so it took a bit longer to get where they needed to go.

Bob and Dave decided to get some shut-eye so that they would be awake and present at Hannah's speaking engagement. Dave had a crew already setting up at the venue; the footage was needed to cut into the show. Mindy and the driver made fast friends, talked amongst themselves, and thankfully left Sam alone.

Maybe it was the smooth ride or Inez's satisfying beverage, but the head of steam Sam had entered the car with had dissipated by the time she got out. Allison was spared a dressing down for leaving from her original text seminal information about traveling to a different part of Long Island with network people who put Sam on the spot by talking shop that she wasn't ready for.

She wanted a clear head for this event. This was research. *Go with the flow*, Katie had texted, and indeed Sam was ready to get to work. It was time to get involved or get left out. Whatever vulnerability she'd been experiencing since living outside of her milieu needed to be pushed aside.

Because she didn't know how long it would take for her to get her hands on the Applause footage, Sam decided to document the whole talk on her iPhone. Even before Hannah hit the stage, Sam was filming the crowd wearing Hannah's for-purchase merch: "Ban marriage" banners and t-shirts that read: "I'm an Anti-Wife," and the more aggressive ones depicting a middle finger with the saying, "Put a ring on this."

Allison came running up to Sam and, in all her passive/aggressive glory, asked Sam how her trip was, then when Sam's guard was down, Ms. iPad informed her that Hannah had a strict no filming policy. "'K?"

"No, it's not okay. That rule is so no one fires it up on YouTube, which would cut into the ticket sales of future events. I'm filming this for myself to help do my job."

A hesitant Allison tried to explain, "Um, no. And if you continue, I'm going to have to let Hannah—"

"Allison, you do you, and I'll do what I have to. And another thing, where's my place in all this? You know, where do I watch from?"

A Cheshire cat grin crossed Allison's face as she hugged her iPad and squealed as though she were about to announce that Sam was the state's ten-million-dollar lucky lotto jackpot winner. "You're in the front row, smack in the center."

Now it was Allison's turn to be unprepared. She was used to those who got that news to start screaming and lunging for a squeeze-the-life-out-of-her hug.

Sam's death stare was accompanied by inhaling then exhaling in such an exaggerated manner that Allison thought she was going to be blown away. Sam then expressed that if she was going to be there, it would have to be on her terms.

"I want to be backstage watching from the wings so that I can not only see Hannah, but the reactions of the audience, their responses, their faces when they ask questions, and more importantly, when they get their answers."

"Well . . ."

"Well, please get it done. Or shall I go to Hannah myself?"

Allison's biggest fear was of being replaced at any level, so she and her mighty Apple product started to back away, nodding her head to acknowledge that she would indeed "get it done."

When she turned to flee and find her boss, Allison did her own deep inhale/exhale, realizing that she was no match for Sam when the marketing consultant was firing on all cylinders. And even though she'd never dare say it out loud, Allison wondered if even Hannah would be.

*****

"I love men. I really do," pronounced Hannah, who began speaking even though the applause had yet to die down. "People say there are no good men out there. Well, I say they're wrong. There are fun, interesting, kind guys out there who are worthy of spending an evening or a weekend or some indefinite amount of time with, but we're not enjoying their company because when we first laid eyes on them, we didn't hear a choir of angels and get struck by a lightning bolt like in a cartoon; we didn't see 'the man I'm going to marry.'"

Hannah then hugged her chest in a mock imitation of a rom-com woman in love.

"If this were a Disney movie, there would be hearts flying out of my shirt every time I said the word 'marriage.'"

"Marriage," she repeated for emphasis. "The scourge of our society. Imagine a world without it. Where the government didn't have to get involved and declare your relationship legit; where you didn't end up feeling trapped by some piece of paper you signed; where you don't end up feeling like you just did it to get your mother and grandmother and Aunt Betty in Boca off your back because 'all your cousins are married.'"

The crowd was rapt. Sam had not seen such enthralled faces since she and The Man stood in Rome's St. Peter's Square with a hundred and fifty thousand of their closest friends as the Pope spoke to the crowd from the central balcony of the Basilica at the Vatican.

"Marriage is a construct of the patriarchy to pit women against women for a rose," making a pointed and disdainful reference to *The Bachelor*.

"We're always giving each other the finger—the fourth one on our left hands, meant to separate the desirables from the undesirables, the delineator being a sparkly gem atop a platinum band. But how many times do those promises of forever not last until death do we part?"

"Let's unpack that last bit, shall we? Anything that anyone is told that they have to do 'forever' automatically turns into a chore. And who wants to do chores? Marriage might have a chance—and I reiterate 'might'—if it had a time limit, like a passport or driver's license. Every, what? Two, maybe five years tops, you decide to renew. Or not."

Hannah was saying everything they wanted to hear and some things they didn't.

"I hate when people say, 'But if you don't get married, what happens when you're old?' Me, personally? I'll hire an eldercare companion; that's what'll happen. Like it's really the selling point for getting married to know that when you're sick, wrinkled, and toothless, you'll take care of each other. The reality is that women outlive men, so the real reality is he'll be dead, and you'll end up alone anyway."

Wait, where had Sam heard that before? The book? No, last night at dinner. It was what her brother and that guy Mike (or was it Ted?) had said.

Sam flinched, though not understanding why she was so bothered. Maybe because using the sentiments of others seemed inauthentic. This was Hannah's philosophy; why was she borrowing other people's words?

She immediately shook off her negative feelings. To sell the Applause show, Sam had to be positive about the product. Hannah does this talk how many times a month? She probably just needed to change it up for her own sake. Like musicians on tour or Broadway actors who perform the same show every night, Hannah must add a bit of new material each time just to keep things fresh so she didn't get bored, which could affect her performance.

Suddenly, Sam realized that the sage on the stage wasn't the only one being watched. She turned her head and was startled by an uncomfortably close cup of hot coffee.

"I thought you might need this," said Mindy.

"Uh, thanks."

Sam kept recording with her iPhone even though Mindy started talking. Sam was intrigued by her look: jet-black hair and pale white skin. The look wasn't goth, though. No, not at all Vampira, more like corporate Snow White.

"Here, let me," offered Mindy as she removed the phone from Sam's hand. "Take a break. I'll do this so you can drink in peace."

"Thanks, again," said Sam, grateful but confused.

Assistants often resented bringing coffee to even the people they worked for, let alone those they didn't.

"So, you like working at Applause?"

"It's a great opportunity for someone who just graduated. I majored in communications at Penn, and I minored in digital humanities, and my goal is to someday run a network like Barry Rogers."

Sam was able to gulp down most of the coffee while listening to Mindy's elevator pitch. Before she could give the younger woman an atta girl, though, Mindy revealed her true motive for the beverage delivery.

"Your reputation precedes you, and I just wanted to say, wow. I'm really impressed by you, you know, your whole 'so young, so accomplished' thing, and even though Bob is getting better about letting me get involved beyond answering the phone, I'd prefer a female mentor. May I call you some time, you know, for advice or whatever?"

"I think that would be—"

"Here." Mindy quickly traded the iPhone for Sam's empty coffee cup. Apparently, the entry-level aide had spied her superior in the distance crooking his finger for her to hop to it.

"And thanks," she yelled back as she ran off.

Fueled by caffeine and flattery, Sam turned her attention back to filming Hannah and her disciples.

The Anti-Wife was now giving the spectators a history of marriage.

"Romantic love is a fairly recent concept. Before that, it was this business agreement. The boy's family got someone to produce an heir, and the girl's father got cows. Even on *Downton Abbey*, remember, Lord what's-his-name admits to Elizabeth McGovern's character that he only married her to get her money to save the estate? What'd she get? Some BS title? Then he tells her that along the way, after they had three kids together, he did actually fall in love with her. Gee, big of him, huh?"

A thunderous ovation with a nice sprinkling of whoops and shouts of "Preach," and "Word" ensued.

"Not only that, but marriage came to be when people only lived to thirty-five—no one expected to stay together for fifty, sixty, seventy years."

Hannah's spiel about the saga of the institution with actual facts and a timeline projected behind her on a screen mesmerized the crowd, as though the magician had just revealed the secret to every trick in the illusionists' arsenal.

The Anti-Wife went on for another hour, then finished up with a standing O. Sam was shocked everyone didn't wave their iPhones' flashlights demanding an encore.

"Live life like you mean it—single AF."

Sam thought the mic drop was juvenile, and blasting Beyoncé's "All the Single Ladies" was cheesy, not to mention predictable, but it only made the audience clamor for more.

Still high on the sound of her own voice, Hannah left the stage and walked right past Sam as though she wasn't there and into the figurative arms of iPad Allison and a phalanx of admirers who'd left their comped, primo seats to rush backstage.

Allison turned to see Sam being left in the dust and texted her: *C'mon.* Miffed at her after-thought invite—actually order—Sam followed defiantly at her leisure at first but then picked up speed out of necessity. She didn't want to be left behind in Riverhead.

The car assignments stayed the same, except the Applause team arranged for their own ride back to Manhattan. They were gone by the time Sam got to car two, which she now had all to herself so she could check in with Katie via FaceTime.

"Was it great?"

"I'll say, very worthwhile. It had a Tony Robbins meets tent revival preacher meets *Sex and the City* episode where Carrie & Co. bitch about men over dinner. But I will say this: The woman has a presence. The audience..."

"Oh, I know," agreed Katie. "And you know, if I didn't have anyone, I might buy into that marriage-shouldn't-exist excuse to make myself feel bet—" And then the underling realized to whom she was speaking. "Although I mean, you don't have anyone, and you don't believe..." Like most people who put their foot in their mouth, once it's wedged in, it's hard to get it out. "I mean, you almost got..."

Sam was embarrassed for Katie and decided to come in for the save. "We're going through an area notorious for dropping calls. Before I hang up: Take tomorrow off. It's been a long week. Have a good long weekend. Talk Monday."

And with that, she hung up.

All week, Sam had been out of sorts. All week, she had blamed it on being under Hannah-house arrest, of being a guest in limbo; then the surprise speaking event and the arrival of the Applause people. She started to envision another ten days of more of the same ahead of her: Allison and her iPad. The stream of wild child groupies. The impromptu dinner parties. Sam was also anticipating a weekend that would rival some Gatsby-esque affair with wall-to-wall freeloaders and, as in the movie remake, Fergie singing, "A Little Party Never Killed Nobody" as its soundtrack.

But as atypical as this work experience had been for her so far, the peaceful, head-clearing drive back to Chez Randolph made Sam finally reconcile that things really hadn't been all that terrible. The house and food were amazing. The people she had socialized with, even Hannah, if nothing else, were entertaining and unlike most she knew. She had gotten other work done, spent time on the beach, which she otherwise would not have had, and been sleeping "like the dead," as her grandmother used to say.

At first blush, one would assume that the real reason for her angst had to do with Sam the Man, but oddly enough, she wasn't as broken up as one would expect. She couldn't put her finger on why his new life with another woman wasn't driving her crazy, and in fact, hadn't been top of mind since she got Allison's late-night text about meeting with Hannah.

Katie, though, was another story. Her assistant's engagement was beginning to rock her harder than that of Little Evie's. At least with her sister, the marriage meant the lifting of her caretaking responsibilities. But what did she gain with Katie's new situation?

Even if she never morphed into a bridezilla, and the newly betrothed spared Sam being kept in the loop about cake tastings or the bridesmaid dress challenge (same dresses/same colors, same dresses/different colors or different dresses/same colors), Sam would still hear her on the phone making appointments with catering halls or inevitably arguing with her mother over flowers or buttercream frosting. There would, of course, be a *Modern Bride* peeking out of her Coach tote, and every time she handed something to Sam, the small yet significant diamond ring would rear its glittery head.

Up until Katie's return from Bora Bora, they had had so much in common. Katie was also an outer-borough girl—from Queens, though, and had lived at home while studying at her NYC school. They both worshipped at the altar of prepdom and were romantically involved with guys they'd met in college.

Sam had secretly always thought how much easier life would have been if Katie had been her little sister; they were practically twins. And now that fantasy was gone.

One thing, though: they had never crossed the line into girlfriend territory; it was always clear who was the boss and who was the subordinate. Now, the idea that Katie might feel sorry for her, or worse, think herself above Sam because she had "Mrs." before her name gnawed away.

The CEO would have to lay down some ground rules. She didn't care whether it came off as sounding jealous or resentful, they worked in close quarters, and she just couldn't have Katie's personal life distracting either of them from Sam's business. She would work this out in her head and deal with it at another time because she was finally "home."

Car two was the last one to arrive at Chez Randolph, and, as suspected, the gang was all there and then some. The DJ's jam could already be heard from out back by the pool, and Sam felt a headache coming on as she slogged into the house. Just as her hand touched the banister, iPad Allison ran up and tapped her shoulder.

"Okay, so there's a buffet by the pool. You must be starving. Better hit it before the wolves devour everything."

Sam forced a smile, and just as she was about to continue on with her journey upstairs, Allison said, "Wait, before I tell you about tonight, what'd you think of the event? Hannah was great, wasn't she? Inspiring, right?"

Sam was tempted to ask which flavor Kool-Aid Allison favored but instead kept it professional.

"Yes, it was. I was so glad I had the opportunity to attend. If you'll excuse me, though. I need to change and collect my thoughts."

"One sec. Now tonight, as you can see, it's going to be a free-for-all, so Hannah just wants you to relax and par-tay down," said Allison while doing a little wiggle-in-place replete with raise-the-roof hand motions.

Trying with every ounce of what energy she had left to keep her head from blowing off, Sam, in an eerily calm way that frightened Allison just a bit, offered: "Thank Hannah for the gracious invitation, but I'm going to go to my room and make some notes gathered from what I witnessed today and perhaps even start the strategy for the campaign."

"But—"

Sam put her hand up, palm out like a crossing guard instructing kids to wait at the corner and said: "Excuse me," then continued upstairs.

Allison knew enough not to say another word and backed it up.

Or at least that's what Sam thought. As she mentally combat-crawled to the second-floor landing, she heard footsteps behind her. That was it. Allison and her iPad were goin' down—literally. She turned with daggers shooting out of her eyes.

"Miss Sam?" said Inez.

Sam felt ashamed of the harsh look that had been reserved for Hannah's assistant and immediately readjusted her expression, then dropped down a few steps so she and Inez would be face-to-face.

"Do you need me, Inez?"

"You must be hungry."

Even though she'd only had two cups of coffee so far that day, the last thing on her mind was food.

"Actually, not . . ."

"It's no good not to eat. I'll bring a plate of fruit and a bottle of water. Just a little something."

"You're very kind, Inez. I appreciate that."

As Sam changed clothes and felt the relief brought on by her shorts and t-shirt, as well as three Advil, she wondered about this affinity she had for Hannah's housekeeper.

In some way, Inez reminded her of her mother. Granted, she was a lot more subdued than Evelyn but cut from the same working-class cloth, looking older than her years because life had been far from accommodating. She was just a regular woman trying to earn her daily bread, putting up with a lot of nonsense to do so. "Lean in" and "#MeToo," even "Anti-Wife"—grand, life-changing concepts designed to help women in the long run meant little to the Inezes and Evelyns of the world who just tried to get through the day unscathed and for whom payday could never come soon enough.

When the housekeeper arrived at Sam's bedroom door, the fruit plate had been garnished with cheese as well as crackers.

"Thank you, Inez. You're very thoughtful. Would you come in for a minute?"

"Is there a problem, Miss Sam? Do you need . . . ?"

"No, no, nothing like that," Sam reassured, as this woman was usually only spoken to when someone needed an amenity. "I just want to chat."

"I'm sorry, Miss Sam, I have to get back . . ."

"Just for a minute. I promise."

Inez was self-conscious about being in Sam's room with the door closed and would not enter any farther than an inch from the wall.

"How do you like it here?"

"Oh, I have a very good job. I'm grateful."

"No, I understand," Sam said as she gestured to the beauty of their surroundings. "This is an awesome place to live and work. But," she continued, gesturing with a hitchhiker's thumb to the outside world, where the volume from the music and tumult was worthy of a visit from the local police, "I mean, that. How do you deal with all that all the time?"

"That's not my business. I just do my job. I really need to get back downstairs now. I'm sorry. Later I will bring you dinner. Something nice."

Inez was the last person Sam wanted to see screamed at by Hannah, so she grabbed the doorknob and held the door open.

"No, Inez. I'm sorry for keeping you. And thank you for the plate and for offering dinner."

Between bites, Sam riffed into her iPhone's voice-activated Notes app. She liked seeing her words type across the screen as she dictated. She had seen and heard more than she'd realized and was motivated to keep working through the evening, exhilarated by the feeling of being on a roll.

Before she knew it, Inez had returned with lobster tails, corn on the cob with some kind of chipotle sauce, and salad with Chef Kenny's special dressing that Hannah had mentioned she was going to help him bottle and bring to market.

"Thank you, Inez."

The maid smiled. She liked Sam, who was a cut above most of the people who passed through the place. Just as she reached for the doorknob, though . . .

"So, Inez."

Still facing the exit, Inez closed her eyes and asked Jesus why this lady would not leave her alone, then turned and said, "What else can I do for you, Miss?"

"Would you tell me how you got here? I know it's not my concern, but I'm interested in how Hannah finds the people she surrounds herself with. It's quite a mix. Do you mind?"

"I really don't like my business all over the place."

"It'll never leave this room. You have my word."

And with that, Inez gave Sam the *Reader's Digest* version of how she came to work for Hannah Randolph.

"I came to this country from Guatemala when I was nine. It took a while, but my brother, parents, and I became citizens. I didn't get far in school. I had to help my family pay bills. I cleaned houses like my mother. I got married when I was sixteen. My husband was older and had a good job with sanitation. When he died a few years ago, I took a job with a family who came here in the summers. They were just okay.

"One day, I was in town speaking in Spanish on my cell phone, and a man told me I should go back to where I came from. I told him I came from Brooklyn. He started yelling terrible things at me. 'Get out of my country,' like that. Out of nowhere, Miss Hannah came over and called him a racist and other curse words I don't say. People were cheering her on, and the man backed off. She asked me what I did. I said housekeeper. She asked me how much I made. I told her, and she said if I came to work for her, she'd triple my salary, and no one would ever talk to me like that again. I moved in that day."

"And you don't mind . . ."

"I mind nothing, except my own business. I have children; my four sons are grown; my daughter lives in Brooklyn with my mother. I see her on my day off. My girl will have people clean her house someday. When she graduates high school, she wants to go to Columbia University and then become a lawyer. I need to go back to work now."

"I went to Columbia. When she applies, have her get in touch."

Sam reached in her bag for a business card.

"I'd love to meet her and give her a recommendation. Anything I can do to help."

The usually stoic Inez did not speak until she knew she would not sound choked up.

To break the silence, Sam said: "Thank you, Inez. Sorry I kept you, yet again."

"Thank you, Miss Sam."

After the door closed behind Inez, Sam thought it best to re-watch the day's event for good measure and did so while she ate, stopping the footage to make written notes, which she took with the precision of a surgeon. Then she got to the part where Mindy came bearing gifts.

The video was fine, but the audio had been eclipsed by the recent grad's solicitous comments, which Sam replayed a few times. It was the second time in a week that her credentials had been met with a "wow."

That was who she was. That was what she had made of herself. And that would be her last thought of the day as she got into bed and went to sleep.

14

S am woke up slowly, one eye at a time. This was the first morning she hadn't had to register where she was. In fact, she had actually gotten used to waking up in what she began to jokingly call her "white castle."

Sam breathed in summer, but before she had a chance to exhale, there was a rap at the door. She checked her phone, and even though it seemed later, the digital display showed 8:30 a.m.

For the first time that week, Sam didn't look at the clock and leap out of bed like the Mad Hatter, worried that she was "late for an important date." She was not about to again rush down to the foyer only to be ambushed by iPad Allison, who would relay that Hannah was sleeping in/in a meeting/ out of town or simply that she took Fridays off.

Assuming the knocking was the ever-thoughtful Inez bringing her a cup of her sense-filling coffee, she rolled out of bed and opened the door, wearing her PJs and a grateful smile, which immediately turned to shock.

"Want to have breakfast?" Hannah said as she blew the face-framing tendrils that had escaped her messy bun out of her eyes.

Sam was experiencing yet another first: a barefoot Hannah wearing a Tory Sport leggings and bralette set in a stance that did not scream "power pose," but more that of a bashful teenage boy asking a girl out on a date, body turned a quarter-way around in order to make a run for it in case the answer was no.

"Sure, sure," Sam agreed awkwardly. "Just let me get dressed. I'll be right down. Um, are we eating on the patio or ...?"

"Carl's driving us into town. Some of my revelers never left, and, well, the place is just a little too crowded for my taste."

For the life of her, Sam didn't understand why Hannah never demanded her house back from these slackers with the old bartender edict, "You don't have to go home, but you can't stay here." But whatever, she was hungry, and as long as she ate, Sam didn't care where.

She washed her face, pulled her hair back into a pony, and since she never embraced the whole athleisure wear fashion trend, pulled on her faded Levi's, a cropped white t-shirt, and white Keds.

Sam headed downstairs with a little more difficulty than usual, as there were people passed out on each step. They were also unconscious on the floor of the foyer, and a quick peek into the library revealed dead-to-the-world bodies in there, too.

The kitchen was clear, though, but on the other side of the patio doors and around the pool of Hannah's multi-million-dollar home, it mirrored a cheap motel the morning after homecoming.

The former Bronx girl began to have a deja-vu of eighth grade. Her friend Joanie had slept over because her parents were away for the weekend, and her high school–age brother, Brian, had decided to take advantage and have a party. He invited everybody from his junior class as well as half the neighborhood and told Joanie to get lost for the evening.

The next morning, it was Sam's job to take two-year-old Little Evie to the playground. Joanie said she would tag along if they could stop by her apartment to change her shoes for more park-friendly sneakers. The two girls—and Evie in her stroller—entered the home, and the first thing they noticed was the floor was moving; the teen party guests had passed out, forming a wall-to-wall human carpet. There were so many bodies that the girls couldn't see the actual rug.

Surveying the pizza boxes, bags that once housed chips and pretzels, as well as countless empty beer bottles, Joanie said, "I hope he doesn't make me help him clean this up."

"How could he let them do this?" Sam observed, not being able to process the scene.

Joanie, who was embarrassed by the state of the house her mother was always cleaning, yet at the same time, angry that Brian hadn't let her stick around for the festivities, suggested, "Maybe you should wait outside."

Sam countered the proposal with, "We'll meet you at the park."

That time, Sam wrote off her surroundings as, *Well, I guess that's what high school parties look like*. But now, she couldn't begin to explain what she was seeing. These people were adults, for Christ's sake. Why would they greet Hannah's hospitality by disrespecting her magnificent home this way? Harkening back to wonder, how could someone let people treat their home this way?

Suddenly, Hannah appeared in the door jamb of the kitchen. She had added Tory running shoes as well as a zip-up pullover to her earlier ensemble.

"Ready to roll?"

Not since the day she arrived had Sam been more ready to get out of Chez Randolph.

****

"Candy Kitchen, Carl, and step on it."

Hannah, using a voice reminiscent of a "dame" in a 1940s movie, said it as a joke, but both Carl and Sam knew the driver indeed better get a move on.

"So, Sam, do you know the Hamptons?"

"Well, I know what it looks like from driving through it on the way to Montauk."

"Ah, 'The End' as all the t-shirts say."

"Yeah," acknowledged Sam, "I like it out there. Or, at least, I used to."

"It's nice, but a little too far out for me and rural. But it's gotten more happening in the last several years."

"Much to the chagrin of the locals."

"So, did you have a summer share?"

"No," said Sam, bashfully, although she didn't understand why she should be embarrassed. "Whenever I, um, came out, actually, we came out, my boyfriend and I, um, actually fiancé, we took his boat out and lived on it after we docked at the Westlake Marina. We did that for years. They knew us, we knew them, it was, you know, literally like our home away from home. His family has a place on Martha's Vineyard, but, um, you know we wanted somewhere that was, like, you know, ours."

Um? You know? Literally? Was it Sound Like An Inarticulate Teenager Day? Sam finally got her big moment with the Holy Grail; it was her time to flex, but instead of being in control and impressive, she was acting nervous and insecure, hence the verbal crutches.

"Oh, so you're engaged?" Hannah asked, almost sounding accusatory.

"Not anymore."

"Well, I bet that's a story," Hannah said, hoping one would ensue and sounding a little too relieved at the demise of her guest's relationship to suit Sam.

"Not really."

Hannah looked at Sam skeptically but decided to drop it for the moment.

"So, do you like the Hamptons?"

Sam smiled and proceeded to give her host her view of Long Island's hot vacay spot, the whole time thinking, *C'mon, Carl, step on it.*

There was a line to get into the popular, old-school diner. They didn't take reservations; they also didn't serve alcohol and catered to a family-friendly crowd. Sam was shocked Hannah would even set foot in the place.

The restaurant was renowned for serving an eclectic mix of locals, posh summer people, and the occasional celebrity. Today, that was Hannah. Yet even she had to wait.

While they did, Sam was happy to be spared more chitchat, thanks to fans coming up to her host and asking to have their copies of her book signed—it seemed like every woman in the place had one—and to ask the Anti-Wife herself relationship questions, which she was more than glad to answer with the go-to, "Don't get married."

All the while, Sam hung back, watching in stoic amazement. Although she was not used to being anyone's second banana, in fact, Sam herself was an It Girl—coming out of internal meetings or client presentations and having colleagues or superiors approach her to say, "Amazing work," "Great job," or "Wow, you nailed it,"—but for this display of hero-worship, she was content to watch from the wings. Her only regret was not having popcorn for the show.

There was vying for Hannah's attention like second graders feverishly waving their "teacher, pick me" hands, tugging at the hem of her garments to feel close to her or perhaps by osmosis transfer to themselves some of Hannah's magic. People were sobbing, some because they confided to their idol (notwithstanding before a crowd) a story of their heartbreak or because they were so overcome to witness their guru in the flesh. For Sam, it was simultaneously awe-inspiring and frightening, and to some degree, ludicrous.

As this went on for a good forty minutes, Sam's initial astonishment waned, so she used the rest of the time to pull herself together and get her mojo back in gear. She'd been thrown by the spur-of-the-moment invite, which was probably Hannah's intention, and the confines of the albeit spacious car were just too close for comfort.

When they finally got seated and Sam, alas ,got her moment for a face-to-face sit-down with Hannah, she wanted it to be as productive as possible. Sam was going to dissect the Anti-Wife movement like a frog in bio lab.

After the waitress took their like-minded order of black coffee and French toast, Sam reached into her bag, pulled out her iPhone, and said, "I hope you don't mind, but I think I'll record our interview. It's a lot easier for me than sitting here taking notes, especially if I'm also trying to eat my breakfast, which I think now we can safely call brunch."

Hannah picked up Sam's cell from the table, powered it down, and then tossed the thousand-dollar piece of electronic equipment back in Sam's Goyard as though it were a used tissue.

Sam was one expletive away from giving this rude, abrasive, presumptuous woman/child how-to-act lessons, then, as usual, remembered she needed to remain professional because Hannah was the client.

She cleared her throat and said, "Well, okay then, I guess I'll be taking notes, after all."

Hannah sat back, with arms crossed and eyebrows raised, the way Little Evie used to do whenever Sam didn't give the tyke her way.

"What?" Sam wanted to know. "What am I missing here?"

"When I invited you to get exposed to the whole Anti-Wife zeitgeist, it wasn't really so that you could get to know me; it was so I could get to know you; sure, Barry thinks you walk on water, but I had to see for myself that you were legit. I mean, you look great on paper, but some people's resumes could make it onto *The New York Times'* fiction bestseller list.

"By the way, I know this was a major inconvenience for you, taking you away from your business and all. Allison told me how frustrated you've been, so I paid two weeks of this month's maintenance on your apartment. It'll be reflected on your next bill."

Hannah spewed this mouthful as casually as she would later mention that she was picking up the tab for their meal.

"You . . . you . . . you," Sam stammered. She finally experienced first-hand what gobsmacked felt like. "Did what?"

"Oh, don't get your thong in a bunch. I knew it was a hassle, and so I just wanted to let you know I appreciated your coming out here."

Sam felt as though she'd just found out the FBI had a wiretap on her phone.

"How in the world did you know how much . . . ?"

"Oh, you know, Allison. She could launch a missile from that iPad. I think she reached out to a realtor connection or something and asked what the maintenance was in a building like yours in an apartment your size, and we just guesstimated. Don't make a big deal out of it. It's just something I wanted to do."

Sam was going to have to let this line-crossing, albeit generous, gesture go for now.

There was absolutely nothing she could do about it, sitting in the restaurant, waiting for her food, but she would be returning the money.

Instead of sharing that decision, which would only take the conversation off track, Sam just said, "Well, thank you. I heard about your big-heartedness from some of your guests the other night, and I'm flattered that you extended it to me as well."

"So, let's talk about you," Hannah grinned while resting her chin on her hands and elbows on the table.

Let's not and say we did. "Sure, what would you like to know?"

"Begin from the beginning. Family?"

"Yes."

"Describe."

"Mother, father, younger sister."

"Parents still married?"

Sam managed to contain herself and matter-of-factly said: "I was raised by a single mother."

"Aha," blasted Hannah as she smacked the table. "Abandonment issues."

Whether it was the embarrassment of being glared at by other patrons, who were blaming her not their idol for disturbing their breakfast, or having a virtual stranger expose part of her psyche she had been in denial about for over two decades, Sam braced herself by gripping the edge of the table to keep her hands from double-fisting Hannah right in the rhinoplasty.

Expressionless, she replied, "I don't have abandonment issues."

Loud and proud at getting the opportunity to "shrink" Sam, Hannah continued: "Anybody who has a parent who leaves has abandonment issues."

"I never felt abandoned," Sam said, cold as the fresh ice with which the waitress was filling her water glass. "Without getting into detail, trust me when I say he did us a favor."

Hannah, who was used to being the intimidating one in the room, sensed it was a good time to drop that line of questioning. She, though, would find a different way to get to the chewy center of this story.

"So, you and your mother—besties?"

Feeling some triumph over her host, Sam turned up the temperature on her end of the conversation.

"We are not. In fact, we have always been in a long-distance relationship, even when we lived in the same house. Now that we don't, it's more of a 'touch-base to make sure you're not dead' kind of thing."

"Let's talk about the little sister."

"Her name is Evie."

"Okay, Evie. You get along?"

"Yes."

"You know," sighed Hannah, "if I wanted to pull teeth, I would've become a dentist. So, are you like BFFs or what?"

"I'm more like her mother. We're ten years apart."

"Got it. What was it like always having to take care of her? How badly did you hate that? How much did you, or do you still resent her?"

This woman could out-interrogate Olivia Benson.

"I don't resent my sister."

"Okay, I call BS. Look, this is never going to work if we blow smoke up each other's crop tops. As you can tell from my rallies and my book and my TV interviews, and the fact that I let a camera follow me around for a reality show, I'm as transparent as Saran wrap. I expect the same from others in my life."

Sam swallowed hard, Barry's words echoing: *Everyone who works on this potentially rewarding project will placate her.*

"Now, you said Evie is ten years younger. So, okay," continued Hannah, scrunching her face as she did the math in her head while looking up as though some virtual calculator would appear to aid in the subtraction. "That's roughly like me and my sister, Cecile. You know, by the time I was born, my mother was kind of exhausted, and so she charged Cecile with raising me. My mother, of course, made all the final decisions on everything, but for the day-to-day, Cecile was indeed 'the boss of me.' I was a little confused at first, you know, my sister instead of my mom showing up at all the things that my other friends had their mothers at, but I got used to it, and then I started to like it. I thought it was cool. I was always with the older girls; I thought they were my friends, and I thought it was a blast to hang with my sister. Two of my other sisters are twins. They hung around with the same crowd and were best friends. For some inexplicable reason, I saw mine and Cecile's relationship the same as theirs. Yes, I was an idiot.

"But anyway, as I got older and started to think back, I realized my poor sister was always having to tote me around, never having a minute's peace with her friends. She couldn't even get into normal teenage trouble because she'd be afraid I'd run back and tattle—and I would have. She always had to make sure I got my homework done, that my lunch was made for school. My God. Your teen years are supposed to be fun. Hers sure weren't. When I got famous, I bought my parents and sibs houses, but Cecile's was the biggest and even better than the one I got for my mother and father. I handed her the keys and said, 'I'm so sorry. I hope this makes up for all the years you lost having to take care of me.' I thought for a minute that she'd say, 'Don't be silly; it was all good.' Instead, she nabbed the keys and said, 'No, it doesn't make up for it, but it's a start.' So how badly did it suck taking care of Evie?"

Sam could not explain the myriad of feelings happening simultaneously: embarrassment that Hannah, all in one breath it seemed, had nailed her youth, amusement at how ridiculous and just plain crappy it sounded, and a strange sense of relief that Sam had not been the only one who spent her formative years as a nanny.

Sam contemplated that maybe when this gig was over, Hannah could set up a lunch for her with Cecile. It sounded like they'd have a lot of notes to compare.

The ad exec could honestly say she had never met anyone like Hannah

Randolph in her entire life. This woman could bring out the best and the worst in people, and at that moment, Sam, who had never been one to overshare, not even to Lena, had an overwhelming desire to go all Hans Christian Andersen and tell the Anti-Wife the story of her life.

******

"OMG, I feel like I'm sitting here listening to Cecile," said Hannah. "Little Evie owes you a house."

Breakfast was long done, and both women were on their fourth coffee refills.

"I don't need a house. I need her to stay married to her husband. Let him be her mother from now on."

Did that nasty remark just come out of Sam's mouth? She never said anything against Evie, not aloud anyway. Rarely even to herself.

"So that's why you were cool with your younger sister getting married before you; it got her off your back."

Sam would have never put it so bluntly, but no matter how you couched it, the answer was the same: "Yes, the timing left something to be desired, but that aside, her getting married was a good thing for both of us."

"What was the problem with the timing?" a curious Hannah asked innocently.

Sam didn't answer right away. She took a beat, the kind that lasts a second but feels like an hour. Once she let Hannah tug that thread, she knew this pit bull with bleached-blonde hair would never let go until the whole garment was unraveled and left on the floor in shreds.

For some reason, though, she wanted to bare her soul and show Hannah that she too had graduated summa cum straight-shooter from the school of tell-it-like-it-is.

"I was left at the altar," Sam said, then just let the sentence hang there, like a king-size sheet flapping on a clothesline, too big to ignore.

It was refreshing for Sam to witness Hannah's mouth open but with nothing coming out of it.

Hannah's eventual response was to move away from the table and suggest they walk and talk, as they could not justify sitting there any longer. Sam agreed, whipped out her Amex, and grabbed the check as apropos any client meal.

"They don't take cards," said Hannah, as always, taking pleasure when she knew something—no matter how trivial—that others didn't.

"Don't stress. I got this. Besides, I invited you."

As Sam returned her credit card to its slot in her wallet, Hannah reached in her pocket and threw two hundred-dollar bills on the table, approximately $150 of which being the tip.

"Thank you."

"Don't thank me yet. We have to have their homemade ice cream for our walk."

Sam was still full but decided not to argue with this woman who was starting to feel like, what? Fam?

******

"You called him Sam the Man? Excuse me while I vomit. I would've never pegged you for cutesy?"

"I didn't make it up; our friends did."

"Find new friends."

"I did. Actually, they all up and went with him when we split." *Who wouldn't*, she thought. He was the one with the boat, the private club membership, and the family home on The Vineyard. "I guess they were always kind of his friends in the first place."

Sam had spent the past twenty minutes spewing the play-by-play of their relationship like a chock-full whirring blender with the top off. And now came the grand finale.

"And then I got left at the altar, not literally, but close enough. After over a decade together, we planned a wedding, then six days before the big day, he sent me an email saying he wouldn't be going through with it."

She said this with such candor that the usually unflappable Hannah was taken aback more by Sam's tone than her story.

"So, this explains your comment the other night at my barbecue. The guy who didn't want to get married is marrying someone else?"

"He is."

"Okay, wait. I need you to elaborate on one part. So, after you got the email and you saw your life making a hard-left turn, what did you . . . ?"

"I contacted my people and said, 'Wedding's off.'"

"No, I mean when it came to him. What did you do next?"

"Oh, I called. But when he started excuse-making, I realized I didn't want an excuse and just hung up. Then I sent his family heirloom engagement ring back to him."

"Did he send you the monetary equivalent . . ."

"No. I got the apartment instead."

"What about the honey—?"

"We were going to his family's home on Martha's Vineyard, so there was no hotel and all that to cancel."

"I'll go out on a limb here and assume you had a gown?"

"Returned to Rent The Runway."

"But what did you do?" Hannah said, sounding like a parent who was told of some scuttlebutt at school and was trying to get to the bottom of her kid's part in it.

"I just told you." *Does this woman have comprehension issues?*

A frustrated Hannah let out a silent scream as she slapped both her cheeks so she resembled Macaulay Culkin on the *Home Alone* poster.

"No, you gave me bullet points; you recited your to-do list. What I'm asking is, did you not get out of bed and cry for a month; throw his shit down the garbage chute; go crazy AF?"

Even more even-toned than before, Sam said, "No. No. And no."

"So, since you and your mom aren't BFFs, whose shoulder did you cry—"

"I didn't cry. I talked to my friend Lena."

"What'd she . . . ?"

"She said all the things women tell other women after they get dumped: His loss. He was probably threatened by your success. And the ever-popular, he was always an asshole."

"Did you stalk his new babe on social?"

Sam shook her head, proud that she didn't know the identity of the future Mrs. Winston.

"I'm not fifteen. Or a masochist. If I had one piece of advice to give, especially young people who come out of the womb tech-savvy, it would be don't follow up on the exploits of an ex. Every time you do, it's like you're asking to have your heart broken all over again.

"Look, no one likes to be rejected. No one wants to realize that the person you thought was there for you made other plans. I was shaken up at first and confess I had a mini-freak out that involved a hospital visit, which

I don't want to get into, and I've had many sleepless nights, and I still get teary now and again, but when it happened, I was in the throes of having my own business and threw myself into that. It saved me, you know, having something so all-consuming on my plate."

With that, Sam expected Hannah, an entrepreneur in her own right, to nod understandingly, perhaps say something consoling to which Sam would assure her that it was "all good." Instead, Hannah eyeballed her with the skepticism of someone who'd just listened to a used car salesman pitch a clunker as "practically new and only driven on Sundays by a little old lady."

"Hmmm, well, I don't think you threw yourself into your business as a distraction. I think you just went about your business as usual. I think your ego was bruised because he beat you to the punch, but I don't think your heart was broken. I'm sensing that the reason you handled the situation so well is that you never really wanted to get married in the first place. You're a dyed-in-the-wool Anti-Wife, and you don't even know it. Or won't admit it."

"No, I always wanted to . . ."

"Okay, I thought we had bypassed the BS portion of our program?" said Hannah as she popped the tip of her waffle cone in her mouth and tossed her crumpled napkin into a nearby garbage can before she continued with, "The way I see it . . ."

Oh, this should be good, thought Sam as she returned the skeptical gaze.

Hannah ignored Sam's cynicism and kept going: "You wanted to revenge marry. Your parents had a bad one, and you have a hate bag on for your mother because deep inside, even though you know what your dad was, you still blamed her for his leaving. The best way to get back at her for that and her turning you into a 24/7 babysitter was to do what she couldn't: get a roman-numeral guy, have his kid while maintaining a successful career, then have her over at the holidays to show her how a real wife and mother gets it done. You latched onto this guy from the get-go, not because he was the one but the one who'd fit the suit. And you could cross 'find a man' off your to-do list."

The smirk was gone from Sam's face. She opened her mouth, not sure what she was going to say, but she wanted to say something just to make Hannah stop talking.

That'd be the day. The youngest of half a dozen kids who'd spent most of her childhood being shouted down by older siblings as well as her parents had vowed that as an adult, no one would ever shut her up again. She held up her hand like a young Diana Ross singing "Stop in the Name of Love" and said, "I'm not finished.

"I also don't think that you've ever had baby fever. You already raised a child, and quite frankly, I don't think you liked it all that much. Now don't get your back up, I'm not saying you don't like or love your little sister, but you didn't like being her mother, and that kind of turned you off to ever doing that job again.

"Then, after, what'd you say, over a decade of being with this guy, he backs out of the wedding, and you don't want to throw yourself or him off a building, or fall into a covers-over-your-head depression or even wonder how much a hitman would cost? No, you got up, put on one of your little suits, and went all kick-ass on your own business, to which all I can say is kudos on your hustle. And somewhere in there, you participated in Evie's wedding without going postal. Gurrl, you may not want to admit it, at least not outright, but . . ."

As she summed up, Hannah poked the center of Sam's chest as though it were a hive, and she was deliberately trying to incite the bees and repeated what Sam had said about her father: "Deep inside, you know Sam the Man did you a favor."

This was a record scratch moment if there ever was one.

They had stopped walking when Hannah began her tirade and were standing in the middle of the sidewalk so passersby would have to walk around them. Sam had long finished her cone but was fisting her napkin as though it were a grenade, and if she loosened her grasp, she and everything around her would explode. She had never thought of herself as being someone who had baggage, but now she felt as though she had more than the carousel at JFK.

Who needed a team of Viennese specialists when there was Hannah Randolph? What this firecracker lacked in formal education, intellectual prowess, and social graces, she made up for by being able to get down to the studs and make people see and hear the truth whether they wanted to or not.

Suddenly, Sam felt a lightness, like Atlas finally having the world taken off his shoulders, and she didn't know how to respond, so she settled for, "Can we walk, please?"

Hannah answered by just starting to move, and sensing some instability on Sam's part, linked their arms. After a few steps, though, Sam said, "I have to sit down," and so they did on a bus stop bench.

Everything her client-cum-therapist had just spouted made her fear that perhaps she didn't know her real self.

Perhaps Sam had been playing the role of the woman who saw the natural progression of life being girlfriend, wife, then full-time mother and part-time businesswoman until the children were old enough, then she would go back to business nine to five.

She knew how that woman operated. She knew how to play her. But this other woman? The one Hannah just described to a T, who did not want a husband or children? Sam did not know how that woman carried herself. She realized, though, that she better figure it out if she was ever going to start living what she now believed, thanks to Hannah's objectivity, might be her truth.

"Carl will be here in five. I also texted Allison to book you on the next Blade and have Inez pack your things. The helicopter goes from East Hampton to East 23rd Street. Including the cab ride, you'll be home in about an hour," announced Hannah.

If she'd been wearing her pearls, Sam would have clutched them. She couldn't even focus on the almost thousand-dollar copter ride back to New York City that she was being treated to; she was too fixated on the bum-rush out of the Hamptons. *This is all my fault*, Sam thought, blaming herself for crossing the line from professional to personal.

"Why? You said you wanted me here for two weeks." Trying to reclaim her professionalism, Sam stated, "I'm committed to the two weeks."

Hannah shook her head. "No, not necessary. I had estimated that I would need that long to size you up and decide if you really understood the whole Anti-Wife thing. But now I know you're more her than I am."

Just then, Carl pulled up. Sam dove into the backseat, nestled against the headrest and closed her eyes. Hannah stayed quiet as well; the two women had talked enough for ten car rides.

When they pulled up at the mansion, Carl got out and helped Inez load Sam's luggage into the trunk. As Hannah slid out of the car, Allison handed her Sam's printout for the flight. She in turn reached through the back window and handed the paperwork to Sam.

In the tone that seemed to forget the past soul-bonding hours had ever happened, Hannah said, "I expect to see some fabulous AF work when I meet with you, Barry, and the rest of the marketing group."

Before Sam could even nod her head, the Anti-Wife was strutting up her front steps with iPad Allison in tow.

15

Sam had traveled extensively for business, and during their relationship, she and The Man had gone to Europe a number of times and Bora Bora once, which she christened the most exquisite place on earth, hence the reason she suggested it to Katie. A helicopter, however, had never before been on the transportation agenda. It was at once both exhilarating and terrifying.

Before either emotion could win out, Sam had landed. Her Uber zipped up the FDR Drive, indeed returning Sam home from the south shore of Long Island in less than an hour.

Her excursion had been so whirlwind that when she reached her building and Jimmy greeted her with, "Welcome back, Miss Dennehy. Where were you off to this time?" Sam opened her mouth, but nothing came out. She had to think, really think, *Where have I been?*

"Oh, uh, the Hamptons."

The past five days had been like an out-of-body experience so for a moment she couldn't discern whether her previous workweek had been real or imagined.

Any other time she would have immediately announced her arrival home by texting Lena and popping into the office. She'd then relay every detail, and revisit with head-shaking mockery the highlights of her time at

Chez Randolph and tell of her entrée into Blade travel.

The minute she shut the door to her apartment, though, Sam drank in the silence and wanted it to envelop her for what she thought might be forever. No television would blare. No Apple Music would thump through Bose speakers. Sam even turned the volume all the way down on her phone.

For the rest of the late afternoon and evening, all Sam could think about was what Hannah had said to her earlier that day; was it really only this morning? It had seemed like a lifetime ago. She binge-watched the conversation in her mind, sometimes responding to her now imaginary friend with a defensive chortle of the "You don't know what you're talking about" variety, and sometimes with honesty, agreeing with Hannah's assessments and backing them up with, in some cases, painful examples.

By midnight, her thoughts so exhausted her that Sam ended up falling asleep on the sofa and did not wake up until dinnertime the following day.

She had missed Saturday day and thought it best to at least do something Saturday night, even if it were to simply get the air.

The born-and-bred city girl walked the promenade that overlooked the East River, first going south down to 72nd Street, turning around and heading north all the way to 96th, then back home to 86th.

She tried to use the time to actually work up a sweat, not just physically but emotionally, over the fact that Sam the Man was going to have a wife who was not her. She wanted to give one last attempt at proving Hannah wrong; that Sam had wanted to get married and that it bothered her that another woman would be living her life.

Thanks to her caregiver duties, Sam never had much of a social life in high school, so she had been determined to have one in college. That first day when she met Samuel, and he was not only double-take handsome in his light blue Ralph Lauren Polo shirt and khakis but had made the first move, she thought, *jackpot*.

"How'd you get him?" her mother asked with a saucy sneer when Sam finally brought her boyfriend around at Christmas of freshman year. Apparently, the fact that her daughter was the real catch had been lost on Evelyn.

Truth was, Sam had not had to lift a finger to "get him."

The athletic prep with the movie-star face and sparkling green eyes that were the standard against which emeralds were measured, with which he used to make intense eye contact, had pursued her from the moment their gazes locked. He even put down his lacrosse stick long enough to introduce himself with a lingering handshake.

"Hi, I'm Sam."

Fighting the urge to run her fingers through his straight, light brown bangs that were brushing his eyelashes, she remained as calm as possible and tried not to stammer: "Hi, I'm Sam, too. Samantha, but everyone calls me, well, as I said."

Her initial excitement gave way to wariness though, after he mentioned he was a native of the Park Avenue ilk. Even though she could pass for one of the debutantes she was sure he was used to dating, her pedigree was a 180 from that world. But Samuel seemed relieved upon hearing her lay it on the line with, "There's no one in my family named Muffy, and we don't know which end of the Cape is up. By the way, I'm from the Bronx."

"Yea, I could tell by your accent," he assured her.

At that moment, Sam set her freshman year goals: make the Dean's List both semesters and lose from her speech any trace of from whence she came.

Not long after their meet-cute, the two Sams became inseparable.

Everyone gushed over the same name coincidence and created the moniker for her other half, which added to the cachet of their eventual campus couple status.

Because The Man was so popular, she suddenly was too. There was no denying it was quite a kick to go from high school hermit to college social butterfly.

So caught up in the whole gestalt of friends and being part of a two-some, Sam never stopped and thought, *Do I really like all these people? Was Sam the Man Mr. Right, or merely Mr. Right Now?*

His family also added to the appeal of the relationship. What a far cry the Winstons were from what she had known growing up in her outer borough. The first time she and The Man pulled up in a taxi in front of 1088 Park Avenue, Sam thought she had died and gone to *Gossip Girl* heaven.

It was not so much the money that impressed her but the breeziness by which they lived. She had grown up in a home thick with anxiety and anger. But these people had a calm about them. True, their serenity had a lot to do with not wondering where the funds were going to come from to settle the Con Ed bill, but Sam found it refreshing just the same.

The father, Samuel Winston, Jr., was the stately, salt and pepper version of The Man, who could have easily adorned the catalogue pages of Brooks Brothers. A distinguished man of few words, he seemed to just sit back and watch his world fall into place around him thanks mostly to his wife, Clare, a slightly older "Lily," aka Kelly Rutherford's *GG* character. The Man's forty-something mother had a patina of sophistication Sam had never experienced in day-to-day life and was as condescending as her son had said she would be.

"Where do Bronx people summer, dear?" was meant to embarrass Sam rather than get to know her. But the younger woman from humble beginnings was so taken by the seasoned woman's glamour that she let it eclipse the haughtiness. Sam just liked to watch Clare go about her business dealing with staff, speaking on the phone, presiding over meals. She couldn't even imagine what it must have been like to have a mother so poised.

Sam had grown on the Winstons. They had her out to The Vineyard and invited the young couple to dinners at Daniel and 11 Madison Park. If nothing else, experiences like these helped Sam strive to better herself socially, gain composure, and act more dignified. Modeling Clare could only help her when she entered the business world.

Sam fell out of favor, though, when the scion dropped out of college to pursue cooking for a living.

Clare had asked Sam out to a fancy lunch at the Colony Club that had not gone the way the matron had predicted.

"Young men do what they do, and it's the women in their lives who are responsible for getting them back on track," said Clare as she stirred her G&T.

Sam just stared at her and nodded, overawed by her surroundings. She knew if she darted her eyes away for a second, she'd get so distracted by the goings-on at the city's most exclusive and prestigious private women's social club, Clare would think her guest had ADHD.

"We want him back in school, as in Columbia. We have bigger plans for him than being a short-order cook. So, what I need from you, my dear . . ."

"That's not what he wants, or actually what he is," interrupted Sam, thinking that if she clarified things, Clare would be more understanding. "His dream is to be an executive chef at a Michelin-starred restaurant. The ones you usually go to. Then the end game is to open his own place."

"As I said, we have other plans for Samuel, and I need you to help us talk sense into him and get him back where he belongs. I'll buy him a recipe book. He can slave over a hot stove in his spare time."

Sam was about twenty years old then and no match for the likes of Clare, but stood by her man, calling him an artisan, saying that being a chef, not a "cook" was his calling and that those who cared about him should support his dream.

Sam stopped seeing the Winstons because Sam the Man did. Then when he reconnected after graduation, he wouldn't bring her with him to Park Avenue because the visits always ended in an argument about his restaurant job on the line. Sam didn't see them again until the food stylings of Samuel Winston started getting written up in magazines, especially their bible, *Town & Country.*

But by that time, Sam had developed her own grace and style, as well as garnered her own success, so she no longer felt they were deigning to invite her in.

The Man had done her a favor all right. As well as now accepting as gospel Hannah's assessment that Sam didn't want a husband or baby, she realized in-laws were unwanted as well.

16

Sam puttered around and slept most of Sunday, so her weekend had offered a well-needed actual vacation from her mandated work vacation at Hannah's. But it was Monday morning, and she needed to get back down to business.

Her vision for *The Anti-Wife* show had to get down on paper and out to the Applause team in the next day or two, so they could begin creating the promotional materials to be approved by her at the beginning of the following week. Then they would present to Barry. The week after that, a theatrical production worthy of Broadway would be put on for Hannah.

Sam grabbed the Anti-Wife mug she'd brought home as a souvenir for Katie and went next door, ready to hit the ground running. That plan was thwarted when she couldn't see the flooring. As she entered her empty office, Sam was literally stopped in her tracks by all the detritus spread out on the parquet.

Pages ripped from bridal magazines with fabric swatches beside them were next to travel destination printouts and, "Is that a vision board?" said Sam aloud to no one. A piece of oak tag the size of a throw rug had at least fifty little cut-out pictures of houses and furniture and children and . . .

"Oh, you're here. What happened? Why . . . ?" said Katie sheepishly as she slid in the front door.

"Let's start with you answering my questions. What is all this?"

"Okay, let me explain . . ."

"While I was away, I trusted you to keep the office running, not turn it into your wedding-planning studio."

Trying to remain in check and professional, Katie cleared her throat and began what she thought Sam would see was a reasonable justification: "I did take care of the office. Everything you needed doing got done. Even though you gave me last Friday off, I came in because, as you know, I have two roommates, so there's just not enough space in the apartment to spread stuff out. So, I took the liberty of doing what I had to do here."

Sam started to lose patience with this story, especially when Katie got to the part where around 4:30 on Friday afternoon, her fiancé showed up to whisk her away for a surprise romantic weekend in Maine.

"He hurried me out of here so quickly that I figured I'd just clean up this morning. I mean, I didn't think it would matter because you weren't going to be here anyway."

"Well, I am here. It turns out that I'm a quicker study than Hannah gave me credit for, and when she saw that I had a handle on the Anti-Wife movement, we agreed there was no reason for me to be there 'deep diving' when I could be here, getting the campaign done. Now, I'm going back to my apartment to make my coffee. When I return, I want this all put away so we can get to work."

Sam changed her mind about gifting Katie the keepsake cup, turned, and walked out.

As she drank her brew from her new mug, wishing it was Inez's blend, her cell rang.

"Hey, Lena. You back from Vegas?"

"Indeed."

"I'm back too. I didn't have to stay the full two weeks, after all. Have I got a story for you."

"And I one for you. Ben and I got married."

Crickets.

"Hello? Sam?"

"I'm here."

"Oh, I thought the call dropped. Did you hear me? I said . . ."

"How could you?"

"What? This is the part where you say, 'Congratulations.'"

"For what? Entering into this . . . what do you always call it? The institution that you're not ready for? You're the last person . . ."

"Okay, my friend. Perhaps I caught you at a bad time. But regardless, why don't we begin again. I say, 'I got married,' and then you say—"

"I don't need what-to-say lessons from anyone."

She regretted her words straightaway, and with tears in her eyes, whispered, "I'm sorry," and offered Lena best wishes.

"Listen, I've got to get into the office. Katie's waiting. I'll call you back later, and you can tell me all about it."

Sam hung up before even finishing her sentence.

The list of people she saw falling for what the Anti-Wife had called "an antiquated life choice" had grown by yet another one, and it was one Sam couldn't bear.

Until Sam met Hannah, Lena was the lone person she'd ever met who was super-confident in who she was and what she wanted. She had been married and was never going down that road again.

Even though Lena professed to hate the whole Anti-Wife philosophy, she lived it.

When Sam the Man called things off, Lena was the one who said, "See, this is what making it legal does. It spooks people. It takes a perfectly good relationship and turns it into a cell that people feel they're trapped in and want out of." And there she was, going back to prison.

Sam suddenly stopped seething, though, when she stared at the logo on her mug. A calm came over her, as though the ceramic object was a healing crystal. The spirit of Hannah was there with her, saying that if her friend wanted to live the fantasy that a second try at a losing game was going to end in happily ever after, Sam should actually feel sorry for her.

The doorbell rang, getting Sam out of her own head. She opened the door and found a repentant Katie in the hallway.

"The office is ready for—you okay?"

"I'm fine." And she meant it. "There's a lot to do. Let's get going," Sam commanded, letting the apartment door slam behind her.

Sam prided herself on being able to shut everything else out when it was time to get down to business. She was as pumped up as a newly changed tire to get her strategy and creative vision for *The Anti-Wife* solidified.

Her blinders, however, came off when, late in the day, Little Evie reached out via text: *Call me—news.*

Even though she was no longer her married sister's caretaker, a force of habit made Sam respond immediately.

Problem? U? Joe? Mom?

Nothing like that.

Sorry, then it has to wait, was her final text.

Sam, however, felt bad about the blow-off. She didn't need the lingering visual of Evie's quivering lip accompanied by a giant teardrop falling on her cheek, a la a Margaret Keane painting.

Rather than texting, Sam wanted to add a human touch.

"Katie, call my sister and tell her I'm slammed, and I'll get to her in a few days when I'm freed up."

Without responding, Katie just picked up the phone. She was in super-assistant mode, hoping to reclaim her status as Donna on *Suits*.

****

In line with her timetable, Sam's brief was done and approved in record time by the Applause brass.

The creative people at the network dove into getting the print and social media ads as well as TV storyboards assembled. As work was completed, PDFs were emailed to Sam for her comments with the goal of everything having her as well as Barry's okay by the following Friday, so the presentation to Hannah would happen the Monday after that.

Sam was sure the Anti-Wife would shove her two cents in there someplace, so if revises could be made by the day after the presentation, then production could get going. Sam found herself out of breath from anticipating her campaign blanketing the airwaves, internet, and print—especially billboards. She also began to envision all the new business that would roll in after the Applause PR people sent out the press release, citing her firm as the spearhead.

With *The Anti-Wife* project off her plate momentarily, Sam spent her day focused on another client. She gave a grateful Katie, who had been working until eleven for the duration, the next day off.

"Thanks for another long weekend. I've got wedding stuff to catch up on."

Katie was immediately sorry she tacked on that second part as she saw Sam's face go from a smile to a wince.

"It's almost five. You can go now if you want. I have some personal phone calls to make. Have a good one."

With that, Sam began to dial while Katie scooped up her belongings and quietly slipped out the door.

She felt guilty about not putting family first, but Sam owed it to Lena and decided not to just call but FaceTime.

"I was wondering if we were ever going to speak again," said Lena through teeth so gritted, Sam wondered if she'd had her jaw wired shut.

"Again, congratulations to you and Ben. Let's talk in person."

The two friends agreed to meet for Friday brunch almost halfway between their two apartments at Sarabeth's on Park and 27th Street.

17

*B*oth women arrived at the restaurant at exactly the same time.

But as they neared each other, Sam couldn't help but feel like she was participating in a gunfight at the OK Corral. It was hard to believe that these two were closer than sisters; the casual familiarity that usually existed between them was nowhere to be found. They warily approached one another, neither knowing whether she should say hello first or if a hug would be welcomed. They fumbled to embrace, each mumbling an inaudible greeting.

"So, should we go inside?" Sam said anxiously.

"Unless you want to eat right off the pavement."

But Lena's joke, delivered with her usually much-appreciated sarcasm, didn't go over.

"No, I think we should go inside," said Sam in all seriousness.

They both looked at the ground and entered the eatery.

Immediately after the waitress took their orders, Lena began to fiddle with her utensils, and Sam started drinking her water to occupy her mouth so Lena could begin the conversation, which she did because she could no longer deal with the uncomfortable silence.

"So, Hannah Randolph and the Hamptons—how did that go?"

"Really, really well. I got all the information I needed to work on my campaign and finally got a handle on the whole Anti-Wife thing. So, I didn't have to stay the whole two weeks." That had become Sam's story, and she was sticking to it.

"Well, that's good. Too bad, though, that you couldn't take more time off and hang out at the beach. I don't necessarily mean with her. You know, check into a bed-and-breakfast or something for a little R&R. You really haven't taken time off since—"

"Yeah, I know what you're saying," said Sam, cutting Lena off before she could mention what Sam now believed she had successfully moved on from. That would've been nice, but I had to get back—you know, nose to the grindstone."

Unable to stand another minute of the awkward pleasantries, Sam decided to get to the point in an unusual sing-songy voice that made Lena recoil. "Hey, but more importantly, you are married." Sam pulled an envelope out of her bag and slid it across the table.

"What's this?" Lena said as she removed the card with a picture of a young and WASPy bride and groom driving off in a light blue convertible, the bride tossing her bouquet. At the top were the words: "As your journey begins . . ."

Before Lena peeked inside, she raised her eyebrows, questioning: "Who are these two supposed to be?"

Sam swallowed hard and looked down at her placemat, like a student awaiting her mother's reaction to an iffy grade.

Lena opened the card, and a Bed, Bath & Beyond gift card fell onto the table. She ignored it while she read the inside saying: "Remember to always enjoy the ride."

Albeit a lovely sentiment, the design and messaging reflected the personality of neither the giver nor the receiver. Lena put down the card and picked up the gift card.

"And what, pray tell, is this?"

"A wedding gift."

"We are two adults in our forties who now have two of everything in one apartment. I don't need anything for my bed or bath, and I've never been able to even fathom what beyond entails."

Sam's nostrils flared.

"I was trying to be nice. I was doing what people do when other people get married, and since you weren't registered anywhere, I just figured you could pick something out."

While Sam was talking, Lena did one of her four/four/four breathing exercises. It was a short amount of time but long enough to recapture her civility, sort of.

"Thank you for this," said Lena as she put the greeting card into her purse. "You can have this back, though," then slid the gift card across to Sam.

Sliding it back toward Lena, Sam said, "I don't want it. I bought it for you. It's a present."

Once again, Lena sent it back Sam's way.

"I don't want a present. All I wanted was for you to be happy for me."

Sam slid the card back across the table, keeping the tips of her sinewy middle and index fingers firmly on top of it to make it clear she was putting an end to this game of gift card knock hockey.

"This is me showing happiness. Just say thank you."

Lena then turned Sam's words from the other day back on her.

"I don't need what-to-say-lessons from anyone."

With a "so there" look, Lena picked up the gift card and tossed it in her purse, where it landed atop the wedding card.

Sam felt tears behind her eyes but wasn't quite sure what she was about to cry over. It certainly wasn't anything that had to do with Bed, Bath & Beyond, so she blinked them back.

"I just don't understand how you could do this," said Sam, stopping short of adding, "to me."

"Well, I'll tell you. We . . . Ben and I were driving around last Saturday and we saw a chapel, not one of those cheesy ones where an Elvis impersonator officiates, but a pretty little white one, and as we were about to approach it, Ben looked over at me, put his hand over mine, and said, 'It's now or never.' You would've thought my first instinct would have been to say, 'Never,' as in never again, but then I thought, *I love this man. I've been happy with him. He's good to me.* Like really? Am I going to let one mistake I made as a young woman—now I'm ranting. In a nutshell: I believed him when he said, 'Never.' So, we went in. I just happened to be wearing white shorts and a white tank top. How's that for bridal karma? The couple ahead of us—they were from somewhere in Indiana—we stood up for them, and they returned the favor. The bride was a little more prepared than I, so she lent me her bouquet, and that's all she wrote."

Lena picked up her phone and showed Sam her new screensaver: the bride and groom from the waist up, posing behind a bunch of white roses courtesy of Mrs. Hoosier.

"See."

Sam smiled. Her friend was genuinely happy.

"The only thing that's really changed is that we live in the same place now. We're wading through all our stuff. So far, Ben's made three trips to Goodwill and one to a dump."

Lena said this with a laugh, and Sam mirrored her friend's reaction, even though she didn't find anything she'd said all that funny. Sam just wanted to give the impression she had not only been listening with interest but was accepting of Lena's new situation.

"Well, good. Yeah. I understand now, and it sounds like you, and by you, I mean you and Ben, know what you're doing, and it's good. It'll . . . it'll all be good."

Sam must've been convincing because suddenly Lena seemed more relaxed and conversational.

"So, dish about your brush with celebrity. This Randolph chick, is she as cray-cray as she comes off? I saw her on Colbert or Fallon, one of those late-night shows. I couldn't help but think she's either really bitter over a breakup or she saw a niche in the relationship self-help market that hadn't been filled—if that's possible—and decided to make it her MO. I mean, everyone acts like the cosmos has granted her the sole ability to guide single women through life, but really, by what metric does she actually know anything?"

Sam took umbrage, not only with Lena's judgments but her ridiculing tone. Even though Hannah wasn't technically her friend, Sam began to defend her as though she were going to the mat for Little Evie.

"She's not bitter, and it's not an act. Hannah really does practice what she preaches about marriage being archaic, and she's got historical facts to back it up. She really has nothing to be bitter about, by the way. Hannah says she never wanted to get married. She says she has her work, her home, food on her table, a hella lot of friends. She doesn't hate men. She enjoys their companionship, but she doesn't need one to take care of her."

"Sorry to interrupt, but who does she date? You know, these men whose companionship she enjoys? I'm a *Page Six* reader. I always see her reported on but never see her with a man."

Come to think of it, neither had Sam.

"Well, you know, she's a private person. And I'm sure because none of them are permanent fixtures in her life, she doesn't want to be linked with them in the gossip rags."

Lena nodded skeptically.

"OK, like I said, sorry to interrupt. So, continue."

"Well, there's a line from her book I absolutely love. Hannah says, 'I can stand my own company.' Isn't that a great line? I told the Applause creative people I wanted to see that as a billboard headline. I mean, that's how I feel, too. I can stand my own company; that's why I didn't down a bottle of pills after my wedding was called off or go psycho when I found out that my ex got engaged."

Lena sat up and leaned in.

"He…he's getting married?"

"Yeah," Sam said with the nonchalance usually saved for describing the nuptials of a distant cousin whom you don't even have to send a card to, let alone a present. "That's how little it mattered—I forgot to tell even you. Hannah says my taking it all in stride is because I've never really wanted to get married in the first place."

"Let me get this straight. You told Hannah that your former fiancé is engaged before telling me? Or telling me at all, which I would have thought to be job one after finding out."

"Right. Well, it was a proximity thing. I found out when I was out there, and you know . . . anyway, just let me finish. We had this really great talk. Hannah says . . ."

Lena then sat there for the next forty-five minutes listening to Sam begin practically every sentence with "Hannah says," fearing the phrase had found a permanent home in her friend's vernacular, now that she'd Velcro-ed herself to his C-list celebrity.

When Sam finally finished, Lena responded, "I guess now I know why they call her an influencer. She's certainly influenced you."

Lena held back, though, by not adding, *I also know why they call her a disruptor; she's disrupting our friendship.*

"What's that supposed to mean?"

"It means you were there to find out about the Anti-Wife, but instead she found out a whole lot about you and seems to have been, um, let's say, opinionated on the sub—"

"Insightful. She was really insightful."

"Right," said Lena. "You know, it appears to me that that woman, what was her name? The assistant? Allison? Yeah, she isn't the only one who drank the Kool-Aid."

Sam didn't understand why Lena was so negative. Maybe she was jealous because she had always been the person Sam considered insightful. Maybe her back was up because she felt she was being replaced, and maybe she was. Hannah was a decade and a half younger than Lena. Sam appreciated her fresher, hipper take on . . . well, everything, so this was the hill she was willing to die on.

"I went into my new assignment with a closed mind. I thought the book was just another one of those relationship how-tos like *The Rules* or *He's Just Not That Into You*. I went there to listen to her, then listened to the people who believe in her, who really know her, and I indeed did a deep dive and ended up finding somebody who finally understands me."

Sam wasn't sure if this assessment was real or imagined, but it had become a narrative that she was growing comfortable with.

"Finally? Really? Understands you? Okay, can we walk this back a minute? When exactly did I not understand you?"

"I'm not saying you didn't. She's just so honest, very tell it like it is. Hannah says what other people are afraid to even think."

"So, was the Kool-Aid she served sugar-free?"

A frustrated Sam heaved a sigh that produced enough wind to rival the output of a Dyson fan. Just as she was about to shoot back a response, Lena's cell rang.

"I have to get this; it's my husband."

Oh no, Sam thought. Lena had already turned into one of those women who uses the phrase "my husband" every five minutes to remind everyone that she has one. She began to fume as the new Mrs. spoke on the phone.

"Hey you. At lunch with Sam. No, we had that two nights ago. Don't worry about it. I'll figure it out. Just give me the heads up when you're leaving work, and I'll time it so dinner is ready when you get home. Okay. Love you too. Bye."

When Lena's attention returned to her lunch companion, Sam, who'd been patiently waiting to lob a zinger apropos the Kool-Aid comment, said, "So, Betty Draper, do you have to leave now to make sure hubby's dinner is on the table by five? Make sure to take your apron off so you look pretty when he walks in."

The tension between them was as thick as the pumpkin waffle topped with sour cream, raisins, pumpkin seeds, and honey that Sam had barely touched.

"Okay, I insulted you; you insulted me," established Lena. "Can we call it even and be normal again?"

Sam agreed as she signaled for the check.

"I'll get this. It'll be part of your wedding present."

"Thank you," said Lena, "for the card as well as the gift card. Ben and I should probably have something in our home that can't be labeled either 'his' or 'hers.' I'll use the credit to buy something that's 'ours.'"

Once outside, they gave each other their usual squeezy hug, and Lena said, "Love you."

"Love you too."

This was the first time Sam had ever said those words to her friend without them coming from the heart. She watched dolefully as Lena walked away, then waited for an Uber to take her to her second "date."

18

Sam was a fan of double, triple, even quadruple booking when it came to business, especially when her marital status changed to absolutely solo. Having every minute accounted for was preferable. But in her personal life, she didn't like a chock-full schedule. There was no envy of those who bragged, "Well, I had breakfast with this one, then I ran to lunch with that one, afternoon coffee here, cocktails there, then a late dinner with ..." believing it made them appear popular. That agenda had the opposite effect on Sam. She thought people who lived that life sounded desperate for company, and each friend they visited with got shortchanged.

So, no one was more surprised than her when she arranged to follow up her Lena visit by bolting up to Riverdale to hang with Little Evie in the afternoon. Sam chose the proverbial two-birds-one-stone thing, as not to have obligations to either her friend or sister hanging over her head on Saturday or Sunday.

The plan was to join her sister and Dr. Joe for dinner. It was probably about time she got to know her brother-in-law a little better. Aside from when he asked her permission to marry Little Evie and, of course, the day of the wedding, Sam had only seen him briefly when she'd first come to see their home because he'd gotten an emergency call from a patient.

Joe had recently started closing the office on Fridays during the summer so he and Evie could go to Wildwood each weekend. He had grown up in Staten Island, and like a lot of people from that borough, he had a thing for the Jersey shore. They were skipping this weekend, though, because he was speaking at a conference.

"I have to tell you in person," said Evie when Sam finally returned her call.

"What's going on?"

"I'll tell you when you get here, Sammy."

Good grief, this girl is married and still such a baby.

"Okay, whatever you want."

In what seemed like record time, Sam's Uber got her up to the bucolic Riverdale section of the Bronx where Evie and Joe lived in a red brick four-bedroom, four-bathroom house with ivy crawling up the side, which could only be described as storybook.

Their four-thousand-square-foot home was a light-filled open space where the kitchen, living, and dining areas took the entire first floor and were well-suited for gracious entertaining. The gleaming inlaid hardwood parquet floors, a wood-burning fireplace, and bay windows set an elegant tone throughout. The kitchen had custom cabinetry, granite countertops and a massive island, and state-of-the-art appliances.

All the bedrooms had enormous closets, but the master had a skylight, and the en-suite bathroom was filled with top-of-the-line amenities, including a glass rain shower/steam room.

On the garden level, there was a large-windowed family room that opened onto the granite patio and landscaped yard with stone walls and a jacuzzi. The couple's home also had a mudroom and garage. Joe had purchased it when he was still a bachelor in anticipation of the wife and family he wanted so badly to have, and now Evie would benefit from his dream house.

Joe was born in Bedford, New Hampshire, and had been orphaned when he was four due to a fatal car crash. He was sent to NYC to be raised by his mother's single sister, a middle-class good time girl who loved him and treated him well, but her whole "life's a party" philosophy didn't exactly offer stability.

When Joe discovered Evie streaming the Fox TV show *The Mick*—about a free spirit who inherits her incarcerated sister's children—he turned to her and said, "You know how you're always asking me about my upbringing?" Then he pointed to the show's lead character and said: "She's who raised me."

He was an easygoing guy but put his foot down about that trigger of a show never being on in his house.

Loco parentis at boarding school, where he began attending in seventh grade, and which his guardian paid for with his parents' savings, investments, and insurance payout, was the closest he ever came to a family. Joe knew, though, that if he was ever to get back what he'd lost, he'd have to create it for himself. The house would be the foundation.

If she were starring in a romantic comedy, this would be the scene where Sam got aggrieved that her younger sister had all this, plus a doctor husband and a Lexis in the garage as the jealousy cherry on top. But all she could experience was her usual feeling of liberation that Little Evie was well taken care of by someone other than Sam.

"The place looks good," said the older sib as the younger gave her the grand tour. "But you're acting like I've never been here before."

"Well, it has been seven months."

Sam regarded her sister incredulously.

"No, I was here like three, maybe four—"

Evie shook her head assuredly.

"There was snow on the ground, remember? I couldn't believe that you wore your fancy designer boots, and you said it didn't matter because you were taking an Uber door-to-door."

Recollection suddenly appeared on Sam's face, but she refused to feel guilty about not seeing Evie for so long. After all, she ran a company, and truth be told, she had spent more time with her sister during grammar and high school than some siblings spend together in a lifetime.

"Running a business takes a lot of time. It's not a snub. It's just the way it is. I've got a big project now—promoting a reality show based on the bestselling book *The Anti-Wife* by Hannah Randolph."

Evie scrunched her nose.

"Yeah, I've seen her on the talk shows. But what a terrible thing to want to be: not a wife."

Sam let the comment slide.

"Right, but hey, you're super busy too," she said, trying her darnedest not to sound patronizing. "You've got Joe and a job, and I'm sure you've made friends."

"Well, that's why I invited you here because things are going to get busier."

They were moving across the upstairs hallway, Sam poking her head in each room and nodding in approval, which is what she knew her sister wanted.

"Is Joe expanding the practice? You renovating the house? What?"

Little Evie stopped in front of the only room with a closed door, then flung it open with ta-da flair, and Sam found herself peering into an empty room, which had been painted pale yellow. She looked at her sister like "and . . . ?"

"You're going to be an aunt."

The mother-to-be splayed her hands over her tummy, grinning ear-to-ear and waiting for Sam to do the same.

But all Sam could do was stare at her until she started shaking her head.

"You're having a baby?"

"Actually two." Little Evie nodded her head with the quick, jerky movements of a bobblehead doll. "Twins."

Sam took a few steps backward.

"Are you kidding me?"

This was not the reaction that the younger woman had wanted or expected, but she was so in denial that Sam wasn't happy for her; she just kept the conversation going, playing it out as she envisioned it would go.

"One for me, and one for you. But sometimes on the weekends, like if Joe and I want to have a date night, because, you know, everything I read says new parents should have a date night to keep the romance alive, you can come babysit, and then you'll have them both to yourself."

"Seriously? This is what you think I have time for in my life? If I wanted to take care of a baby, or babies, in this case, I'd have my own. How dare you? My God, nothing's changed. You're an adult; you're a married woman, and you still think I exist to be at your beck and call."

"You always took such good care of me that I thought you would want to do the same for my babies."

"No, you didn't think at all, except, of course, about yourself."

"Please stop, Sammy. This was supposed to be a nice visit."

"Sure, nice for you. What was the nice part supposed to be for me? To be told I was going to get to give up my life again to take care of a child when its mother didn't feel like it? You thought I could relive my teens when I was toting you around when everybody was hanging out and didn't invite me because they knew it meant you'd be tagging along? What did you think? That it was fun for me to have the responsibilities of our absentee father and neglectful mother heaped on me?"

"Grandma was there. I remember her taking care of me too."

"She took care of you? Well, if your definition of 'taking care' means leaving you in the playpen all day while she watched Lifetime movies and slept on the chair until I got home from school, that's a pretty low bar for caregiving."

By now, Evie was watching Sam pace in circles.

"Honestly, what was the rush? You could've taken the first ten years of your marriage to travel, maybe not work with your husband. Maybe get a job in a different type of office, interact with different types of people. Jesus, get a hobby, see what you're capable of. Give your children a mother who's a woman, not still a little girl."

Sam tapped feverishly on her phone and then, seconds later, headed downstairs toward the front door.

"Where're you going?"

"My Uber will be here in three minutes."

The lady of the house, who, moments ago, was on the verge of a crying jag that would've resembled the outpouring of a broken drainpipe, threw her shoulders back, put her hands on her hips, then raced down the stairs after her older sister.

"Oh no. Those days are over where you yell at me and give me a time out, not because I really deserved one but just to show me you were in charge. Well, you're not in charge now. This is my house."

Little Evie took a beat to catch her breath, which allowed her to continue a bit less shrill.

"I'm sorry things didn't work out for you, I really am, but don't take it out on me."

"That's what you think this is about?"

"Seriously, I don't know what it's about. It could be about that, or it could be about that you're still holding a grudge toward Mommy. I don't know, and at this very minute, I don't care. All I know is that I couldn't wait to tell you that I'm pregnant, and this is what I got instead."

Her voice started to break at the same time Sam's Uber app trilled. Evie grabbed the phone, glanced at it, then pushed it horizontally into Sam's chest as though it were a switchblade.

"Here, I don't want you to keep Joaquin waiting."

Little Evie opened the door, inviting her now-unwelcome guest to go.

Taken aback by her sister's sudden backbone and feeling too out of control to fight back, fearing that worse things would fly out of her mouth, a shaky Sam hurried down the front steps, out to the street, and into the car. She didn't look back, hoping that that simple gesture would help her put not just this afternoon, but the entire day behind her.

19

*A*fter her wedding was called off and Sam focused on her startup, dating wasn't just put on the back burner; it was taken off the stove. Yes, it was because she was raw after going out with someone for so long and having it end so abruptly. But it was also because she didn't have the energy to hustle for clients and a new man at the same time.

From what she'd heard over the years from single friends and colleagues, the dating scene could really kick your ass. The few terms she'd heard had entered the dating discourse since last time she was out there—"ghosting," "benching," and the oxy-moron "love bombing"— seemed juvenile. People sliding into each other's DMs sounded intrusive, and quite frankly, a little scary. Not to mention that the blind date who was the perfect gentleman in the restaurant could turn into anything but once he was alone with you in your apartment.

Right off the bat, Sam confessed to Lena that she'd rather write three marketing strategies simultaneously than create an eHarmony profile. She also committed to herself that she'd only agree to fix-ups but never really asked anyone if they knew anyone, and if they did, she was never available to go out due to working around the clock. But it had paid off, and she was proud of herself, not to mention relieved, there was something positive in her life.

Even though she wasn't yet on the verge of burnout, Sam sensed that it could very well be just around the corner. From her time in the Hamptons, she realized how a little R&R—when she finally succumbed to it—could work wonders.

Although Sam really didn't have the constitution or desire to be a party girl like Hannah, what she did admire about the successful author/lecturer/businesswoman and soon-to-be reality TV fixture was how she always seemed to manage to carve out me-time. Always believing in the credo that if you want to be successful, watch and do what successful people do, Sam decided that this behavior was something she was going to emulate.

While still in her Uber on the way back from Riverdale, Sam had ordered dinner from Uber Eats so it would be waiting with Jimmy when she arrived home. After her meal, she freshened up with a quick shower, got dressed, and ran around the corner to Arthur, her neighborhood stylist at Hair Décor, for a blowout. By around seven, Sam found herself heading up the steps of the Metropolitan Museum of Art.

Start your weekend at MetFridays! There's something happening every Friday evening until 9:00 p.m. Curate your own evening from a host of events: see an exhibition, experience a concert, drop into a drawing class, or enjoy a cocktail with friends on the Cantor Roof Garden Bar.

Sam had seen this ad in *New York Magazine* for years, and although she always wanted to go, Sam the Man, who used to call museums "mausoleums" and whose grandfather had been on the board of The Met, always refused. "There, The Whitney, The Guggenheim, The Frick, well, just all of them; I spent my youth going to fundraising galas because my family always bought tables. If I never step foot . . ."

All right, already, Sam thought and so stopped asking. Now she didn't have to ask anybody anything; she was going to participate. It seemed like a civilized way to get out into the world with a little culture thrown in.

Sam slipped into a black slip dress and a never worn pair of Giuseppe Zanotti five-inch sandals procured at a sample sale.

Lena had dragged her there for some retail therapy shortly after the split and insisted she buy the ankle breakers "to get her sexy on."

Now's as good a time as any, thought Sam as she laced the straps around her lower leg.

Sam hadn't been to the American Wing in quite a while, so she wandered through, thinking perhaps, as she was admiring one of the recreated colonial rooms, someone would make conversation, but no one did. But she had better luck once she hit the roof garden.

"Cranberry and club with lime, please."

As the bartender poured her soft drink, a man sidled up next to her and said, "And barkeep, don't spare the horses."

The bartender laughed and nodded as he handed Sam her virgin beverage: "Here you go, Miss."

After thanking him, she responded to (as well as sized up) her new companion, who was Jon Hamm-esque, not quite as good looking, yet still tall, dark, and handsome in his own right.

"What can I say? I'm a teetotaler."

"Well, teetotaler, I'm Jason."

"Samantha."

"So, Samantha, have you seen the view? It's really great from over there."

In an effort to be gracious and enjoy easy banter with a seemingly lovely man, Sam suppressed her innate New York defensiveness and didn't blurt out that she was a native who knew what everything in Manhattan looked like from just about every angle.

"Let's go, then."

And with that, they headed to what he'd declared the "best" place to see the Central Park South skyline before doing a lap around the outdoor garden, then planting their flag by the wall ledge that faced the art-deco buildings of the Upper West Side.

Sam was relaxed and chatty, talking matter-of-factly about her business, yet never once felt as though she were monopolizing the conversation. Jason seemed genuinely interested in her and anxious to tell her about himself and his work in finance.

"I've lived in New York going on two years now. Before that, I was in Rome for five, after getting my MBA from Stanford."

Jason had left her side only once to refresh their drinks. When his phone rang, he didn't answer, but as he apologized for having left on the ringer, he noticed the time.

"8:40. I'd love to keep talking. Want to head over to the bar at The Carlyle?"

"Thank you, but I need to go."

"But we're having such a nice—"

"We are. You have been great company, and this evening turned out better than I imagined, but I just need to go."

"Let's exchange—" he said as he readied his phone to enter her number.

"I'll just take your card," Sam said and to which Jason acquiesced. "Thanks. Good night, and again, lovely meeting you."

She headed toward the exit, without even the urge to look back to see if he was watching her walk away or see the confused look on his chiseled face. She was too busy feeling better than she had, not just all day, but in forever. Sam had gone out and met a nice man, who seemed genuinely glad to make her acquaintance, proving to herself that she still could, and would when she was ready.

Sam credited her good time to the Anti-Wife who once surmised: "Being intimidated by your single life can destroy your social life," as well as remembering Mimi's contribution at the barbeque: "I'm so glad those days are behind me when every guy I dated made me say, 'Am I gonna marry him?'"

Now that, thanks to Hannah, Sam had taken marriage off its pedestal, she didn't come off as needy, automatically liking a man, in that evening's case, Jason, simply because he seemed to like her; there was no considering, after a few moments of cheerful repartee, whether he could be "the one," and hoping that if she played her cards right, he'd be introducing her to his mother in no time. Not giving off the scent of *eau de désperation* made her more attractive to be around. No wonder Jason wanted their evening to continue.

Instead of attempting to teeter down the famed steps of the Met, Sam exchanged her Zanottis for a pair of flip-flops she'd been smart enough to toss in her clutch before leaving the house.

Her only misstep that whole night was not taking 82nd Street all the way across to East End, then walking north for four quiet blocks to her building. Without rhyme or reason, Sam turned up Second Avenue, the bar-hopping mecca, where, after two blocks, she reached Dorian's Red Hand, and a group of women in an array of pastel bandage dresses came stumbling out and almost knocked her over on the way to their awaiting white stretch limo.

"Sorrrrrry," they took turns slurring, then all pointed to their friend wearing a white sash that read "Bride" over her white, micro-mini dress, and screamed, "She's getting married."

They made two rows, and between them, the betrothed shimmied her way to the curb and got into the car. As the rest piled in, one turned and said, "Wanna come?" to which the rest yelled out of the windows, "The more, the merrier." For the grand finale, the bride-to-be popped her head out of the sunroof like a jack-in-the-box and hollered: "Join the party."

Sam smiled, offering best wishes, but assured them, "No thanks, I'm good." And she meant it.

Once at home, she fished around her bag for her phone and also found Jason's business card, which she kissed goodbye before tossing it in the trash.

20

S aturday, Sam rented a Citibike, something she'd never done before, to again feel out in the world and get moving.

On Sunday, she bought a matinee ticket to the ballet and sat next to two women with season subscriptions. One owned an art gallery in SoHo, and the other was the stage manager at an Off-Broadway theater in the Village. They welcomed her into their conversation during intermission, and Sam accepted their invite to join them for dinner after the show.

The following workweek was manageable, talking to clients and, of course, going back and forth with the Applause marketing group about the following Monday's presentation to Hannah.

Lena had texted to get together, but Sam texted back that she was too tied up with the Applause stuff and didn't have time. Not long ago, she would have made time, but the truth was, she just didn't have anything she wanted to say, and Sam didn't want to risk rehashing their "you got married behind my back" conversation or listen to stories referencing Lena's "husband."

That Friday morning, after she and Barry Rogers and the team did a final run-through of the presentation, Sam headed back to the office. Before she even put down her Goyard, her mother called.

Although Sam was letting Katie go early, the younger woman had loose ends to tie up, so Sam left the office and went next door to her apartment for privacy, as speaking to Evelyn usually took an embarrassing turn with an oft-accusatory remark leading to an all-out screaming match worthy of a *Real Housewives* reunion show.

"Hi Mom, just give me a sec."

"I just wanted to—"

"I said give me a second. I just came back from a meeting. Okay, I'm in my house now. What's up?"

"I eloped."

Sam knew she heard what she heard, but between hearing it and responding, what flashed before her eyes was a *60 Minutes* segment about older women being romanced by young con men who marry them to steal their homes and life savings.

"What. Have. You. Done?" the daughter said in a low, controlled tone, her eyes squeezed shut so tightly that when she opened them, she saw stars. Sam held her breath and braced for the answer.

"I told you, I eloped," Evelyn said with the casualness with which she might announce she had just had her hair done. "You remember Albert the butcher? He's my husband."

Sam remembered Albert as being a nice man whose establishment had been a staple in her Bronx 'hood. Whenever she went to pick up the family's meat order—after she had gone to the dry cleaner and picked up a few groceries, always with Little Evie by her side—Albert made sure to say, "Tell your mom I said hi."

She recalled even once thinking that Albert would probably be a good man for Evelyn to go out with if they both had not been married. It wasn't until Sam was a sophomore in high school that she found out her mother wasn't anymore, prompted by the news that the parents of one of her classmates were getting divorced.

"How come you never got divorced, Mom?"

"What are you talking about? Of course, I'm divorced," said Evelyn.

"When did that happen?"

"I took care of it long ago."

"But you never said—"

"I never wanted to talk about it, and I don't want to talk about it now."

A decade and a half ago, when Sam was treated to a surprise revelation about her mother's marital status, she shrugged it off as yet another piece of family drama. That afternoon, alone in her apartment, though, her thoughts were on a grander scale.

Has someone put something in the water?

Lena, now her mother, plus her sister, with Katie on the cusp, not to mention the flurry of random acquaintances and strangers she'd been crossing paths with, all had rings on their fingers.

Sam just did not have the emotional reserve to deal with this bombshell. Suddenly, a noise so guttural began at her toes and raced up her body like a feral animal trying to escape out her mouth. By the time the sound was unleashed, it had reached operatic proportions: "What the fuck?"

As though she were listening to her daughter being murdered, Evelyn was stunned into silence, unlike Jimmy, who began buzzing the intercom feverishly.

"Hold on," barked a breathless Sam into the receiver.

She picked up the wall phone and assured the doorman she was fine and he should alert her complaining neighbors that they would not be disturbed any further. While she was still talking to him, the doorbell rang in long and short bursts, akin to a Morse code distress signal.

Sam hung up on Jimmy and returned to her cell.

"Hold on again," she said once more to Evelyn, as she opened the door to a horrified and stammering Katie.

"Oh, geez, you're okay. Thank . . . what . . . wha—?"

"I'm fine," assured Sam. "Go home."

Sam slammed the door and reverted her attention back to her mother.

"You still there?"

"Sorry to say I am."

"Let's begin at the beginning. You're now Mrs. Albert the Butcher. But wait, he has a wife. Edna or Edith or—"

"Enid. She died six months ago."

"Six mon—? What, did he ask you out at the funeral?"

"Could I tell my story, please? Albert and I have been together for almost twenty years."

In a tone that practically achieved her previous screech: "You were cheating with a married man since I was like twelve?"

"Yes," Evelyn said flatly. "Al was in a loveless marriage, but Enid suffered from MS so he'd never leave her. And I didn't want him to. I was a single mom who wasn't looking for another man whose socks and underwear I'd have the pleasure of picking up off the floor. We just kept each other company when we both could get away at the same time. It's not everyone's idea of a relationship, clearly not yours, but it worked for us. After she died, and not at the funeral, he said, 'We're old now. We earned the right to be together out in the open.' Once that happened, we decided to make it official. Little Evie and Joe came down to City Hall with us and—"

"You invited them and not me?"

"That's right. Your sister told me how you reacted to the news about my first grandchildren. I didn't want to deal with that kind of nonsense on my special day, and from the way you just acted to my news, I obviously made the right decision."

"You two are chums now? When did this happen?"

"Life changes, Sammy. People change. I decided I didn't want to spend the last half of my life the way I spent the first half: angry, overwhelmed, and resentful."

****

When Sam was ten, Evelyn got pregnant. Even at her prepubescent age, Sam knew it had to have been an accident, perhaps brought about by an alcohol-fueled evening, because her parents rarely spoke, let alone made love, since her father spent most nights sleeping on the living room sofa in their modest Bronx home. When she got up in the morning to go to school, she had to be extra quiet as not to wake him.

Sam learned at an early age that in order to not feel ashamed, angry, scared, embarrassed, or just plain sad regarding her home life—or eventually anything—she'd have to learn to stuff her feelings way down, and, as she'd seen embroidered on a pillow, keep calm and carry on.

It wasn't long after the new addition to their home had arrived that her parents stopped giving each other the silent treatment and just started screaming at one another, fighting over everything and anything. "There's not enough salt in the potatoes!" could begin World War III.

Fearing that her mentally abused mother, always in a state of anger, anxiety, and one Valium away from a full-on nervous breakdown, might take it out on fragile, innocent, and colicky Little Evie, Sam took it upon herself to become the baby's caregiver as well as protector.

"I'll do it, Mom," immediately became Sam's go-to, whether it be in reference to feeding (regardless of the hour), bathing, or just rocking the baby to sleep. Her first summer job, if you will, albeit non-paying.

When Little Evie was a newborn during those hot months with never-ending days, Sam found composure in being in charge. However, when she went back to school that September to start sixth grade, she prayed as the key slid into the front door each afternoon that Little Evie was okay. Yes, Sam was free-range while her friends were being helicoptered by their mothers. Luckily her school was only a block away.

No mother was as happy to see a child as Evelyn was to see Sam each day at three-fifteen because that meant she could relinquish her maternal duties for the rest of the day and night, available to contend with her husband when he eventually came home from the loading dock.

One day though, he didn't come home ever again.

At the time, Evelyn was bordering on thirty-one, but the wear and tear of her trying marriage made her look almost fifty (and not in the "fifty 'n' fabulous" magazine copy way) and feel even older. It didn't help that her undiagnosed depression revealed itself in the way she let herself go: never wearing makeup, always hiding her often-dirty hair under a baseball cap, and making a brown, Juicy Couture sweatpants and matching hoodie set her go-to all-occasion outfit.

Evelyn had been a beautiful girl, an auburn-haired pin-up. People used to compare her to Jaclyn Smith during the *Charlie's Angels* years. She met her future husband at a Knights of Columbus dance when he was still in his naval uniform, a few years older than the guys in her Inwood neighborhood. She was dazzled. Then drunk. Then in his bed. When he was discharged three months later, he returned to the neighborhood and was informed Evelyn was pregnant, and there was no doubt that it was his. She was too innocent for it not to be. They got married a few days later at City Hall. That was the last time Evelyn would ever see her husband as the prince who had not only come but come back.

He passed out drunk on their wedding night and every night after that.

A little over a decade later, after always being dismissed unless her husband was looking for a fight or sex, Evelyn was permanently dissed and, for the most part, relieved. The only thing she would miss about him was his paycheck.

Suddenly without an income, Evelyn would have to get a job, but she would be competing with younger, more educated women and other stay-at-home mothers returning to work with resumes that had impressive, pre-mommy employment.

Even as a pre-teen, Sam had an inherent understanding of marketing, branding, and packaging. She bought a glossy magazine and pointed out to her mother that even a non-permanent rinse like Clairol's Loving Care could boost her now-mousy brown with strands of gray hair to a vibrant mahogany, and a minimum amount of makeup could get the pretty back. Sam also convinced her that a small investment in clothes from the low-priced H&M would be worth it. They were going to have a new life, so she should look the part.

Evelyn was taken aback by this role reversal and touched by it as well. She was not used to being supported, even from her own mother, whose take on Evelyn's marriage had always been, "Well, you made your bed..."

When Evelyn returned from shopping with two new pairs of pants, two blouses, a sweater and blazer purchased on sale, L'Oreal (because she was worth it) permanent color, and Covergirl makeup from CVS, she gave Sam a long, wordless hug.

Sam participated in the embrace but quickly pulled back. Although that rare moment was welcomed, it was awkward, then anger-inducing. It forced Sam to face what she had learned to ignore: her lack of a mother's loving touch.

Teen Sam finally may have been able to boast about having an attractive mom, but Evelyn was still Evelyn. The depression she was lifted out of, the one that had made her too tired to do laundry, show up for parent/teacher conferences, or consider anything but McDonald's a dinnertime staple, was replaced by high anxiety over having to support two little girls.

"You gotta learn to take care of yourself," Evelyn told Sam repeatedly, never stopping to think that in broad terms it may have been good advice, but day to day, it made Sam feel neglected, but nothing like the way Evelyn ignored Little Evie. Just looking at the little girl brought on palpitations for her mother. Sam quickly learned that whenever her mother swore she had a heart attack, it was really a panic attack and questioned whether Evelyn really wanted her to "call 911."

Sam's single mother decided that to save her sanity as well as support her family, she needed to be out of the house as much as possible. Evelyn began working two jobs—a relatively easy office receptionist position during the day for the benefits and a hard-on-the-back-and-feet waitress gig in the evenings for the fancy restaurant tips.

Much to Evelyn's chagrin, her elderly mother moved in with them to care for Little Evie until Sam came home from school. Grammy often only made it until after lunch, falling asleep on the living room's wing chair, where Sam would find her, with Little Evie standing up in the playpen, peering over the top railing like a prisoner contemplating a jailbreak.

Sam would put her sister in the high chair so the child could watch her prepare a basic dinner. The older woman, rejuvenated from her long nap, would clean up the kitchen while Sam did her homework beside the crib so big and little sisters could keep each other company until it was time for bed.

It had to be this way, as daycare was an added expense the Dennehys could not afford. Sam just took it in stride; she would rather be denied hanging out with friends after school in order to watch her sister than have her father around. And sad to say, the less she and Little Evie saw of their mother, the better.

Another thing that Sam was grateful for was Evelyn's decision never to marry again. If her father was any indication of this woman's mate-picking skills, the next one would be the same horror show, only taller with a different color hair.

Things got easier once Little Evie started going to school full-time. By then, Grammy had passed away, so Sam became fully responsible for taking care of her sib, which gave her a sense of purpose. Unlike her friends who had little sisters and complained, referring to them as brats and didn't want to be bothered with them, Sam actually liked hers. Little Evie was adorable and giggly and easy to be around. Sam didn't find those qualities in most people.

Her decision to not go away to college wasn't a demand made on her; she came to it all on her own because Little Evie, then eight, still needed her watchful eye.

Although her mother was older by then and down to working only her day job, where she had been promoted several times from receptionist to secretary to executive assistant, she was still an emotionally fragile, sometimes volatile woman. Evelyn and Little Evie had never really bonded. Sam, as co-parent, had done all the heavy lifting and knew she would probably always have to in one way or another.

Sam the Man had been understanding of Sam's family dynamic, even though his was much more traditional. She considered his floating bachelor pad her home away from home, as she still lived with her mother and sister well into her twenties. Lena once called Sam "Helicopter Sister," to which Sam shot back: "Baby, I'm the whole damn air force."

Sam had promised herself that she would move out when Little Evie started high school but extended that to when her sister started her junior year. At sixteen, Evie had her own life with lots of friends and learned—thanks to Sam—to stay out of their mother's way.

*****

"Your sister wasn't conceived out of love. It was a drunken act that girls today would call date rape even though it was with my husband. She was lucky I let her live. When I looked at her, I saw him. After he was gone, well, he was never really gone because she was there. If I kept my distance from her, it mentally kept him away, too. At least that's what I told myself; that and that putting clothes on her back, food on the table, and a roof over her head was enough. It wasn't, and I have a lot of shame about how I behaved toward my beautiful little girl. Albert convinced me, though, that it's never too late to make amends. So, I did, and she welcomed me with open arms."

"What about me? What about what you did to me?"

"What did I do to you? You were old enough to know the score."

"I was a little girl. You turned me into her second mother."

"You know, if you want to waste your time walking down memory lane, at least remember correctly. You wanted that job. We were partners, not equal partners, but . . . you liked being in charge when I was at my office and the restaurant, and even when I was at home. It was your choice, and I think it's what made you the boss you are today."

Tumbleweeds.

For once, Evelyn was lucid and rational, but Sam's head was just not in a place where she could appreciate it.

She realized that she had not moved since her mother started talking. Sam was just standing in the middle of her foyer, staring across the living room at the baseboard under an accent table that displayed a Venetian glass vase she and The Man had picked up on their trip to Italy.

Both Sam and her mother became painfully aware of Sam's shallow breathing.

"Sammy? Samantha?"

"I've known you all my life, yet I don't know you."

"Likewise."

"You've been independent so long. How could you choose marriage again after it was so awful? You know firsthand, it doesn't work."

"Who says it doesn't, that jackass who got cold feet at the last minute after wasting years of your life? I told you when it happened not to let it make you bitter."

"I'm not bitter. He did me a favor. I concluded I never wanted to get married. I don't know why anybody does. Hannah, Hannah Randolph, you've heard of her, right? She wrote that book *The Anti-Wife*? Well, Hannah says—"

"Who? What are you . . . Is your sister, right? She says you're not yourself. Maybe you should have gone to talk to somebody, like a therapist, after . . . Do you need to talk to someone?"

"I don't know, but it probably shouldn't be you."

"Fine, Sammy. I just called to let you know that if you call the house and a man answers, it's not the wrong number. Goodbye."

Sam remained statue-like with the phone to her ear, unable to even blink, let alone budge. A siren passing under her window jarred her out of her daze long enough to walk zombie-like into her bedroom, where she laid down and went to sleep.

She dreamed that she was atop a snow-capped mountain. Mistress of All She Surveyed. Sam had her hands on her hips like the Jolly Green Giant, feeling powerful and independent. Then she looked down, and her white snowsuit had morphed into a wedding dress, and the snow was actually white goo. Panicked, she scanned all the other mountains and saw brides and grooms. They were not mountains after all, but massive wedding cakes, and she was stuck atop hers alone, sinking into coconut frosting.

Her eyes popped open, and Sam jutted up in bed, feeling the sheets to make sure they were not indeed gooey.

She got up, sipped some water, went to the bathroom, and returned to bed. No sleep would be on the agenda, though. So, Sam stared at the ceiling until she couldn't remain horizontal another minute.

21

Sam welcomed Monday the way a paroled convict greets freedom. Her only discomfort was with how comfortable she felt not calling Lena to clue her in about her mother's nuptials or Little Evie for a concerned "How exactly are you okay with this?" exchange. But she didn't want to talk about it. She didn't even want to think about it.

All day Saturday, Sam had busied herself with chores and even did her laundry in the building's basement instead of sending it out, just to burn off her excess energy. She popped a Lean Cuisine in the microwave and called it dinner. Then, even though she had plenty when it came to professional garb, Sam spent date night at Bloomingdale's buying something new to wear to the big Applause meeting.

What started out as a quick retail therapy session for perhaps a new shirt ended with said shirt, a new suit, shoes, and a bag—all by Tory Burch.

To keep Sunday from feeling never-ending, Sam forced herself to sleep in, then read every article in each section of *The New York Times*. In the very late afternoon, she practiced, more than she needed to, her preamble to the presentation and answers to what she anticipated would be many questions, aka challenges, that Hannah might have.

For inspiration, Sam spent the evening re-reading underlined passages she'd marked in her copy of *The Anti-Wife*. She read with interest—over and over—one in particular: "A man can put a type of stress on you that you won't have with a woman friend, as long as she's the right friend— someone with the same outlook."

That used to be Lena. Now, who? There was only one person to whom Sam felt she could relate.

****

Presentation day had arrived. Before she left for Applause, the exec went into the office to touch base with Katie.

"Morning. I'm headed over. I don't know if it'll go past lunch or if I'll be going to lunch with Barry and Hannah and whomever, but I'll text to let you know how things are shaking out."

The whole time Sam was talking, Katie was nodding her head and saying things like "got it" and "noted," but she was actually preoccupied with giving Sam's outfit the once-over.

"You look different, by the way. That suit is new, isn't it?"

"Yes, it's Tory," she said, referencing her navy A-line skirt and coordinating navy and ivory tweed jacket.

Spying the logo on both Sam's navy belt bag and pointed-toe heels, Katie noticed, "Those are Tory Burch, too."

As cheerleading was as much a part of the job as office management, Katie knew a compliment was in order; Sam was dressed nicely, even though she seemed to be wearing someone else's clothes: "Well, you look great. Knock 'em dead."

An hour after the meeting had been scheduled to begin, Sam, Barry, and the marketing team stood around the conference room, anticipating Hannah and inventing new words for "tardy." While most everyone surmised that the reason must be 495 Expressway traffic, Sam knew it was a power play; their client was making them wait on purpose. Sam wouldn't have been surprised to find out that Hannah was sitting outside the building in her car, perhaps making Carl circle the block more than once.

Forty-five minutes after that, a pigtailed Hannah Randolph bounced into the room, sucking on a lollipop like a teen-with-'tude character on a Disney Channel sitcom.

Pink, blue, and silver hair strands were weaved into the childish hairstyle, which reminded Sam of the multicolor handlebar streamers that she'd long ago put on her two-wheeler to make it look new before handing it down to Little Evie.

Hannah swaggered through the room full of suits, wearing blue denim overalls with a red bandeau top peeking out from the bib, and red Havaianas. To the naked eye, her who-gives-a-damn hoedown outfit seemed to be chosen by rolling out of bed, picking up whatever was on the floor, and stepping into it.

The optics made jaws drop around the room, except those of Sam and Barry, who nodded knowingly at each other. The very non-Tory ensemble was meant to throw the group off its game.

For this meeting, she was not just the Anti-Wife; Hannah was anti-pushover; a brat who was not going to eat her vegetables. She would not be buying what they were selling, at least not right away. They were going to have to work for it. And they did.

Four hours later, even though every proposed digital and traditional piece of promo material had the Hannah Randolph sign-off, the marketing team appeared as empty and picked over as their catered lunch trays. Even Barry was exasperated at how his cash cow had nitpicked and argued every point, clearly not because she believed in what she was saying but just for the pleasure of being oppositional. Even more irksome was how Hannah then sat back and watched with a curled lip as everyone in the room jumped through hoops to convince her of what she already knew— the advertising for her TV series was on the money.

Yes, everyone was peeved, except for Sam; she felt she understood where Hannah was coming from.

Sam remembered a passage from *The Anti-Wife* where Hannah wrote that whether it was a one-night stand or long-term relationship, she wanted the other person's best; only then could they bring out the best in her. That's what she was looking for from the group who was going to handle her show, as well.

While the others exited the room like battered prizefighters stumbling from the ring and Barry confabbed with his assistant, Sam made her way over to Hannah, who, to Sam's delight, was already walking toward her.

"Good meeting," said Sam.

"Oh, don't get all corporate on me, gurrl. How've you been?"

Having bought into her illusion that Hannah was her new BFF, Sam widened her eyes and casually tossed off, "You don't want to know," while actually hoping Hannah did and would ask.

When she didn't, Sam quickly added, "But I'd love to sit down with you. I really enjoyed our talk at Candy Kitchen. Maybe we could go back again this weekend. I've got a hotel reservation at Topping Rose House in Bridgehampton."

This bald-faced lie rolled off her tongue so easily it actually frightened Sam, who had always prided herself on being a forthright, the-truth-will-set-you-free type of person.

"Cancel it. If you're out in the Hamptons, you're staying with me. And don't waste my time with some 'Oh, I couldn't impose' BS."

In the invitation lottery, Sam had just won the Mega Ball—time to bond with Hannah as well as plans for the last weekend in June.

"You're the client."

Barry approached, inviting Hannah to his office to chat before she left and patting Sam's shoulder, offering, "Great job. We'll be in touch."

As he ushered his star out of the conference room, Hannah turned, and in lieu of goodbye, said, "Do me a fave? Text Allison and tell her you're coming on, when? Friday? Saturday?"

"I was actually going to be out on Thursday. You know, make a really long weekend of it."

"Okay, see ya Thursday. Nice outfit, gurrl. I've got that bag in red."

****

Wht my Thurs like? Sam texted immediately to Katie, then watched the three dots moving but could not wait for Katie's message to materialize, texting: *Whatev - move to either Tues or Weds - on way back*

Katie's three dots disappeared, and the thumbs-up emoji took their place.

Sam's cab ride from Midtown Manhattan back to the Upper East Side was a string of unbroken green lights, which she chose to see as a metaphor for her life at that moment. She was moving forward unencumbered by family and faux friends she decided had been holding her back.

This time, when visiting Hannah's Hamptons retreat, she would do so more broadmindedly and more receptive to the other housemates she'd once labeled as sponges.

Sam walked into her office already talking, giving Katie a play-by-play of everything that happened at Applause.

The whole time she'd worked there, Katie'd never seen Sam so excited, actually nerve-racked, over a successful meeting.

"Congratulations," Katie said. "By the way, you had two meetings on Thursday. I moved one to tomorrow and one to Wednesday. Both clients were fine with seeing you sooner rather than later. So, what's up for Thursday? New client?"

"No, I'm taking off. I'm going to the Hamptons."

Not used to Sam being so social, Katie hid her surprise.

"Nice. I, of course, will be here on Thursday, but can I work from home on Friday?"

Only half-listening while perusing her call sheet, Sam mumbled, "Sure, why not?"

"Thanks. Oh, and I have a billing question."

But before Katie could state what it was, Sam pointed to *The Knot* magazine peeking out of the Coach tote perched on the window ledge.

Did I not predict this?

"I told you I didn't want this junk in the office."

Trying to overlook the word "junk" being used apropos her wedding, Katie offered a gritted-teeth smile with her explanation.

"Right, well, technically, it is in the office setting, but it's inside my bag. It's not like I'm reading it or anything."

Sam opened her mouth to respond but then realized she had no right to tell anyone what she could carry around in her own purse, so she just changed the subject.

"I'm going to return these calls. While I'm at that," said Sam as she picked up her Anti-Wife mug, "make me a cup of coffee," waiting a beat before adding, "please."

Katie had reminded Sam who was a bride, and so Sam reminded her who was boss.

22

Sam took the 6:00 a.m. Hampton Ambassador, hoping there would be no traffic at that hour, but no such luck. The minute they hit the Long Island Expressway, she could tell it would be a four-hour ride.

She brought her laptop to do her usual mound of work but was determined not to open it while at Hannah's. She would not even look at it again, though, until the ride back on Sunday night. Nor would she check her phone. Well, at least try not to. Sam was resolute to be all-in and present.

She also had to remember her second suitcase stowed beneath in the bus's storage compartment. Sam, a seasoned traveler, prided herself on being like George Clooney in *Up in the Air*, able to pack everything she needed in one satchel. She couldn't do it this trip, though, because of some new last-minute acquisitions.

Her Tuesday meeting had been down in the West 30s, aka the Garment District. Afterward, as she headed to the subway, passing one wholesale store after another, Sam got caught up in a sidewalk traffic jam because there was a stream of people lined up single file, waiting to enter a prewar building. Like most New Yorkers, Sam couldn't walk by without asking, "What's the line for?" When three or four people chimed in unison, "Tory Burch sample sale," Sam took the information as a sign that the universe was supporting her wrangling an invite from Hannah and that if she was going to mesh with her new friend, she needed to dress the part.

By the time she got upstairs, there were indeed slim pickings left, but she was still pleased with what she ended up with: a black canvas beach tote, orange logo sandals, a navy gingham romper, and navy terry pullover.

Although she got out of there at almost three o'clock, and Katie had been texting like a madwoman because they had to prepare for the Wednesday meeting, Sam made a pit stop at Bloomingdale's for a pair of Tory's patterned flip-flops, as well as travel ballet flats that fold into their own little pouch, which Hannah had raved about and carried with her everywhere. Schlepping the extra weekend bag was worth it.

Carl met her at the bus stop, just as before, except this time, for the whole ride to Hannah's, she was speed-talking like one of the *Gilmore Girls*.

"So, it was quite a trip even though I left early thinking I'd beat traffic, and on a Thursday, no less, but I guess everyone wants to come to the Hamptons, and I'm sure Hannah has a full house as usual. I can't wait for a cup of Inez's special coffee although I'm so excited to start my weekend you probably think I don't need caffeine . . ."

For the whole drive, Carl kept glancing at her in the rear-view mirror to monitor whether this animated woman was going to shoot into space via the open sunroof. He had not remembered Sam being quite so effusive. Every time he tried to address a question or statement, she'd go off on another tangent, so he just ended up nodding his head as she jabbered. At one point, he sped up, going faster than the speed limit because she was giving him a headache, and he wanted her out of the car as soon as possible.

No one was more surprised by Sam's friendliness than Allison, who almost dropped her iPad when the returning houseguest—previously in a perpetual state of "put out"—hugged her and pecked both cheeks.

"Um, hi. Good to see . . . yeah, okay." She gestured like a prize model to the mansion, offering accommodatingly: "After you. Hannah's waiting by the pool."

When Sam headed up the front steps, Allison turned to Carl, who was making the same baffled *What's up with this one?* face back at her.

Sam scurried into the house and mistook Inez's welcoming smile as an invite to embrace, but when the reserved housekeeper saw Sam approaching with arms extended, she held the vacuum she was carrying out in front of her for the block.

"I'll be right with you, Miss Sam, just let me put this away," she said before disappearing down the hall where her cleaning supply closet hid.

Like a museum docent, Allison directed Sam through the kitchen out to the patio where Hannah was reclining on one of the black and white striped chaise lounges. The lady of the house heard chattering yet barely lifted her head and slightly raised her sunglasses to see what all the racket was about.

"Oh, hey," she groaned, then returned to her prone position with eyes once again shielded by her oversized shades.

Not quite the howdy-do Sam had hoped for from this bottomless pit of energy, but Sam had come to understand that unpredictability was part of Hannah's charm.

"So, I thought I'd never get here," Sam began breathlessly, but her "Lorelei Gilmore" routine wasn't playing with her hostess.

"Stop. I'm hungover. The rustling leaves sound like bombs going off. Go put your swimsuit on. I'm getting overheated just looking at you."

Sam was feeling a bit warm herself in her jeans and Lily Pulitzer floral velour hoodie.

"Right, I'm dressed for the bus. They had the AC on full blast."

To make her disinterest even clearer, Hannah moaned Inez's name, and within seconds, the attentive staffer appeared with some green, iced concoction replete with bendy straw so that Hannah would not have to pick her head up too high in order to sip her drink.

As she served her employer, Inez said, "Miss Sam, may I help you unpack?" emphasizing the word "unpack," which Sam understood to mean get up and leave Hannah alone; she also got the impression Inez was doing it more for Sam's benefit than her boss's.

"You know, I'm good. I'll do it myself when I change."

Sam was assigned the same room as last time, which made her feel at home.

There didn't seem to be any other guests, not yet anyway, and since her hostess was in no shape to receive her, and Allison, Carl, and Inez were on the clock, there was no hurry for her to do anything.

The inviting balcony called out to her, and she stood staring out at the peaceful ocean. Her anxieties, which made her come off as a college kid during finals on a six-pack of Red Bull, were beginning to subside. There was a downside though. With the deafening quiet brought thoughts of Lena, Evie, and Evelyn, which led to a feeling of loneliness.

Sam shook her head as though she were trying to ward off a cloud of gnats. She was not going to let anyone, especially Macbeth's Three Witches, ruin her time.

Using what was left of her nervous energy to hang up her clothes, Sam began to feel organized and ready to take on the day, so she shimmied into her Solid & Striped blue and white one-piece, went down to the pool, and headed toward the deep end, inching gingerly on the balls of her feet like a cartoon cat burglar passed the sleeping giant. She was now officially part of the squad who spent its waking hours tip-toeing around Hannah Randolph.

23

*H*er laptop did not open once on the way home Sunday evening. When Sam got off the Ambassador at Third Avenue and 85th Street at 1:30 a.m., she couldn't believe how the last four and a half hours sitting in traffic had flown by.

Staring out the window of the luxury liner, Sam hadn't seen what was on the other side of the pane. It was as though she had been looking at a screen, upon which played out the story of her long weekend, like a Netflix movie.

The usually reserved non-partier had not had such a time in . . . she wasn't even sure if she ever had one like that.

Thursday night, after a couple of Inez's magic green elixirs, which turned out to be green tea smoothies with the hair of the dog, Hannah came to and was ready to entertain her usual maddening crowd of hangers-on, of which Sam was now one.

This time around, Sam jumped at Hannah's hospitality and worked the room like a politician, re-introducing herself to Mimi, Mike, Susie, Bobbie, and some of the others she felt forced to mingle with during her deep dive visit. Sam even flirted with a C-list TV actor, who was sandy-haired and ripped like an athlete on a trading card.

The next morning when Sam didn't go downstairs for coffee by 10:00

a.m., Inez popped up with a cup to see how she was doing.

"Oh, Inez, you're so kind. Thank you. I figured Hannah was sleeping in, so I would just hang in my room till lunchtime or so when she'd be by the pool."

Before Inez left, Sam asked about her daughter and let her know the offer to meet with the girl for that Columbia recommendation still stood.

Alone in her room once again, Sam was grateful for the peace and quiet. She took Inez's special brew onto her balcony, closed her eyes, and let the crashing of the waves mentally take her to a place where it didn't matter that she wasn't married or how it came to be that she wasn't married, or who else was. Just as the serenity was enveloping her like a lover's hug, feeling all's-right-in-my-world, it became apparent that not all was right in the world of some others.

"Everybody out. I said, get out. You, you, you, you, you. Get your stuff and get out. Don't make me call the police."

The minute the word "police" was uttered, Sam became alarmed and headed downstairs to see what all the ruckus was about.

She hadn't even reached the bottom of the stairway when she realized there was not a real problem. As usual, revelers from the night before had passed out by the pool and then just decided to invite themselves to stay for Friday's festivities as well.

Apparently, Hannah had peeked out her bedroom window and asked sarcastically if *The Walking Dead* was filming a scene in the backyard because "it looks like the aftermath of a zombie apocalypse." iPad Allison was then tasked to "get rid of the bodies," to which she invariably responded, "On it."

Sam stood at the foot of the stairs and watched as the unwanted guests clomped out the front door like job applicants who'd been turned down.

The second she slammed the door behind them, Allison saw Sam and proved she'd have great range if she were ever to switch her profession to acting by promptly transforming her scowl into a wide, bright smile worthy of a Colgate commercial.

"Good morning. Did you enjoy yourself last night?"

"I did. Is Hannah available yet?"

"Absolutely. She's out back. You know the way," and with that, she and her iPad disappeared down yet another hallway Sam had yet to investigate.

"Hey gurrl," said Hannah with a Cheshire-cat smile. She was sitting at one of the tables under the awning, reading the *New York Post*.

"Hey girl, yourself," Sam chuckled.

"I was watching you last night. I'm glad you decided to come out of your shell."

"Me too. I actually had a very nice time."

"Even though you don't drink," Hannah added with a headshake.

"Even though."

"And you talked to that cute guy from that show, yet didn't take him to your room."

"No, I didn't."

"Well, maybe you'll have better luck tonight."

Sam smiled but felt a little uncomfortable. What business was it of Hannah's? Then she realized that what had really made her uncomfortable was the awareness that she hadn't even considered taking the handsome actor to bed.

Truth was, she was afraid. Sam was thirty-two years old and had only slept with one man her entire life. She suddenly felt embarrassed for herself. Although she knew she could attract men, she didn't know how to date, nor how to act on one, especially at the end of the evening when the guy might want to come upstairs.

As though Hannah had been reading her mind, the brazen blonde lifted up her sunglasses, looked her houseguest in the eye, and said, "In all sincerity, Sam, it's time. Tonight, you need to get busy."

Hannah had never called her by her name before in conversation. That personal touch was so flattering, like being a high school freshman acknowledged by a senior, Sam couldn't wait for that evening's goings-on just to please her new pal.

"So, are the same people from last night coming back tonight?"

"It's Friday night; we're going off-campus—Carl's taking us and Bobbie, Mimi, Mike, and Jessie Quinn—"

"Wait—the A-list movie star Jessie Quinn?"

"She's one of my BFFs. Anyway, she's in from LA, and we're going out to Montauk to The Surf Lodge. That's okay, right? Going to Montauk won't be some trigger for you because you and 'Sham the Man' used to go there? Too soon?"

Sam couldn't help but laugh at Hannah's twist on her ex's sobriquet. Why had she never equated the ridiculousness of his nickname with their relationship and gotten out sooner?

"I think I'll be fine. In fact, when he and I used to go out there, we could never get a reservation at that place. Then when it got kicked up a notch into 'the place to see and be seen,' we didn't even try."

"Well, the owners have been begging me to come, but anyway, hang out, go to sleep, read a book, do whatever relaxes you because tonight we party. Oh, and FYI, the crew will be filming our night on the town. You really ought to reconsider signing the waiver. I mean, their focus is on me. If you're on screen at all, it would be for split seconds at a time. It would just make my life easier."

"Yeah, we'll see. It'll probably be okay."

"Hey, you guys," said Mimi as she poked her head out of the patio double doors, hoping she'd be welcome. Hannah waved her over to the table, and Mimi and Sam now flanked Hannah like backup singers. "I just wanted to stop by and say I'm really looking forward to tonight."

Hannah turned to Sam to give her the 411: "I introduced Mimi to Jessie, and in turn, Jessie gave Mimi a small part in her next movie." Then to Mimi: "You guys start filming next month, right?"

"I'm so excited. I mean, I only have one line, but who cares? I'll be on the silver screen with this super high-powered star."

"Congrats," said Sam, more impressed with Hannah's facilitating a break for the young comic than with the actual film part.

"So, Mimi, if you're so happy," asked Hannah, "what's with the puss?"

Relieved by the invite to finally spill what she had really come over to share, Mimi explained that while on her recent comedy tour, where she had been on the bill with several other female stand-ups who were older, married, and had kids, she felt ganged up on.

As Mimi told her tale of woe, Sam began to get the impression that this young woman was one of Hannah's STRAYS.

"Honestly, it was like being with my mother, my grandmother, and my aunts. They kept harping on the fact that not only was I not married, but I don't have a 'real' boyfriend, and you know, it's all in the tone—that pitying tone. 'You're so pretty. Why can't you find anybody?' and it seems they're all in agreement about how much happier I'd be if I had a baby. I wanted to say, 'Actually, what would make me a whole lot happier is if you would stop asking me why I don't have a boyfriend, let alone a baby.' Geez, can you imagine? I have a hard 'nuf time caring for me."

"But you didn't, right?" said Hannah. "You didn't say anything."

Sam observed sadly, yet started to feel angry because Mimi's story triggered her Lena/Evie/Evelyn trifecta of grief.

"No, I chickened out."

"Well, that's a legit issue. You've got to find your voice, gurrl."

Mimi sighed a sigh of resignation. "I'm just one of those people other people think they can mess with, you know, boss around."

"I'm one of those people other people like to antagonize," said Hannah, "just to see if they can get me to lose my shit or to prove they're not afraid of me."

Mimi looked at Sam. "Something tells me people don't say stuff to you. You're one of those people other people like to impress."

"Well, thank you for saying that, but I have a few people in my life who don't think twice about reminding me of what I don't have, and at the moment I'm estranged from all of them."

"Paint me a picture," said Hannah, and Sam did. By the time she got to the part about her new stepdad, Hannah dropped her fork as though it were a mic.

"Whoa gurrl, you're surrounded."

"Yes, I am."

"You know what ladies, we all are." In a grand gesture of solidarity, with Hannah as the connective tissue, she took one of Sam's hands and one of Mimi's. "That's why we surround ourselves with each other. We're Anti-Wives, and we're not going down the marriage road because we know where it leads, and it's nowhere good."

****

Hannah & Co. were given the VIP treatment at The Surf Lodge, and the added bonus was that Jessie Quinn had brought with her Lars, a twenty-three-year-old thirst trap. The former model with surfer-dude looks, when not stepping and fetching for Jessie, was trying to break into screenwriting.

"He is legit delish. Go for it," Hannah whispered to Sam.

"Him? No, he's too young and not my type."

Exasperated, Hannah said a little louder than a whisper, "Gurrl, first, let's remember where 'your type' got you. Second, you're not looking for a husband anymore. You're looking for a good hang, and in this case, it's only for one night, so don't overthink it. Just go for it. Besides, maybe your ex will be watching my show with his basic bitch. Imagine when he sees you with Mr. Hot AF over there? He'll know you're not thirsty. Ever hear the expression, 'Living well is the best revenge'? Let Lars be your revenge."

Sam, with Hannah as her wing woman, took a long look at the Scandinavian heart-melter and responded, "Maybe I will. And oh, I signed the waiver."

The waiter returned to see if the group wanted another round. This time, Hannah told Sam she should add a shot of Stoli into her cranberry and club.

"I told you I don't—"

"Look, it's not like you're on the wagon and I'm trying to get you to break some hard-earned sobriety. You've just chosen to never add alcohol to your repertoire. But that was then; this is now. I'm not suggesting you drink a bottle of Jack through a straw. It's only one shot in one drink. The rest of the night, you go back to your usual. You just need a little liquid courage to loosen up. Which reminds me, I've been meaning to ask, what do you do for fun?"

Too embarrassed to answer, "Nothing," Sam turned to the waiter and ordered: "Cranberry and club with lime . . . and a shot of Stoli."

Even though she hadn't gotten drunk, she knew the vodka had had an effect, and after the initial anxiety she had over feeling buzzed, as Hannah promised, Sam felt relaxed, so much so, she "went for it."

The next morning, around 10:00 a.m., Sam awoke and peeled Lars off of her, slid from his bed, picked up her clothes, which she held in front of her naked body as she tip-toed quickly back to her room, which was only two doors down. The house was silent, and just as Sam thought no one would be the wiser, Inez appeared from who knows where and almost dropped the stack of towels she was carrying. Figuring the housekeeper wasn't seeing anything she hadn't seen before, Sam just gave her a what-can-you-do shrug and entered her room.

Once behind closed doors, she let go of her Blue & Cream slip dress and Jack Rogers sandals, then stood in front of the full-length mirror. It was all she could do to keep herself from high-fiving her reflection. Sam had turned a corner. Whether the vodka actually had anything to do with it or not, Sam had moved on in her personal life and was giddy. And she had Hannah to thank.

She showered, dressed, and did her hair and makeup. Always the strategist, Sam wanted to be the first downstairs so that she would not be walking into the Hannah/Jessie/Lars troika, which would have made her feel like an intruder. Her way, she would be by the pool, reading the paper, thereby welcoming them into her space.

The newly minted party girl was taken aback when she got to the pool area and found Hannah alone.

"Jessie and Lars headed to her apartment in Manhattan. She's got pre-production for her movie, and blah, blah, blah. I don't remember what she said. She had to leave. Whatever."

"I slept with Lars," Sam blurted out, not sure whether she was bragging or confessing.

"Good for you. So tonight, the same crowd from Thursday night, with a few additions, will be by. That actor you flirted with will be back. Maybe you'll get lucky again."

Make that definitely. Saturday night, she followed Friday's routine: one of her drinks had a shot of Stoli, then "go for it."

Sunday morning, Sam woke up as Mr. C-List was putting his pants on. He kissed her goodbye and said, "I'll hit you up on Insta next time I'm out here."

For what? It's not like she was auditioning him to be her better half. But she nodded, even though she actually hoped to never see him again except on TV.

Feeling emboldened, Sam spent the day with Hannah by the pool, reading the papers, talking about fashion, entertainment, hot topics, just really shooting the breeze as gal pals do.

When it was time for her to catch her bus back to NYC, Hannah hugged her hard.

"Don't forget, next weekend is July Fourth. I'm having a mandatory red, white, and blue party. Anybody not dressed like our flag gets kicked out."

"Stars and stripes are the new black. Noted."

With her fun weekend behind her and new outlook on life before her, Sam sat on the Ambassador, able to easily tune out the complainers whining to the driver and his bus attendant about traffic. She had plans for the following big weekend, and she was star-spangled excited.

24

S am walked into the office on Monday to find *Page Six* displayed across her desk.

"You're famous," announced Katie.

"What do you know?" was her uncharacteristic response to a public photo of her, Hannah, and Jessie Quinn with their arms around each other at The Surf Lodge.

"Not only that," said Katie, pointing to her computer screen, "but you're also all over Hannah Randolph's Insta."

The assistant offered this last part with hesitation because of her boss's aversion to having her personal life out in cyberspace.

Much to Katie's surprise, though, Sam seemed elated.

"Me? Really?"

This validation that the two women had crossed over from biz contacts to IRL hob-nobbers, well, Sam had to see this for herself. She hovered over Katie's shoulder, examining the contents on the screen with the intensity usually given to a client document that needed her approval.

There Sam was in a candid shot, chatting up Mimi and Bobbie; another, at one of her host's day-to-night-long soirees, with Hannah and her dancing on the beach—a bonfire glowing in the background; she and Hannah holding hot dogs as they flanked Chef Kenny, each giving him a kiss on the cheek; a group shot from the BBQ on the beach evidenced by Hannah's pre-ketchup stained Helen of Troy gown; and finally, with Hannah at The Surf Lodge, a picture similar to the one in the paper but without Jessie. In this one, Hannah had both arms wrapped around Sam, hugging her with her eyes closed.

This last photo gave both women pause. Katie side-eyed her boss, and Sam glanced down, blushing. Their reactions had less to do with Hannah's I'm-young-rich-and-famous mugging for the camera and everything to do with Sam's expression that was nothing short of orgasmic.

Sam took a beat then shook off her self-consciousness. Even though her face was plastered all over Hannah's Instagram, where the Anti-Wife's over 100 million followers would see that an un-famous Bronx girl was as close as two riders on the Q train during rush hour with their idol, the only thing certain other people cared about was Sam's picture on the gossip pages of New York's #1 tabloid.

A text from Lena: *Page6? Inevitable when u run with the beautiful people. This beautiful person would like to catch up maybe over long wkend?*

Sam texted back: *LOL*, with no response to the meet-up offer, which reminded her . . .

"Katie, because this weekend is the Fourth—and I know I already said that we'd take Friday off—but I want to take Thursday as well, so we'll have to get all our work done today, tomorrow, and Wednesday."

The assistant's jaw dropped.

Sam reacted with exasperation.

"I thought you'd be happy to have the extra time," and, making air quotes, added, "for wedding stuff."

Katie was chagrined, not just with a break-neck week or even with the wedding dig, but the mocking tone Sam added to her voice. Channeling "Donna" and the TV character's never let 'em see you sweat façade, Katie changed her tone to über-professional, and said: "No prob."

Another text, this time from Little Evie: *Wow! Page 6. Ur famous!*

Sam texted back a smiley face emoji, as the sisters had not officially made up, and Sam was not ready to start communicating again.

She drew the line when it came to answering her phone as Evelyn's number came up, but out of morbid curiosity, she listened to the voice-mail: "Sammy, you're on *Page Six*. Albert went to buy me a frame."

She recalled that Evelyn hadn't been as excited—or impressed—or interested in framing her diploma, when Sam graduated from her Ivy League university.

For the next three days, Sam and Katie plowed through, servicing clients with what Sam believed to be her usual diligence but what Katie felt was the short shrift. One, itching to be signed, was overlooked completely.

"Your former colleague Sarah left yet another message."

Sarah had quit BrideMe to work at Lifetime as the showrunner for some "Bridezilla Says Yes to the Dress" type of series and wanted Sam to consult.

"Oh, and she added congrats on *Page Six*."

"Right now, I just don't want to deal with her and her show. Tell her I'll call her after the holiday weekend."

Katie had never known Sam to turn down work or treat a client, especially a prospective one that fell in her lap, so cavalierly.

"Are you sure you can't just touch base for . . .?"

"I have a life," she reminded Katie. "I may not have a ring, but I do have a life. Next week."

And with that, Katie turned her back on her boss and, for the first time ever, ignored Sam's directive and responded to Sarah's request for a meeting.

****

Sam's long weekend at Hannah's was one never-ending party and even more fun than the previous four-day visit because this time, there were fireworks. The usual suspects showed up, plus Barry Rogers and several of the Applause people she knew from the marketing group, who were all excited about the mid-August launch of the new campaign. They were also interested in her hookup with Lars.

"What a hottie," said Barry.

"How did . . . did Hannah . . . ?"

"We saw the footage," Barry admitted as his Applause staff snickered. "If I ever made out like that, it would take a case of Chapstick to get my lips back to normal."

Everyone, including Sam, laughed because everyone always laughs at what the boss says, but she was so embarrassed, one would think a sex tape had been circulated. Thank goodness that picture didn't end up in the paper.

The next afternoon, the sun had one job and did it with gusto. Hannah moved the party from her backyard to the beach for topless volleyball. Even though Sam didn't play, she was an enthusiastic spectator/cheerleader, now seeing her host as colorful, hence, not looking on aghast as Hannah & Co. disrobed shamelessly.

At one point, Hannah stopped the game to read what was being written on the cloudless sky: "Marry Me, Meg!"

With the same dismay shown by the Scarecrow, Cowardly Lion, Tin Man, and girl in the ruby slippers when the Wicked Witch of the West flew across the heavens, scrawling "Surrender Dorothy," Hannah shook her fist at the puffy white letters and screamed, "Don't do it, Meg. You'll be sorry."

The whole beach, including Sam, followed the lead of the Anti-Wife, fist-punched the air, and chanted, "Say no, Meg," until Hannah spiked the ball declaring game-over and headed back up to the house.

Sam's Stoli shots—still in moderation—had become customary. As usual, she waited until the evening to enhance one cranberry concoction, then invariably hooked up.

She was also flattered that Hannah finally noticed she'd "Tory-ed up" her wardrobe.

Katie had remarked as well and almost seemed disappointed that they'd lost their sartorial simpatico.

"I've been dressing like, well, you since I was in high school. At a certain level in your career, it's time to raise the bar," Sam countered, insensitive to the fact that she'd just offended the younger woman.

Another person who noticed a change in Sam was Inez. They didn't chat anymore. Sam also noticed that Inez was not as mindful of her as the housekeeper once had been. Perhaps, that was because the perennial guest started to believe the mansion was hers, incorporating into her vernacular phrases such as, "Inez can you get me . . . Inez, I need . . ." and the *coups de grâce* of orders: "Inez, here's what I want . . ." All were given with the entitled tone used by Hannah, who actually was entitled since she paid the woman's salary. Henceforth, Inez only spoke to Sam when she was spoken to. Even then, her monotone words were, "Yes, Miss," before the request was filled.

The only downbeat moment was when Sam got a call from Lena while she was taking what she hoped would be a recuperative morning walk on the beach.

"Hey, Lena, what's up?" Sam shouted over crashing waves and seagull screeches.

"Where are you?"

"The beach?"

"What beach?"

"I'm in the Hamptons at Hannah's."

"I thought you already finished that tour of duty."

"I'm here as a guest."

"Oh, I was calling to invite you . . . well, never mind. You're not around, so . . . Ben and I are having people over for . . . like I said, you're not around. So, how is it there?"

"Well, I'm kind of a regular here now, and I gotta say, I'm having the time of my life. I'm even learning the difference between vodkas. The other night we ran out of Stoli for my cran and club, and someone suggested Ketel One so—"

"What? Vodka? You drink now? What brought that on? Or should I say 'who'?"

"I'm sorry, are you my mother? I take a shot to loosen up before the evening's festivities. It's really helped me be more social, especially when meeting men. Let me tell you who I slept with. You know that actor who's like the fifth lead on that cop show starring—"

"You get drunk so you can go to bed with guys? Wait, do you blackout and then wake up, having had sex? Do you even remember if you consented? Oh my god. This woman, your new friend, I would think twice about . . ."

If Sam's whole life were not on her phone, she would have chucked it in the ocean with the determination of a pitcher in the bottom of the ninth throwing a no-hitter.

"I do not get drunk. I have not been sexually assaulted."

"Have you been using protection? You know, you're going to have to start getting AIDS tests. And then there are STDs to think about."

"I'm having new experiences, thanks to Hannah. She helps people, you know. She's so generous with her contacts and her money and just being there for others. And now she's helping me. When Sam left me, he changed the course of my life. I used that forced change to build my business. When I met Hannah, she changed the course of my life again. Now I'm using this change to build my social life, which I'm going back to now.

Thanks for the invite. Have a great party."

Click.

Later that evening, or actually in the wee hours of the morning, the house was eerily quiet, even though it was still filled with people, albeit passed out. Sam couldn't sleep and stepped over bodies to make her way to the kitchen. Chef Kenny, who lived in Hannah's guest house, was cleaning up.

"Oh, I thought I was the lone awake resident," said Sam.

"Inez is in charge of keeping the house clean, but I take charge in the kitchen. I like things a certain way, and well, as you can see from the mess, I often have my work cut out for me."

"I can help. I don't mind."

With that, Kenny pointed to what could be thrown out and what she could cover with a lid or Saran wrap while he unloaded then reloaded the dishwasher. They worked in silence at first; then, Sam broke the ice by asking the proverbial question: "So, how'd you get this gig?"

Like Sam the Man, Kenny had graduated from the Institute of Culinary Education.

"I got a job in a fancy Brooklyn restaurant. Truth be told, though, I didn't like the city or working in a big place. I decided that instead of where I worked dictating where I lived, I'd figure out where I wanted to live, then move and find work. I grew up in Massapequa and spent summers out here. So, I got a place in Amagansett and eventually became the executive chef at a moderately priced cafe. Hannah came in one night and demanded to meet me. I thought she had a complaint, as the staff told me she was kind of ranting, like 'get the guy who made this out here.' Very Hannah, as you can imagine. She said it was the best thing she'd ever eaten, wrote her phone number on one of the cloth napkins in lipstick, if you can believe it, and I'm sure you can, and told me if I ever wanted a gig as a private chef to call her."

He then said that two weeks later, the owner sold the place and he needed a job.

"And here you are."

"And here I am."

When they finished their respective chores, Chef Kenny made Sam a three-cheese omelet, and she savored every bite while he finished restoring his kitchen to his precise standards.

"My ex went to ICE, too."

She then told Kenny of Sam the Man's career track, which was the opposite of his own.

"Different strokes, I guess."

"But he's yet to have his own line of, what is it? Salad dressing?"

"Hannah wants to back a line of Chef Kenny products, a la Paul Newman's salad dressing, tomato sauce, and popcorn. Mine would start with dressing and condiments, you know, flavored mustards, mayo, and horseradish. It's a dream, but Hannah has a way of making dreams come true for people."

"Well, I hope it works out for you," Sam said sincerely.

"And she'll probably hire you to do all that marketing stuff for the brand."

"I don't know about that. But, if she did, it would be my pleasure."

"Seriously, once you're in with her, she's all in for you. She knows so many people. I wouldn't be surprised if, after this show takes off, she reaches out and gets you so many more clients."

"That'd be great, but the famous people she knows are movie stars and models."

"Oh no. She's got her toe firmly in the corporate world. Don't mention this; wait for her to tell you, then make like you don't know, but when really rich women who are married to really powerful business tycoons get the heave-ho for trophy wives, they consider Hannah their go-to. She charges five hundred an hour for consultations on how they should proceed in their single lives, you know, as Anti-Wives, and these women keep her on Skype for hours. Hannah's a really good listener. And because she makes so much off the wealthy, she does those phone consults for free with, you know, lower-income women who need advice. Everyone wants her two cents. She cuts through the bull and tells it like it is."

"I can attest to that."

"I know how Hannah comes off, all ballsy and aggressive, but what you see isn't always what you get. She really is a good girl. I love . . . you know, working for her."

Sam may have been full from her satisfying meal, but she felt lighter for their talk. Kenny was a nice guy, a good man. She thanked him for the food and the counsel, then, to show how earnest she was, Sam patted his hand platonically—just as Hannah walked in.

"Well, what do we have here?"

Kenny regarded Hannah sheepishly, like a boy whose mother had just caught him with a girl in his bedroom.

Sam jumped in to defend their tête-à-tête, though not quite sure why she had to.

"If Ken here ever gives up cooking, he's got quite the career as a shrink."

"Oh," said Hannah, still looking at Kenny. "And here I thought I had the exclusive on your consigliere services."

The chef cleared his throat, stood up straight, and shifted into a show-no-fear stance to offer what he hoped would be a satisfactory account.

"Your houseguest couldn't sleep, so I made her an early breakfast or late-night snack—take your pick, then she watched me put the kitchen back together. Now, what can I get you, Hannah?"

"Nothing," she singsonged. "I'll wait for Inez to make me coffee. She should be up in a few."

"Okay, then," announced Kenny. "Carl should be about ready to take me to the farmer's market for fresh produce, so ladies, see you later."

"Don't forget the corn; you know it's my faaaaaave," she hollered after him, like a kid reminding her dad to pick up Oreos at that supermarket.

"Your wish is my command," he yelled back, giving Sam the impression that whatever that little moment of tension between him and Hannah had been, it was over.

After they heard the front door shut, Hannah turned to Sam and stated bluntly: "He's not for you."

Clearly, not totally over.

"For me for what?"

"I know you have a thing for chefs, but . . ."

"I don't have 'a thing' for anyone. My fian—my ex-fiancé is a chef, yes, but . . . what's the problem?" Sam asked, genuinely confused.

Trying to walk back what definitely began as a challenge and had entered into confrontation territory, Hannah just shrugged and said, "Well, you know, you're a guest, and he's a member of my staff, and you know how it is."

No, Sam did not know "how it is;" she didn't even know what "it" was supposed to be. In fact, she didn't think that even Hannah knew what she was talking about. Sam wanted the conversation to end, though, so she just nodded and said, "Yeah, right, no problem."

Inez entered, and Hannah told her she could bring her coffee when it was made.

"I'm going back to my room. Bring Sam a cup, too; she'll be with me."

The two women sat for the rest of the morning on the veranda outside of Hannah's suite, spilling the tea about all the famous people the Anti-Wife knew and whose exploits she revealed. Later, Carl drove them into town to do a little shopping, and when they returned, Chef Kenny had prepared them a steak and lobster dinner with grilled corn on the cob and salad.

There was no need to take the bus home that night, as Carl was driving Hannah into the city to meet up with Jessie Quinn to go clubbing all night somewhere in downtown Manhattan.

Her host slept the whole way while Sam gazed out the window, anticipating how easily she would fall asleep once she got into her own bed. Her out-and-about lifestyle was still new to her, so Sam couldn't imagine getting home at around eleven on a Sunday evening, changing, dancing all night, then being able to get up for work the next morning. But it wasn't an actual issue that needed to be resolved since Hannah hadn't invited Sam to join her and her movie star BFF.

25

Whereas Sam once lived to work, now she was, as that old Loverboy song goes: "working for the weekend;" accepting Hannah's hospitality was Sam's new normal.

In the meantime, she finally got around to getting in touch with Sarah, but the newly established television producer told her it was too late; she'd found someone else for the job.

Sam reported this to Katie with great relief, explaining that she wasn't interested in working with Sarah again anyway because of how the whole BrideMe thing went down. Actually, she just didn't want to feed the wedding machine by promoting a show that would inevitably boil down to "the happily ever after" myth. Besides, Sam reasoned that servicing Sarah's cable network would be a conflict of interest with Applause.

Lena kept leaving emails, voicemails, and texts, the "just touching base" kind, to which Sam replied with brief and innocuous *all's well hope ur summer is good 2* missives, as though Lena were some vendor with whom Sam felt obligated to keep up a relationship.

Her mother left voice messages. Evelyn was now embracing her role as wife, mother, and soon-to-be grandma, reporting with delight every little happening, such as Little Evie's doctor visit "that went very well," and the barbeque in Riverdale where she and Albert got to meet Evie and Joe's neighbors, who apparently were "such nice people."

It was all so tedious. The only thing that got Sam's juices flowing anymore was heading out east to hang with Hannah.

But right before the last Saturday in July, a text showed up from Allison with the subject line: *This weekend.*

Sam felt an anxiety attack coming on. What if Hannah had had enough of her company? What if Sam was disinvited? What would she do? How would she spend the weekend? She handed the phone to Katie.

"Read this, please. Aloud."

Katie took the phone, wondering where her once cool, calm, collected, so-young-so-successful powerhouse of a boss went, and how long she'd have the patience for the always-on-her-last-nerve neurotic who'd replaced her.

"Sure, let's see: *H got last min AW speak gig says u should come out Sat. morn anyway—her casa es tu casa.*"

As Katie watched Sam wipe her brow like a woman who'd just found out her mammogram came out cancer-free, she thought it a smart idea to humor her boss.

"Hey, sweet deal."

The assistant lost any semblance of her good nature when Sam retorted without a hint of irony: "You know it, gurrl."

****

Sam was elated to be going to the beach as usual and remained on top of the world until she reached the steps of Chez Randolph via taxi since Carl was chauffeuring Hannah. As iPad Allison came scampering down to greet her, something finally dawned on Sam.

"So, Allison, how does this work, you know, when Hannah's not here?"

"FYI: some others will be staying here as well, and, you know, often there's kind of a 'when the cat's away' quality to it," the assistant said with a wry smile and a wink.

Was she kidding? When the "cat" was home, the place had the ambiance of *Animal House.* What more could they do when she was gone—except perhaps burning the place down—that Hannah wouldn't consent to if she were there?

"Oh, and I'm leaving shortly to catch up with Hannah," Allison said, as always, thrilled to be part of the Anti-Wife caravan, then reported, "and Chef Kenny isn't here either, but the fridge is stocked, and Inez will be back late tomorrow evening. So, enjoy your weekend." And she was off.

Yes, Sam was a bit sad that she wouldn't be spending time with her new BFF and felt badly being excluded from the speaking-engagement entourage, but Hannah trusted her with her home, which Sam believed spoke volumes.

Upon entering what had become known as "her room," composure shrouded Sam as usual. If all she did was spend two days in her white palace of a suite with the ocean air sweeping in through the French doors, well, that would suit her just fine.

Sam even brought a suitcase devoted to work with her this time since the hostess was going to be in absentia.

Hannah's casa was indeed going to be her casa for the next couple of days, and she was going to make the most of it—after a short nap.

A few hours later, a conga line, akin to a sorority hazing raid, barged into what was supposed to be her private chamber and startled Sam awake. The line leader explained they were going through the house, looking for "party poopers," of which she clearly was one. Had Sam neglected to lock her door?

Her fellow guests had also begun to drink and roof dive into the pool. "Rosé all day . . . and night" was the battle cry that wafted in from the outside. Sam, still a bit groggy, allowed herself to be pulled from the bed onto the line and followed the gang through the rest of the second floor, down the staircase to the entry hall, and out to the pool, where the DJ had so pumped up the volume that it hurt to listen to the tunes.

Sam did not want to be a part of this. It was one thing when Hannah was there because no matter how wild things got, she had the clout to control the crowd, or at least dispatch Allison to do so. The inmates were running the asylum this time, and it was, quite frankly, a little scary.

Sam read the room and saw some familiar faces, like Mike and Ted, but they were partying, a little harder than usual, and she didn't feel comfortable even with them. Chez Randolph without Hannah was not for her. An executive decision was in order: scoop up your stuff, call a cab, and get the hell outta there.

"Nooo ohhh," Sam yelled suddenly as she began to lose her balance. Thanks to the even longer and more aggressive conga line snaking around the patio furniture, someone had bumped into her, but just as she felt herself about to hit the deck, a hand scooped her up. Sam whipped around to see who was simultaneously saving and manhandling her.

"Thank goodness, a sane person," said Brett.

"I'm about to hit the road."

"Can't say I blame you, but can I beg you to stay just a while longer. I'm supposed to be keeping an eye on things for my sister, but seriously, who's going to listen to me? So, just one drink?"

Brett had Sam stand out of harm's way, and, since he'd heard her drink request during previous stays, he asked the waiter for a cran-club with lime and a vodka shot and for himself, a scotch-rocks, same as Hannah always drank.

Their chitchat turned into an actual conversation that they wanted to continue in earnest, so Sam and Brett headed toward the beach, where it was not exactly quiet but at least not ear-piercing.

"So, who exactly arranged this?" Sam needed to know.

"My sister did before she got pulled away for her last-minute speaking thing. She figured, 'why cancel?' Hannah likes her friends to have a good time."

Both believing there had to be more to talk about than their Hannah connection, Sam and Brett began to ask about their respective careers, then, as people do when getting to know one another, they each shared his and her tales of past romantic love gone wrong.

The waiter found them and asked if they wanted refills. This time, Brett ordered the same, but Sam figured why not have her obligatory shot of Stoli in her drink. She hadn't realized her first one was spiked and attributed her relaxed feeling to Brett's nice-guy, calming effect.

They kept talking, not noticing it was getting dark, and once again, the waiter came back, inquiring if they each wanted another. She and Brett were deep in conversation by then, and Sam absentmindedly handed the server the glass, forgetting to tell him not to add the Stoli this time.

The third drink gave her more than a buzz; she was a little woozy but was having such a sweet time with Brett, she figured she'd just wait out the haziness.

When he leaned in for a kiss, Sam welcomed the chance to kiss him back. He was about three years younger than her but came off as mature, low-key, and respectful, unlike Hannah who was brash and often discourteous. *How were they raised by the same people?*

Brett was decent. Husband material. Not for her, but for someone. Sam felt safe with him, especially in that wild environment, but primarily when she finally realized she was under the influence.

"Um, you know, I think I forgot to tell the waiter not to put vodka in that third drink. That second shot really hit me."

"Oh, no. When I ordered the first up on the patio, I asked for vodka as well. I've heard you order it that way, so . . ."

"That explains it."

Three shots may not really be a big deal to a drinker, but to her, well, it was two too many—especially on an empty stomach. The last time Sam had eaten was on her morning journey, a muffin and coffee somewhere around exit 45 on the expressway.

So, this is what drunk feels like? I can handle this. Until she couldn't.

"You know, I go into Manhattan on business sometimes," offered Brett. "Maybe we could grab din—are you okay?"

"I need to go to the restroom . . . my room . . . just for a min . . ."

"Let's go."

Brett led Sam from the beach to the backyard, around the pool, and through the house with the due diligence of a bodyguard tasked with making sure a rock star got from the arena to the limo unscathed by screaming fans.

When they got to her room, Sam tried to pull herself together long enough to say a proper goodnight.

"Do you need me to help . . ."

"No, no. I'll be fine," she slurred ever so slightly. "I just need to splash water . . . you know, lie down . . . just for a min . . . yeah. So, thanks. I'm glad I stayed. I had a nice—"

He kissed her forehead, turned the knob, and said, "I don't trust any of these people. Make sure to lock the door."

And that's what she did the second she was on the other side of it, as well as grabbing the straight-back chair and shoving it under the knob for good measure.

Sam fell asleep with her cheek pressed against the cold porcelain throne after, of course, she had thrown up from a sudden bout of the spins. In the wee hours, she came to, and afraid to stand up, fearing she'd fall back down, crawled to her bed.

In the late morning, she woke up with a headache, a queasy stomach, and a memory as to why she never started imbibing in the first place.

Once, when Sam was a junior in high school, neighbors with a daughter in Little Evie's first-grade class wanted to take her along with them for a weekend at their second home in the Catskills. This meant Sam was off duty and could actually attend a party.

She was handed a beer before anyone even said hello but stopped short of drinking it, thinking about whether she wanted to emulate a habit of her long-gone father.

What helped her make up her mind about choosing sobriety began with Terry Morgan, the smartest kid in the school, who was so inebriated and incoherent, no one would ever have believed he was a National Merit Scholar. Sam then noticed other girls who seemed as though all their pre-game efforts getting glammed up at Sephora was for naught since, in their boozy states, the cosmetics had melted into raccoon eyes and smeared lipstick.

From across the room, Sam saw a group of friends dancing, but when she went to join them, she noticed that what they were doing was more like swaying to the music because they were in a bit of a stupor themselves.

The clincher, though, which had her putting the brew down on the first flat surface she came upon, was the sight of Karen O'Hara, the senior voted in the yearbook as Most Likely to Win *America's Next Top Model*. She had mascara tears running down her blotchy face while her BFF held back her tangled blonde hair so she could puke in the Hefty-lined kitchen trash can.

Sam finally got to see what she hadn't been missing and decided liquor would never touch her lips.

Sixteen years later, she sat up in bed and saw herself in the mirror across the room. Who was that hot mess of a creature? Well, since she'd heard through the grapevine that Karen O'Hara was currently a ski instructor out in Idaho, Sam had to accept that the mess was her.

Perhaps the "one shot in one drink" liquid courage seemed like a good idea at the time when she needed to start being more social, but that hurdle had been cleared, and so she and vodka would be parting company. Right then, she declared herself once again a teetotaler—or to paraphrase the parlance of some Hamptons 12-steppers: faux-sé all-day.

Sam also realized what a difference there was between one-night stands and spending an evening with a quality man and perhaps having it develop into something that could lead to intimacy. That was where she wanted her social life to go.

After taking the longest shower she'd ever taken in her life, Sam put on her Tory gingham romper and went downstairs with trepidations about what and who she might find. But, the house was in order as though the party had never happened. If it weren't for her thumping hangover, she would've believed it all had been a dream.

"Hey, you," said Brett, who was reading *The New York Times* by the pool.

So relieved to see him and only him, Sam didn't even ask how Hannah's home got cleared out or cleaned up. She would be able to recuperate in peace.

The two new companions spent the rest of Sunday afternoon together. Seeing she was still under the weather, Brett kept giving her water because she was dehydrated, brought her Tylenol, and tried to make his sister's guest as comfortable as possible as she curled up on the chaise lounge, tucking her in with one of Hannah's sheet-size, fluffy towels.

Her thoughts went to Sam the Man, and she realized that in their time together, he'd never been quite so solicitous. Well-mannered? Always. Kind? Most of the time. Thoughtful? Well, he did his best. But never would she have ever described him as caretaking. Perhaps, though, there was enough blame to go around. Maybe he never took care of her because she never let herself be vulnerable, making it clear she could take care of herself.

Sam would not be surprised to find out that his new bride-to-be was, if not a damsel in distress, at least a bit on the needy side.

Although she had to admit that she'd relished her sojourn into being pampered, akin to a spa day, Sam would not trade her independence for anything. Yet another thing that made Hannah's assessment that marriage wasn't Sam's bag even more apparent.

Brett excused himself, leaving the pool area to take a call. Sam, feeling a little better but still looking a bit haggard, went into the kitchen, hoping to find Inez's delicious coffee. The housekeeper had returned early. Guess that answered how the house got fixed up. But when Sam asked Inez if she minded making her a cuppa Joe, the domestic declined.

"I'm sorry. I am busy preparing for Miss Hannah's return."

But Sam wouldn't let her go, and it had nothing to do with coffee.

"Inez, please come back here. Please."

Even though Sam was not her boss, Inez knew that if Sam wanted to make trouble for her with her real boss, she could. And so, the humble servant turned to be addressed but as always, with her head held high.

"Yes, Miss?"

"What's the problem, Inez? We've never spoken to each other like this. You—"

"You said you would help my daughter, and you didn't answer her email."

"Inez, I never got an email."

"I saw her write it. She used the address from the card you gave me. She sent it. You never got back to her."

"Honestly, Inez, maybe it went into my spam, or I missed it." Sam took out her phone. "Give me her number. I'll call her right now and—"

"My daughter got what she needed from other people. Miss Hannah knew somebody who knew a dean at the school."

Before she turned to leave the kitchen, she gave the once-over to Sam in her sorry state and said, "When you first came here, you were different, not like the others. Now you're one of them."

"Inez, no, I'm—"

"Please. I am getting upset and overstepping my bounds. If I talk anymore, I could get myself in trouble with Miss Hannah. Please. I have to go back to my work."

Sam stood alone in the kitchen, embarrassed and guilt-ridden. She was not that person, the one who offers to help then never follows through. But her shame was short-lived, eclipsed by the return of pounding in her head.

As disturbing as her conversation with Inez had been, she took solace in the fact that Inez's girl had gotten the recommendation from Hannah and popped her K-cup into the Keurig.

Sam just wanted to ride out her afternoon until it was time for her bus reservation. Until then, she'd hang with Brett, enjoying both his company and his benevolence.

When it was time for her to leave, Brett said he'd drive Sam to the Hampton Ambassador's bus stop. Just as they got to the driveway, though, Carl pulled up with Hannah and Allison, who gave a quick wave then hurried up the steps and inside.

"Hey gurrl; leaving so soon?"

"I'm afraid so. I brought work with me and got absolutely nothing done. I'm going to have to do it on the bus. If I can."

"Well then, that means you had a great time. Where you going, bro?"

"Diving her to the stop."

"Carl's here now. He'll take her," said Hannah in her done-deal way.

She hugged and said goodbye to Sam and got out of the way so her guest could get in the car. Before Sam did, though, Brett moved in.

"I'll give you a call about grabbing dinner."

As Hannah watched her brother kiss Sam on the lips, her face turned to stone, and after Sam was settled in the backseat of the town car, the lady of the manor slammed the door shut.

Seconds after they started to roll slowly down the driveway, Sam heard yelling. Just as she turned to peer through the rear window and spied Hannah gesticulating wildly at Brett, who was looking down with hands buried deep into the pockets of his shorts, Carl hit the gas.

26

Sam threw up in the bathroom of the Hampton Ambassador. The residual nausea from the booze, plus the upset from what Inez said, and then seeing Hannah's reaction to what was obviously Brett kissing her, turned her stomach.

Even though barfing made her feel a little better, she still didn't feel what one would consider well.

When she woke up the next morning, Sam wasn't hungover anymore, but she did feel sluggish. She took her time getting ready with another extra-long shower. By the time she got into the office, it was a little after ten—and Katie was not there.

"What the hell?"

Sam checked her phone to see if there was a text from Katie explaining why she was late and what her ETA would be, but there was none. Then she saw the letter on her desk, a white number 10 envelope with her name written in Katie's beautiful Catholic schoolgirl cursive. The letter inside simply read: I resign.

Channeling Dorothy Parker, Sam asked out loud, "And what fresh hell is this?" then saw the company's landline message light blinking as if on cue.

"Good morning, Sam. This is Sarah. Apropos the assignment here at

Lifetime, I just wanted to make clear that I approached you because I felt like I owed you for what happened at my previous place of employment and couldn't, for the life of me, understand why you wouldn't get back to me, but I don't care how that cow got in the ditch."

As her speech went on, Sarah became smugger and more self-satisfied; hence the more pronounced her southern drawl became.

"So, sugar, even though you didn't return my calls, which made me madder than a wet hen, Katie did. She convinced me to hire her freelance. So, while you were out galivantin' with that Anti-Wife woman, who, in my humble opinion, is only anti bein' a wife 'cause she can't find a husband, Katie created a strategy that, well, I just have to say is brilliant. She even gave you some credit, saying that she learned at the feet of the master. So, I'm just callin' to say thank you. Thank you for blowin' me off and allowin' this talented young woman a chance to shine so bright as all get out that I had to get her hired as a marketin' manager at my company."

By the time her diatribe was done, Sam thought she had been listening to Reese Witherspoon in *Sweet Home Alabama*.

Sam hit the erase button, then leaned her elbows on her desk and started rubbing her temples with the tips of her fingers.

"I just need to think. I just need a moment to think," she said aloud. "I just need quiet . . . quiet."

Just when she thought her wish was granted, Lena's number came up on her cell's screen, and Sam was tempted to hit the decline button, but out of guilt, picked up: "Hi Lena, what's up?"

"Well, we haven't talked since the Fourth, you know, when you hung up on me. So, I just wanted to check in."

"Okay, then, let's do that. Let me check you in: My little sister is pregnant with twins, my mother got married to my childhood butcher whom she's been having an affair with for two decades, my assistant quit after stealing one of my accounts—wait, she didn't steal the account, it was never mine and, in fact, I didn't even want it because I didn't want to deal with—you remember Sarah, right? From McCann? She's over at Lifetime now and wanted to hire me. I wasn't interested, but Katie worked on the assignment freelance and hit a home run, and got herself hired. Top it. Go."

"Okay, um, do you want me to come up there?"

"Let me finish. Or, as we say in advertising, 'but wait, there's more.' I started drinking, and now I've stopped. I started having one-night stands, and that's come to an end, too. I spent time with a man I liked, and apparently, that's a problem for Hannah, who is now mad at me—oh yeah, the guy was her brother—and I've just got a lot to sort out. So, no, I don't want you or anyone to come up here. I need to think. I should get off the phone."

"Are you really sure? Because it sounds like, well, it sounds like an episode of a soap opera but also like you need someone to vent to and not on the phone."

"I can't. I just can't."

And with that, Sam hung up the phone, her many emotions as tangled as a knot of gold chains.

Sam felt so scattered she needed to list all the things she had reeled off to Lena and then prioritize them.

Dealing with her mother and sister, who seemed to be rolling right along quite nicely without her, went directly to the bottom. Lena was above them—all to be dealt with at a later date.

Katie took the number-three spot. She had to be replaced, but Sam couldn't contend with resumes and interviews at the moment. She would go it alone for at least the next couple of weeks as she did when she was first up and running.

The number-two spot was her social life. She rationalized that perhaps she had done things that were a bit out of character and that she wasn't too happy about but felt that she had to go there in order to figure out how to get out of the place where she had been stuck.

She now would have to find a way to meet the type of men she wanted to see more than once, ones she would only be intimate with after getting to know them. MetFridays was a start, but she needed something more structured, perhaps a class or season ticket to something. Activities where she would see the same people each week, which could lead to new friends.

Number one on the hit parade was definitely Hannah. Sam actually thought that she would be glad that two people Hannah was close to had found each other, not for the long haul perhaps, but, you know, to go out with sometimes, and for companionship. The kind of relationship described in *The Anti-Wife* book.

Sam really needed to hash things out with Hannah, but she did have work to do, and since currently, she'd be doing everything solo, she decided to go right into work mode. *But maybe I'll try Hannah just once.*

By lunchtime, she had gotten nothing done, unless one counted the two-dozen phone calls to Hannah's cell, an equal amount to iPad Allison, a number of texts, and an email to Hannah, which she anguished over as though it were a plea to kidnappers to return her loved one. If Sam ever wanted to give up her marketing consultant business and become a professional stalker, it was clear she had the stuff.

Believing she had embarrassed herself enough for one day, Sam forced herself to laser-focus on the needs of her existing clients, which ended up having her working well into the night. On Tuesday and Wednesday, it took every ounce of restraint not to reach out to Hannah or Allison yet again. Somewhere, there were opioid addicts who were having an easier time resisting bottles of Vicodin right in front of them than it was for Sam to not pick up the phone or type a message.

She knew Hannah and Allison had gotten her many, many correspondences, and when neither of them had contacted her by Thursday, Sam just couldn't control herself anymore.

She sent Hannah another text using the Topping Rose House ploy that had been so successful the day of the Applause presentation: *made reservations @TRH maybe u can come 4 brunch & we can talk or I can come to you.*

Then she picked up the phone to call the hotel and was promptly told they were booked.

Oh no. What if Hannah gets back to me and agrees to lunch? Then what?

It turned out Sam had started worrying for nothing.

Her cell pinged and the text read: *Allison here. H hopes u enjoy ur stay this weekend @TRH if she's free at any point I'LL CALL U.*

At least, she spared Sam the colloquial precursor: "Don't call us."

Sam put her nose back to the grindstone and kept it there until it was time for dinner the following evening. She thought of taking a shower, getting a blowout, and heading once again to MetFridays, but opted to take ZzzQuil and try to escape with slumber the Hannah dis via iPad Allison.

Saturday morning, Sam woke up and stared at the ceiling, aware that there was only one way she wanted to spend the day that stretched out before her.

As she made her way downtown in a taxi to the heliport, Sam convinced herself that purchasing a ticket on Blade was a prudent idea and money well spent.

She just wanted to get to the Hamptons as quickly as possible to clear the air with Hannah. Like Glen Close's character in *Fatal Attraction*, Sam "would not be ignored." Her plan was to march up to the house, ring the bell, and announce, "Hannah, we need to talk this out." Very straightforward. It would be appreciated and admired, not to mention understood by a straight-shooter who started a movement by speaking her unpopular-opinion mind.

After she landed, Sam took a local taxi to Chez Randolph. In the mere seconds it took her to pay the driver, open the door, and step out onto the driveway, iPad Allison had run through the house, out the front door, and flown down the front steps, as though elevated, like a character in *Harry Potter*.

"What are you doing here?" said Allison, her tone lacking the usual phony gracious inflections. "I said, I'd. Call. You."

"Hello to you too, Allison. I came to talk to Hannah."

Allison sidestepped Sam as she tried to get up the stairs, and in the think-on-your-feet, fast-talking-answer-for-everything way made famous by con artists and adolescents caught making mischief, she said: "Um, Hannah's not here."

Seriously, that's the best you've got? "Okay, so I'll wait."

"I don't know when she'll be back," the assistant-cum-sentinel said, again sidestepping Sam and now holding her iPad in front of her like a shield.

"Allison, I'll sit by the pool or in the front entry hall or on these very steps and just wait."

"Hannah really doesn't like people here when she's not here."

"Since when?"

Sam was like Hannah, relentless, and could outmatch Allison, who dropped her shoulders and exhaled like a suspect the cops had browbeaten into submission. She stopped short of putting up her hands and announcing, "I give up."

"Please, you really need to go. If you knew what I'm dealing with—"

"What's going—"

Just then, Sam looked up and saw Hannah looking out the bedroom window. She stood, staring down at Sam long enough to make sure Sam had noticed before she let go of the draperies with a flourish, like an actress snapping closed the curtains to signal the end of Act I.

Thus, Sam's inner battle began to wage: *I want to walk away with dignity, but I also would like to go all Bruce Lee on Allison's iPad and karate kick it in two.*

"So, she's not here?"

Clearly busted and emotionally drained from not just this encounter but the bandwidth needed to do her job, Allison's head dropped forward and her whole body slumped with it, as though she'd just been stricken with osteoporosis. Always the trouper, though, and dedicated to never letting Hannah down, she then stood back up straight while inhaling, immediately letting out an exhaustive sigh, making Sam wonder if the assistant's next move was to have Sam perp-walked off the property.

Instead, with eyes welled up with pity, Allison swallowed hard and resigned: "You really need to—"

"Go." Sam finished the sentence emotion-free, although, on the inside, she was infuriated over being the object of someone's boredom with a side of head-shaking disappointment, which flipped a switch in Sam's brain. This was no longer about Hannah being mad at her; now, it was about Sam being mad at Hannah.

"Yes, I do need to go," Sam reiterated so it sounded like her idea. "Can Carl drive me into town?"

"No, sorry. He's busy."

In her peripheral vision, Sam could see the chauffeur leaning against Hannah's sedan, examining his fingernails like a woman contemplating a polish change.

"Fine. I'll call a car service."

"Great, and if you could wait at the bottom of the driveway, Hannah would appreciate it."

Sam's internal GPS signaled for her to turn toward the road, and without replying, she started walking and dialing. The local taxi service answered but promptly put Sam on hold. During that time, she checked the Ambassador website as she could not waste (or afford) another dime again traveling via Blade. She saw there were no empty seats on neither the luxury line nor the Jitney.

When the dispatcher finally came back on the line, Sam asked if there was anyone available to drive her all the way back to Manhattan. The answer came in the form of an incredulous laugh punctuated by a definitive, "No."

Sam then asked to be brought to the closest Long Island Railroad station, where her day's journey could rival that of Steve Martin's in *Planes, Trains, and Automobiles.*

Sam was assured that the cab would be by to pick her up "in five." Each minute, though, seemed like an hour. She felt relief when she heard a car approaching but became irritated upon realizing that the sound was coming from behind her.

Carl pulled up beside Sam as Hannah rolled down the back tinted-glass window.

"Get in."

Sam resolved right there that the last time Hannah gave her an order was the last time Hannah ever gave her an order.

"No, I will not 'get in.'"

"I thought you wanted to talk."

"I did. But that ship sailed when I saw you hiding in your bedroom as Allison lied to my face about your being not home."

"My brother likes you."

"Did he pass you a note in study hall?"

"I can't have that."

"With all due respect, it's really not your business. We're two adults. We enjoyed each other's company, FYI platonically, and talked about perhaps seeing each other again, not eloping in Las Vegas. So, really there's nothing to get carried away about."

"I'd prefer if you were going to Vegas."

Sam raised a skeptical eyebrow.

"That's right. But I know that's not something you would do because you don't want to be married. He does, though, in spite of all he went through married to that . . . that . . . words fail, he still believes in it, even though when out in public he agrees with my Anti-Wife philosophy. He's looking for a wife. I can't have him hurt again. I can't have him getting his hopes up about you."

The taxi rolled up, and before Sam started walking toward it, as her parting shot, she said, "Hannah, he's a grown man. Like you say in your book, 'Unmarried adults are free to make their own decisions and mistakes.' Right, gurrl?" There, Queen of the Clapback, let's see if you can take it the way you dish it out.

Hannah decided to white-flag it. In a last-ditch effort to keep Sam from going, she got out of the car and stood behind the open door as though it were armor.

"Sam, we need to talk."

Wow, thought the unwanted guest, *she's running two games at once.* First, with the given-name familiarity, a tactic that thrilled Sam so much in the beginning, she ended up sleeping with Jessie Quinn's assistant and drinking vodka. Second, the ol' push-pull. When Sam wanted her, Hannah pushed her away (via Allison, of course); when Sam tried to leave, Hannah attempted to pull her back in. Sam would not be Al Pacino in *The Godfather III.*

"Then we'll talk—during business hours. Have Allison text me to set something up. We can meet at Applause."

As the cab took off, all Sam could think of was a saying she once saw on a t-shirt: "Don't push me away and then wonder where I went."

27

Sunday morning, Sam got up, put on her one-piece under a pair of shorts and a t-shirt, grabbed a blanket from the linen closet, a beach read lent to her by Katie at the beginning of the summer "for the bus ride," which she'd never cracked, and walked over to Central Park, knowing full well the days of enjoying Hannah's hospitality were, without question, behind her.

She was going to spend at least a few hours sunbathing on the Great Lawn with probably four hundred of her closest New York friends, who wanted to enjoy the first Sunday in August on the greenest part of the concrete jungle.

Between chapters, Sam took a break to chastise herself for blurring the lines between business and pleasure. *How could I . . . What was I thinking?* was the basic direction taken by her laments. She'd made few true screw-ups during her storied career and, for the life of her, could not figure out how a seasoned pro such as herself could trip up as she did. There was no way to put a shine on any of this. She was scorched earth, and Hannah would probably—make that definitely—tell Barry to use another consultant for the next wave of promo work.

To talk herself out of an anxiety attack, Sam reasoned that *The Anti-Wife* was just one assignment from one client, not the capstone of her career.

Sometimes business deals work out, evidenced by her long list of successes; sometimes, as in this case as well as with BrideMe, they don't. The important thing was to get up and dust herself off.

Sam had to start focusing once again on her business and current clients—the ones who she had treated like second-class citizens for the past month and a half.

With a clear head, she was now able to grasp how frustrating it must have been for Katie to carry the ball because Sam had one foot in the office and the other in the Hamptons.

To make it up to her, Sam thought it only right that she invite Katie to the Applause party at the end of the week where Barry Rogers was going to pull the trigger on *The Anti-Wife* campaign. She might even extend the olive branch to Sarah, as well.

If I'm still invited, dawned on her while reapplying sunscreen. Hannah might have her banned from the event.

Barry had arranged the merriment for the marketing group in a hotel suite located directly across from the show's digital billboard in Times Square. Just as on New Year's Eve, they would count down to when it went live.

The guest of honor, was told she could bring whomever she wanted. Sam hoped that Barry had ordered enough loaves and fishes to feed the inevitable five thousand who would be tagging behind his money-in-the-bank star.

****

Sam woke up at 6:00 a.m. on Monday morning, feeling more like herself than she had in a long time, ready to shower, dress, and head right next door into the office. There was a lot to accomplish that week.

She had rethought her position on working without help and elevated recruiting a new assistant from LinkedIn to the top spot. But like much of her life of late, Sam had to shift gears at the last minute.

By the time she came out of the shower, there were almost a hundred messages in the form of emails, voicemails, and texts on both her phone and computer.

Sam opened one from Lena: *OMG R U OK?*

"What?" she said aloud, as she shook her head at one of many messages from the usually un-alarmist free spirit and opened the front door to pick up the awaiting *New York Times, Wall Street Journal*, with the *New York Post* topping the pile.

Notorious for its headlines like the legendary "Headless Body Found in Topless Bar," the tabloid had written above the face of a laughing Hannah Randolph the words: "Anti-Wife Takes A Husband."

Sam smacked her hand over her mouth with such force that for a second, she thought she'd loosened her two front teeth.

Well, I guess now I know what she wanted to talk about and what Allison was "dealing with."

Sam had to sit down for what was to follow but didn't make it past the edge of her sofa before she began to read the story of the biggest flip-flop since Havaianas put one of its sandals on a billboard: The woman who became a millionaire several times over by spouting "marriage doesn't work and should be banned," now had Mrs. before her name.

Hannah had eloped the Thursday before Sam made her surprise Hamptons appearance.

Sam's mind was racing, and although her body wasn't exactly shaking, there was a slight shiver up her spine. She couldn't seem to concentrate; her comprehension felt off. The best she could do was skim, picking up on key words to at least get the gist of the report: "anti-marriage … until … love of her life … changed mind … never happier … love wins … new book … marriage works."

If Sam were still a drinking woman, this moment would have justified an it's-five-o'clock-somewhere long pour, but instead, she went for the remote. The morning shows were having a field day, each with its own toothy-grinned variation of, "She said she'd never say 'I do,' but the Anti-Wife has gone and done it. Stay tuned to find out who she said it to."

Sam already knew, as the *Post* had published the cover of *People*, which had been granted the exclusive wedding photos of the happy couple frolicking on a beach, with Hannah looking effortlessly chic in a white sleeveless poplin dress with shirring at the shoulders and leaf-accented ties, which was gifted to her by new pal Tory, who she'd met at some fancy, Manhattan save-the-*whatever* fundraiser. With one arm draped around her groom, the now anti-Anti-Wife waved her bouquet in the air as she once did her bestseller.

"Ah, him." Sam sighed out loud. How had she not figured this one?

Honestly, though, what difference did it make who it was? This was truly a who-cares-how-the-cow-got-in-the-ditch moment. What mattered was that Hannah was married and as ridiculous as it seemed, all too many lives would be affected.

As Sam watched the crawl at the bottom of the TV screen, she hallucinated the words "you lying bitch" replacing all the this-just-in news.

The off button on the remote could not have been pressed hard enough. Sam hadn't even felt this duped when Sam the Man called off the wedding, after having told her from the day they met that he knew she was the woman he would marry.

Suddenly, her spacious two-bedroom with panoramic views started to feel as claustrophobic as a coffin. She had to get out of that apartment.

Sam got up, went to the front door, and broke the cardinal rule she'd made for herself when she hung out her own shingle. The business owner had sworn she would always give her own office the same respect given to other businesses she'd labored in by dressing professionally, ever-ready to run out to a last-minute client lunch or impromptu meeting. That morning, though, she went out into her building's hallway in her robe, wet hair, and bare feet to enter her workspace.

"I really need to calm down," she told herself as she made a cup of coffee. When she realized she'd done so in the Anti-Wife mug, she poured the drink down the sink with the intention of smashing the cup but thought better of that erratic behavior. She didn't want to spend the next month having stray ceramic slivers crunch beneath her feet.

Sam sat at her desk and went through the texts and emails. Some were Google Alerts, others were non-business related, and several were from clients and needed to be addressed—meaning she had to pull herself together pronto. But first, the Hannah-centric messages.

From Lena, there were quite a few of the *WTF?* variety.

From Little Evie: *don't u know her? did u go 2 wedding? any celebs there?*

A phone message came from Evelyn: "Your sister says you work with that anti . . . marriage or wedding or whatever she calls herself. Now that she's married, does that mean you lost your job?"

And an email from Katie. Before Sam opened it, she braced herself for a missive with a meme of someone ROTFL, but instead, the young professional wrote something in the tone and length that she probably should have used in her resignation letter:

Dear Sam,

I just heard the Hannah news. Before I get to that, first, let me apologize for my abrupt departure.

The last month working for you was difficult and made me quite uncomfortable. Your animosity toward my upcoming wedding and negative remarks, coupled with the drastic change in your behavior, especially your unusually slapdash rush to get work done for clients and disinterest in new business, prompted me to want to find a new position elsewhere.

I'm sorry that I had to go behind your back to do so, but Sarah's opportunity was too good to let it get away, and I'm sure if you had been your usual level-headed self, you would have known that.

Now that HR is married, I guess that puts an end to the Applause show and your part in it. Sorry all our great and hard work on the promo campaign will go to waste. Perhaps, though, this is a blessing in disguise. Your troubles began when you got involved with the Anti-Wife.

To prove to you I want there to be no hard feelings between us, I went into PayPal and sent Applause your final invoice for the project.

FYI: I suggest you change all the office passwords.

Sincerely,

Katie

Sam hit "reply" and wished Katie well in her new endeavor as well as her upcoming nuptials. She also couldn't disagree with the blessing-in-disguise part, especially apropos the footage of her cavorting in the Hamptons that would gratefully never air.

Sam then texted her sister: *Yes, I know her. No to the wedding. Pls tell mom my job is just fine.*

To Lena, she wrote: *Dont know whats next 2 rattled 2 figure out what happened.*

At nine on the dot, the office phone rang. Nine? Where had the last three hours gone?

"Samantha Dennehy."

"Hi Sam, this is Mindy from Applause. Remember me? I'm Bob's—"

"Yes, Mindy, I remember."

They're having an assistant call me?

"So, I guess you heard."

"Indeed, I did."

"So, just letting you know, the launch party is off. The show has been shelved; hence the amazing campaign you masterminded has been as well. I'm so sorry to have to be the one to tell you."

"Well, I appreciate that Mindy, and thank you for the heads up, but I assumed everything had been tabled and planned on giving Barry a call, well, now."

"Oh, he's not taking calls. He's behind closed doors all day. His secretary told me on the DL that he's already been on the phone with Hannah. I think they spoke in the wee hours. I probably shouldn't have shared that, but you deserve to know. I mean, our people here do really good work, but what you brought to the party raised the bar. I'm sure they'll use you again. I would definitely bring your name up for future projects, you know, if anybody ever cared enough to ask me what I thought about anything."

"Mindy, how would you like a new job?"

28

With Hannah off her plate and the sense of accomplishment Sam felt when she hung up with her new right hand, she had just what she needed to restart her day.

She went back to her apartment, blew out her hair, put on makeup, but gave pause when she opened her closet and was faced with her Tory Burch wardrobe curated when she fancied herself Hannah's twin flame.

Sam pulled out a tried and true J.Crew shirtdress and slid into a pair of Manolos, added jewelry, and headed back next door.

Mindy was starting the following Monday, so Sam had five days to dive back in and reconnect with clients and make some calls to drum up new business.

By one o'clock, her stomach began to growl, but her real emptiness wasn't coming from her belly. Even though she had scratched off the now top chore of her to-do list, which was replacing Katie, and fell back into her role of business owner without missing a beat, she still felt as unsettled as she had when she got on the train after the driveway altercation two days prior.

The intercom buzzer startled her out of her thoughts.

"It's your friend Lena," announced Jimmy.

The OG of BFFs waltzed out of the elevator, carrying in one hand a cardboard tray holding two Starbucks venti iced teas and in the other a Chop't shopping bag, which no doubt housed a Santa Fe salad for Lena and a Classic Cobb for Sam. She could not even wait for her friend to put down the bromides before giving her the kind of hug experienced by soldiers who return home and surprise their kids at a school assembly.

Sam suggested they dine in her apartment, where they could relax and eat on the extra-long sofa. But as famished as she was, Sam, and subsequently Lena, did more talking than eating.

"Why are you still my friend? The Bed, Bath & Beyond gift card should have been enough to send you packing."

Lena smiled and gave a tiny laugh, "Forgiveness is part of friendship. Ride or die."

A gentle fist bump validated that they were once again the role models for #friendshipgoals.

"I don't know what happened," admitted Sam. "It's like, I lost my mind or control, or I really don't know."

"I do. Look, I've never gone deep into your family shit. I mean, I've listened to you bitch about your mother and worry about your sister, but we've never talked about your dad. I always took at face value the 'he did us a favor' thing. And you know, maybe he did. But the fact remains that he was your first male relationship, and he left you. Then Sam Winston turned around and did the same thing. That's a pretty vulnerable state to be in."

Sam's lip started to quiver. She tried never to think about her dad, ever. And here, first Hannah, and now Lena, made it clear that even though he had been gone a long time, he still loomed large and affected her.

"You were supposed to get married, and when that fell apart, you didn't. I mean, maybe at first, for what, a day? Then, you pulled it together—but it wasn't real. As I recall saying at the time, you needed to feel your feelings. But you wanted to be all: 'Look how strong I am. No man is going to get the best of me. I'm going to turn this negative into a positive and throw all my energy into my business.' And the business thing worked out. But once again, you never gave yourself a chance to grieve the loss.

"On top of that, people around you, especially people close to you like me, your sister, and, well, for comic relief, now your mother, got married. And no one is saying you're jealous—don't even go there. But these are triggers to what happened or actually didn't happen. I mean, even in the first *Sex and the City* movie, after her wedding fell through, Carrie spent a week in bed with the shutters closed."

"I guess meeting Hannah didn't help matters."

"Well, let's unpack that. Remember, what was it, six or seven years ago? The summer your sister was around sixteen and suddenly went wild?"

"Yeah, good times—the drinking, smoking pot, running around Greenwich Village at all hours of the night with those trashy girls she met in summer school and those boys who looked like Shaggy from *Scooby-Doo*."

"And the night I went with you to drag her out of that club on . . . was it Bleeker?"

"The Bitter End. That was the least of it. The worst being when she thought she was pregnant. I ran up to the Bronx, and by the time I got to my mother's house, thank goodness Evie had already gotten her period. I actually scraped my knees when I fell on them in gratitude."

"The point is, she got that kind of thing out of her system and got her life right. Well, this was your wild summer."

"I guess, but—"

"You're one of those people who doesn't like to show her feelings. Okay, you do you. But having your wedding called off, well, that was something that had to be addressed, not ignored. The stress of that had to come out some time in some way.

"Hannah Randolph and her Anti-Wife—pardon me, bullshit—opened the door. She not only said things you wanted to hear, but she also gave you this world to escape to. And you did. But even though you shook off your life for a while, I'm not sure if you've yet to feel your feelings about what happened to you."

With that, Sam felt months upon months (maybe even years) of emotion begin to surface. She took her salad and iced tea, placed it on the coffee table, put her face in her hands, then fell forward into Lena's lap and cried, "How could he have done that to me?"

Lena wasn't sure if her friend meant her ex or her father or both. And quite frankly, neither did Sam, but the dam had finally burst and, with Lena there, she felt safe enough to finally let herself feel.

29

"So, Labor Day plans?"

"Well," said Mindy, "I couldn't afford a summer share this year, but my friend Debby has been in one in Wainscott. Anyway, the house rule was no guests, but they're doing away with that since this is the last weekend, so I'm grabbing the Jitney when I leave here tonight. Who knows, maybe this'll be the weekend I meet my husband."

Sam smiled. "If that's what you want, I hope you get it."

"How about you? What are your plans?" Mindy asked with interest.

"Friday, I'm going to work on that new business venture we spoke about."

Ever the entrepreneur, Sam, unimpressed with the classes and such she wanted to get involved in to meet new people, had an idea. She was going to call the company "Cultured Singles." The group would meet on Saturday nights—because not everyone has a date on date night—at a venue yet to be determined. The fee would cover eight weeks at a time, and in a refined cocktail party setting, there would be a speaker who'd come give a talk about art, music, books, travel, etc.

She had begun talking to business contacts about it, and not only were there those interested in investing, but they also wanted to become members.

"Then, on Saturday, my married friends Lena and Ben invited me to a backyard barbeque. Their friend lives in a brownstone near theirs in Brooklyn and said they could bring me to his party. I smell a setup, quite frankly, but who knows. On Sunday, my sister and her husband—"

"Evie and Dr. Joe," clarified Mindy, trying to show her new boss that she listened when Sam talked and remembered details.

"Right. They're having a cookout as well. I don't know if I mentioned it, but Evie is pregnant with twin girls. She's naming one of them after me."

****

The prior weekend, Sam called to invite Little Evie to Manhattan for lunch. They met at Saks, where they ate at L'Avenue, and Sam started to explain her behavior and apologize, but the mother-to-be wouldn't hear of it.

"Sammy, you've always taken care of me. I could never stay mad at you. I love you. Sisters fight." Evie shrugged. "Let's forget it. Everything is really good now, you know? Mommy was so unhappy for a long time. She made that clear by ignoring me and dumping a lot of crap on you, and by crap, I mean me."

"You're not crap, and she didn't dump you. I volunteered. I wanted to mind you."

"Still, it wasn't fun for you, but honestly, I felt lucky. I got the better part of the deal. I got to be raised by you instead of her. And now, well, you should see. Really, she's a different person. She even looks different. She's lost some weight from walking—that's her and Al's hobby, and her hair's totally salt & pepper, and long, like just past her shoulders. Albert says she looks like this country singer, Emmylou Harris. I Googled her, and you know, it's true. In fact, that's Al's nickname for mom."

Sam did not even try to stifle her laughter at tough-as-nails Evelyn from Inwood being referred to as Emmylou.

"Whatever relationship I didn't have with her before," continued Evie, "well, I'm starting to have with her now. We go shopping, have lunch. Hey, better late than never, right? I'm really happy, so let's just keep the past in the past and eat. I'm starved. I'm eating for three, you know, and one of them is Little Samantha."

Sam was so touched, her tears started dropping into her cranberry and club soda, and she didn't care who noticed.

Afterward, the Dennehy girls strolled arm-in-arm until the mother-to-be couldn't walk another step. They took a cab the rest of the way to Sam's apartment, where she had her laptop set up at the dining room table.

"I know that traditionally I'd throw you a baby shower, but you don't need anyone to give you anything. You have me. Consider this it."

Sam signed on to her Amazon Prime account, and the two sisters picked out everything not-so-little-anymore Evie would need—times two.

****

"Oh," said Sam to Mindy, "and my mother and her husband, I mean, my stepdad, Albert, are going to be at my sister's as well. I need you to call JetBlue and see how to go about using my rewards points to buy open tickets for them to go wherever they want for a belated honeymoon. If the airline can't do it, call American Express and see if we can do what I want with points."

"I'm on it. Oh, wait, what are you doing on Monday, you know, Labor Day?"

"I'm leaving that open."

"Who knows, you might meet someone at one of the BBQs and spend it with him."

Sam chuckled, "Maybe. But I'll also want to prepare for my Tuesday meeting at Applause."

****

"He's one forgiving guy," was the buzz at the network, whispered in dubious tones and accompanied by skeptical head shakes. Everyone, including Sam, couldn't believe that Barry didn't want to kill Hannah with his bare, well-manicured hands.

But forgiveness had nothing to do with it. Barry Rogers was an astute businessman.

Upon hearing the news about the wedding, he made a new lucrative deal with Hannah Randolph, optioning the new book that she was rushing to get ghostwritten, the tentative title: *From Anti to Wife*. That would also be the name of her new reality show.

"The controversy alone will make this television gold, definitely appointment viewing. I want the same marketing team as last time," said Rogers when he called Sam earlier in the week. "And Hannah agreed. She thinks you're a genius, by the way. Same fee as the last go-'round, and I can have the contract over to you immediately. So, you in?"

"Absolutely," said Sam, not believing what she heard herself agree to. This whole experience had proved to her that even a seasoned executive could have a teachable moment.

On the human spectrum, Hannah Randolph was neither a sinner nor a saint. Like everyone else, she tried to make a place for herself in the world by creating a narrative that got her through the day in the best possible light. When that storyline no longer worked for her, she found a new one.

How could Sam find fault with that when she'd done the same thing? What was it she had told editor Amy so long ago on the street in front of St. Patrick's about "the whole piece of paper thing"?

Sam's narrative was that of the ad exec on the rise, who would not marry the man in her life until she'd made it. Then that morphed into successful entrepreneur with no time for a relationship. And now it was time for a new scenario. Sam was not quite sure what that would be yet, but she was excited to figure it out.

In the meantime, it was once again an opportunity to model someone successful. If Barry Rogers, who had many more years of experience and achievement, could chalk up Hannah's 180 to "it's not personal, it's just business, and we're in business to make money," then so could Sam.

She saw this second chance as more than another major payday, though. It was a way to right a wrong. Sam had crossed a line last time, but the reason for that had been dealt with. Now, there would be no blurring; it would be totally professional.

In all her bohemian wisdom, Lena had told Sam that even a bad experience could have some good come out of it. Let the healing begin.

*

Although she still and probably always would embrace her prepdom, Hannah's influence helped Sam graduate to the next stage in her sartorial life. She'd stepped up her fashion game—especially for work.

She would infuse her wardrobe with more varied designers of her own taste. Mindy would be selling a lot of her Torys on Poshmark.

*

Sam's talk with Hannah that morning at Candy Kitchen had actually been cathartic. First, she realized that she wasn't the only sibling ever tasked with caring for a younger family member. Second, she chose to no longer see herself as a martyr. The conversation allowed Sam to admit that sometimes having been a "teen mom" was a real drag—and she was resentful. She took it out on her mother, but the truth was, if her father had stepped up and been a responsible grownup, Sam would not have had to become one sooner rather than later.

*

The best thing that had come out of that tête-à-tête was the question as to whether marriage was right for her. She'd never really had to give it any real thought as an adult since Samuel Winston had dropped the promise of it in her lap, and it sounded like a good idea at the time. Although how their end came about had been humiliating, honestly, not becoming his wife had left her no worse for the wear. Whether she wanted to be a wife at all, well, that was still up in the air.

In fact, Sam wished she could be as sure about marriage as she was about motherhood.

*

What was revealed during her breakfast with Hannah was true. She had already been a mother to Little Evie. Did it, done it, been there.

The only children she wanted now were Evie's twins, to whom she would be the fun aunt—something Joe could certainly relate to—eventually taking them on fabulous trips and to wonderful restaurants and buying them amazing gifts.

Her current goal was to meet new people—women as well as men—and not trash marriage to "cover her loneliness and desperation," as she'd seen Hannah confess to in the teasers for her upcoming, exclusive interview with Barry Rogers himself on the Applause Network.

Marriage could be a good thing for some, not so much for others. Sam was not going to fret over which category she fit into. For the moment, she wanted to focus on companionship.

And when a man was not in the picture, she would set out on solo activities because, as she'd learned from the Anti-Wife, Sam really could stand her own company.

EPILOGUE

On Labor Day, Sam got up and made herself a huge mug of coffee from her china set, as Mindy had sold *The Anti-Wife* mug on eBay for $385—anything AW was a commodity since Hannah had shut down that ecommerce business.

Sam grabbed the paper from outside her front door, perused the headline, then tossed it aside, opting to begin her day bemused by the on-demand program on her TV screen, the Barry/Hannah interview she missed in real time because Sam was at Little Evie's party having a beautiful time with her family and their friends. Her sister had been on the money: Evelyn had never looked better, and Albert, who was as affable as Sam remembered, clearly was bringing out the best in her.

Both her mother and new stepfather were particularly touched by the tickets to "anywhere," as was Evie, who saw something in her sister she'd never seen before: vulnerability. The younger sibling called for a group hug and had Joe take a picture of the three women to document the new era in their relationship as "the squad," as she referred to them. Before Sam and her mother left the house, the doctor presented them each with a print of the photo, as though it were a prescription for something that would make them feel all better. Sam leaned hers on a bookshelf until a suitable frame could be found.

Before Sam got to the must-see TV interview, there was one more bit of closure she needed to take care of.

As she typed "Sam Winston" into the Instagram search box, Sam announced in a clear voice, "I can do this."

After her good cry and soul-baring talk with Lena, Sam finally admitted that the breakup had been hard on her, harder than she was willing to concede. Late that evening, Lena punctuated their afternoon together by sending Sam an eCard that read: "Hey, remember that person you thought you couldn't live without? Well, look at you, all livin' and shit."

Yes, she was. And if Sam could live to tell the tale of her father's abandonment, her mother's lifetime of crazy, her younger sister's marriage to a doctor no less, and being dumped a week before her wedding, she could survive anything, even seeing finally the person who'd replaced her.

Of course, Mr. Live Out Loud did not have a private account. When his photo grid popped on the screen of her Mac Book Pro, Sam was overwhelmed by the breadth of pictures starring himself and her doppelganger.

The Man's woman was elegant, chestnut-haired, and had skin that looked practically fetal. Jessica was Samantha 3.0.

Fearing momentarily that all her healing would evaporate into the ether, Sam plowed ahead and clicked on the shot he'd taken of their *New York Times* wedding announcement. It seemed that "Jess," as The Man had referred to her in all his posts, was a recent grad of Cornell.

"She's not just younger, she's ten years younger, like Evie." Sam announced aloud.

Mrs. Winston would be taking an executive position at her father's real estate empire. They married at the bride's family's compound in Montana and honeymooned at her family's estate on Hawaii.

"And she's one of his own kind," Sam added, along with the observation, "no wonder they were able to do it so fast, they didn't have to book anything." Not even first-class plane tickets. Sam concluded that if Jessica was to ever mar her milky white skin with a tattoo, it would read: *only flies private.*

Of all the emotions she was feeling simultaneously, Sam could pinpoint awkward, uncomfortable, and defensive as the standouts, with just plain weird as a chaser.

Another time and place, she would have fought off her feelings, but now, thanks to Lena's insistence Sam let it all out, she gave herself permission to wonder teary-eyed, "why not me?" flashing back to good times, and shaking her head in disbelief that they were not enough for The Man to want to stick around for any more.

She then hearkened back to Lena's proviso that "if things are meant to be, they will be. This my friend," referring to her relationship, "was not."

Sam also had to remember that even though she'd known Samuel for over a decade, she did not know him as part of this couple, and refused to let her fertile imagination get the best of her, creating some perfect love story a la *The Notebook*, where there might not be one. After all, people looked at the two Sams and thought they were made in heaven, when clearly, they were not.

Sam realized she'd seen enough after scrolling through a few more photos, like the one where the couple was in formalwear at the Met's Young Members party, prompting the raised eyebrow comment: "Never step foot in one again, huh?" Then, last and least, she enlarged one of Samuel and Jessica posing on the porch of the Winton's Martha's Vineyard home. Sam had stood on that porch, and posed for that exact picture five or was it six years ago. It was nowhere to be found though, as all traces of The Man's ex had been wiped clean from his page.

"Right back atcha," and with that, nostalgia was eschewed by reality.

The picture had been a wake-up call for the self-made woman that no matter how beautiful the island off Cape Cod was, how wonderful of a time they'd had, and how welcoming her hosts had been, Sam never felt as though she really belonged. A red flag if ever there were one.

She inhaled what seemed like all the air in the room, then exhaled, "Well, that's done," logged out of Insta and closed her laptop, as well as the book on Sam the Man.

****

Sam once again had proven to herself that if nothing else she was resilient, and now, with the push of a button, it was time to take on the Anti-Wife.

Clap clap clap clap clap went the sound effect that accompanied the Applause Network logo as it faded to reveal a bare set.

"Hannah Randolph," stated a stoic Barry, perched on a stool in front of a publicity photo of the acerbic blonde holding a copy of her first book like a hockey MVP pumping the Stanley Cup into the air.

With the gravitas of Diane Sawyer presenting new evidence in the Kennedy assassination, he continued: "She is the bestselling author of the self-help bible, *The Anti-Wife*, a book that chronicled her philosophy that marriage should not exist because she believed the institution to be arcane.

"As widely reported, this network had planned a much-anticipated unscripted television show around the anti-marriage guru, determined to live by example, so that women, in her words, 'could stop being chattel.' We had to scrap those plans, though, because now, Randolph sports a ring on her left hand, Mrs. before her name, and a new outlook on an institution she once disdained.

"In this exclusive Applause interview, the influencer and disruptor extraordinaire sat down with me to discuss the new direction that her influence and disruption is about to take."

There then was a cut to Barry and Hannah in a friendly face-off in her Hampton's living room.

"So, Sadie, Sadie married lady."

"I'm legit," said a coy Hannah swathed in an all too familiar Tory Burch ensemble, her left hand adjacent to her face to show off her diamond ring and matching band as though she were posing for a Jared's ad.

"This is quite a turn of events."

"I'll say," she guffawed, unapologetically.

Another cut offered viewers footage of Hannah at one of her rallies, which Sam recognized as the one she attended on Long Island, echoing her "marriage doesn't work" credo, with audience members cheering and holding supportive signage. Next, the footage jumped to a frenzied book signing, where her disciples had been so desperate to engage with their fearless leader that entire displays got knocked over, causing the independent bookstore to shut down the event.

"So how do you respond to people who are now calling you a hypocrite?"

"I don't know that they are."

"Do you live in a cave?" Sam yelled at the TV. Hannah's marriage flip-flop had made her catnip for critics, evidenced by the top story on *Newsweek.com* with the words "Anti-What?" over the face of the Anti-Wife. Apparently, Barry agreed.

"Really? All those people who bought not only your book but also into what you were saying about marriage being passé and how it wasn't for you, or anyone for that matter? And then you turn around and—"

"And what?" interrupted Hannah defensively. "Fall in love? Make it legal?"

"And she's off," Sam said to the screen. "Let's see how she spins herself out of this one."

"Look, first of all, haters gonna hate. And second, anyone who doesn't want to get married, shouldn't. It's not for everyone. And the more people admit when it's not for them, the more people will be spared getting divorced. I believed for a long time that I was one of those people. But I was lying to myself. And the more I lied to myself and shared my lie with others, the bigger it got. I was covering my loneliness and desperation to be loved."

"Looking at you, though," said Barry, "it's hard to believe anyone as attractive as you, couldn't find—"

"Oh, I found, all right. There are plenty of men out there who'd sleep with me or mooch off me or pass the time until someone new came along, which is what happened to a friend of mine."

"Oh no, you didn't," said Sam, catching Hannah-the-smart-aleck's dig at the fate of her long-term relationship.

"I just never found anyone who loved me or brought out the best in me. I actually believed no one would or could."

"Where did this lack of self-worth on your part come from?" Barry wanted to know.

Forgetting all about the research she did that brought her to her own conclusion that marriage wasn't in her DNA, Hannah said, without hesitation, "My dad. From when I was about thirteen, he started telling me I wasn't the marrying kind, and I believed him."

An interview with Ralph Randolph came on.

"Hannah said you always told her she wasn't the type to get married."

"Guilty," confessed Mr. Randolph. "So independent. So headstrong. Uncompromisin'. Marriage is give-and-take. With her, it's all take, unless she's givin' you a hard time. People like that . . . who could live with someone like that for a lifetime?"

When the cameras returned to Hannah, she was throwing up her hands, laughing, and rolling her eyes.

"Ya get it, now?"

"I do," nodded Barry. "So, you're rolling along, believing it couldn't/wouldn't happen. Preaching your philosophy, becoming a multi-millionaire, developing a following, and then one day . . ."

"I realized the man of my dreams was right under my nose, or actually, my mouth."

The camera pulled back, and there was her new husband sitting beside her.

"You married your personal chef. Thanks for joining us, Kenny."

At that point, Sam moved to the edge of the couch to get an even better view of the lovebirds cooing at each other. No wonder that with all Hannah's talk of loving men and sex, Sam never saw her with any. Sam also remembered one morning catching Hannah coming out of her guesthouse where Kenny lived and her host acting all flustered, rambling about how they were planning a dinner menu. Sam accepted at face value the explanation she wasn't owed. She also suddenly understood the scene she had witnessed in the kitchen that time. Hannah thought Sam had been putting the moves on her man or vice versa. The dots had been connecting themselves right before her eyes, and she hadn't even noticed.

"How?" Barry asked. "Just . . . how?"

"I realized that during his time in my employ Kenny not only fed my body but my soul. I've always suffered from insomnia, and I'd get up and rummage about in the kitchen. He'd sense I was there and come find me. We'd talk. I would bare my soul to him. But I was so stupid—"

"You're not stupid," interjected Kenny. "You're brilliant."

"No, I was stupid not to realize sooner you were the one."

Chef Kenny nodded his head in acquiescence.

"And this, in a nutshell, will be their marriage," mumbled Sam. "Kenny will say something, Hannah will disagree, and Kenny will go along like Charlotte's ex Trey, with his own version of 'alrighty.'"

The footage then went to an establishing shot of the pool area at Chez Randolph with Allison, Inez, and Carl sitting around one of the patio tables.

Barry, in voiceover, asked on behalf of the audience: "What though does this union of the boss to one of their own mean to the others in Randolph's employ?"

"So, this is like on *Downton Abbey* when the chauffeur married into the Crawley family. How are you dealing with it?" Barry challenged the group.

Carl, looking ever the movie star, began, "Kenny's a great guy. I may be his driver now, too, but when it's just us, he still sits in the front seat with me. But, you know, when he's with Hannah, they sit in the back. It's only right."

The camera moved to Inez, the regal everywoman.

"Forgive me, Inez," said Sam, bowing her head, unable to hold the housekeeper's gaze, even via the flat screen.

"The house is quieter now. Not so many people to keep Miss Hannah company. She doesn't need that anymore now that she has a husband. And he still cooks, so that's good."

Finally, always-camera-ready Allison got her close-up.

"You know, in today's world, a woman has to be so careful about whom she meets. I think it's great that Hannah married someone from within her circle, someone she knows she can trust."

"What about those who might call her a hypocrite?" baited Barry.

"Well, I turn around and call them sexist. I mean, did anyone call George Clooney a hypocrite when he married Amal after decades of saying he'd never marry again? I think all those people who are name-calling and labeling will change their tune when they read Hannah Randolph's new book."

Allison, smiling like a spokesmodel, then held up her iPad with a full-screen cover mock-up of *From Anti to Wife*, which the camera zoomed in on. Needless to say, the visual was a beauty shot of a luminous Hannah.

The end of the segment was a two-shot of Hannah and Barry sitting next to each other, this time on the patio before the glow of the firepit.

"Hannah, any last thoughts you want to share with our Applause viewers?"

Hannah turned and focused directly into the camera, aka Sam's eyes, and it was as though they were back at Candy Kitchen and the one-time Anti-Wife was sharing her thoughts with her former houseguest and her alone.

"Life is a journey of self-discovery. I explored being single and seeing marriage through a negative lens. Now, I'm married and viewing it through a positive lens, and I look forward to sharing my perspective in my next book and our reality show based on my life as a newlywed."

"I haven't yet congratulated you with a hug," said Barry, playing to the camera.

"Bring it in," blushed a choked-up Hannah, not to be upstaged.

Before these two master showmen could intertwine, Sam shook her head and turned off the TV. She started to chuckle, which opened up into snorting, unrelenting laughter so strenuous that it felt like an ab workout. At one point, it became so uncontrollable that Sam was bent over and had to place her hand on the coffee table to keep from falling off the couch onto the area rug.

As she began to catch her breath and her chortling trailed off in spurts, Sam grabbed her phone and texted Lena: *just watched Hannah interview— PT Barnum in heels n hair extensions.*

****

Later, Sam rented a Citibike and rode all through Central Park. When she was exhausted and sweaty enough, she sat on a bench near the 84th Street entrance behind the Metropolitan Museum of Art.

Next to her came and sat a silver-haired woman who Sam estimated was a youthful sixty. They smiled at each other, then directed their attention elsewhere; Sam to the kids playing frisbee on the Great Lawn, dog walkers, and other park-goers strolling by; the older woman to a gentleman her age buying ice cream at a nearby vendor.

"They don't have Creamsicles," he yelled.

"Then get something else. I don't care as long as it's cold," the woman shouted back.

Sam didn't know why, but she was fascinated by them. Never one to be nosy, she shocked herself by asking, "Is that your husband?"

"Yes, my Henry."

Sam didn't think it was a stretch to assume, given their ages, that they'd been together a long time.

"How long have you been married?"

"We're newlyweds."

Again, Sam made what she thought was a logical assumption.

"So, were you ever married before—you know, divorced or widowed?"

The woman regarded Sam, a bit taken aback by this stranger's low-grade interrogation but was proud of her relationship and didn't mind talking about how they met.

"Henry was married. For a long time, in fact. His first wife died about ten years ago. I never married, though. I never found anyone who was really for me and didn't want to get married just to say I was. I kept my life full, but, sure, there were lonely periods when I doubted my choice. I was never so grateful to be single, though, than when my true love came along."

With that, she got up to meet halfway her husband, who was walking toward her with their ice cream.

Sam watched them walk away and whispered, "Never say never."

ABOUT THE AUTHOR

Lorraine Duffy Merkl is a published author, freelance journalist, and advertising creative director/copywriter. Her novels *Back To Work She Goes* (2013) and *Fat Chick* (2009) were both published by The Vineyard Press. Merkl's essays have appeared in the *New York Times, New York Post, New York Daily News, New York Observer, Cosmopolitan,* the Huffington Post, xoJane, Bustle, *Redbook, Woman's Day, Seventeen, Marie Claire, Town & Country,* The Girlfriend, The Ethel, Rachel Ray In Season, *Newsweek,* Shondaland, and *The Independent,* to name a few. Merkl resides in Manhattan with her husband, son, and daughter.